FOXY
TAILS
NATALINA REIS

HOT TREE PUBLISHING

FOXY TAILS

NATALINA REIS

HOT TREE PUBLISHING

Also by Natalina Reis

M/M Stand-alone Romances

Infinite Blue

Lavender Fields

Sleeping Love

Foxy Tails

Of Magic & Scales Series

Of Magic and Scales

Of Scales and Fire

Of Fire and Bone

Of Tails & Mistletoe

M/F Romances

Loved You Always

Blind Magic

Fictional-ish

Her Real Man

The Jewel Chronicles

Desert Jewel

Rebel Jewel

SNOW JEWEL

For information, contact the publisher, Hot Tree Publishing.

WWW.HOTTREEPUBLISHING.COM

EDITING: HOT TREE EDITING

COVER DESIGNER: BOOKSMITH DESIGN

EBOOK ISBN: 978-1-922679-47-5

PAPERBACK ISBN: 978-1-922679-48-2

To my mom and dad, who taught me to be curious about the world around me and love its diversity and wonder.

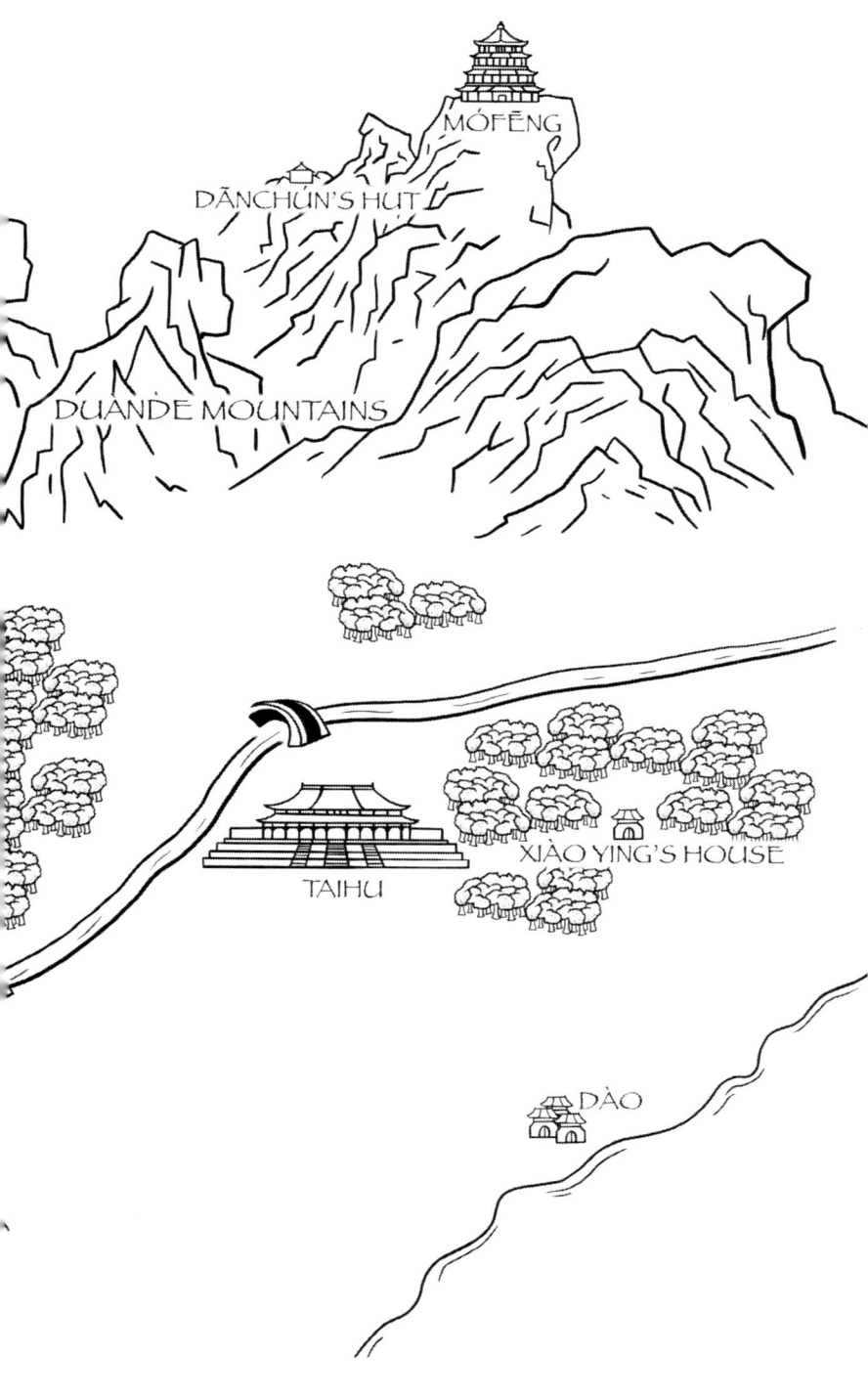

CAST OF CHARACTERS

Húlí = The Fox, also known by his real name Xi Ming Xin (A-Xin = intimate, familiar form of address) - male fox shifter

Xiǎo Yīng = The Healer (A-Ying = intimate, familiar form of address) - male

Ling Ling = female and Húlí's best friend.

Yè Yǐng = dog

Xu Ming = Húlí's first lover

Shūshu = Húlí's master

Gōng Zhèng = (fair) old emperor

Gōng Hǎoxīn = (Kind Heart), emperor's son, crown prince

Gōng Làn = (rotten), new emperor

Lóng Wei = Old Gǒu, monk

Yuèguāng = (moonbeam), Huli's mother

CHAPTER 1

THE CHASE

HÚLÍ

He could almost feel the bite of their sharp teeth as the incessant barking followed him through the forest. Húlí ran faster, his full tails flaring behind him and his furry ears homing in on the growling behind him.

"Damn tails," he spat out. They would give him away if he couldn't get himself under control and retract them.

He tried to slow down his breathing, an almost impossible feat as he bounded around trees, nothing but a blur of light to anyone watching. Except for the hounds. Those would never let go or be deterred by Húlí's speed.

A clearing appeared up ahead, and he let out a

quiet cheer. He'd be able to run faster within it and maybe lose the canines.

It wasn't the first time he had gotten himself into this kind of trouble. Húlí—or Fox, the name most knew him as—was excellent at putting himself in a tricky situation, especially if it involved a good-looking human male. His energy was running low again, and he craved the boost a love tryst always gave him. Unlike on previous occasions, this time the handsome male in question had been fully aware of Húlí's true identity and had taken precautions. Thus the fact that he was now being chased across the Shadow Forest by a team of at least three hungry, magically enhanced hounds.

A small cottage popped into view on the horizon as if a magician had clicked his fingers—or whatever it was they did—and produced it out of thin air. It was a humble abode surrounded by a vegetable garden and a mini orchard. He sniffed the air but couldn't detect any danger as he drew closer.

Behind him the barking continued relentlessly. They'd be upon him soon unless he figured out a way of retracting his tails. Once his tails were out of sight, they'd lose his scent.

Húlí rushed toward the wooden door, hoping it was unlocked and that whoever lived there had vacated the place. Once he was inside, he'd be temporarily protected from the hounds' sense of smell long enough to calm down and get rid of his tails. At least that's what he hoped.

Busting through the unlocked door, Húlí uttered a quiet thank you, the momentum almost throwing him into the roaring fire in the hearth directly across from the entrance.

"Who the hell are you?" a voice exploded behind him.

Shit! The house was not empty after all. Awesome. *Now I have to deal with this human too.*

"Close the fucking door," Húlí begged, bracing his hands on his knees and trying hard to regain his composure. Even a fox like him got winded after such an intense chase.

"Not unless you tell me who you are," the human male said.

Húlí turned halfway to look at him. Couldn't he see his red tails, gloriously—and unwisely—unfurled behind him? Right, he couldn't. Húlí had no control over the scent his tails exuded but he could glamour them from humans.

"I'm being chased," he sputtered, trying to catch his breath. "Please, can you close the door? I will tell you everything afterward."

The male, a tall young specimen with a mop of dark curly hair carelessly gathered into a high pony-tail hesitated for a heartbeat before doing as he was asked.

"Thank you," Húlí whispered, a sigh of relief escaping his lips. Now, he could slow his heart down and cut the trail of his scent. Brushing off the dust from his clothing, he took deep breaths and checked for damage caused by the chase. His arms and hands were scratched and bleeding, leaving a trail of red stains on his light blue long tunic. "Shit. Now I will have to trash my clothes. I liked this *shan yi*." His outrage only grew when he found a large rip on his left side where one of the hounds had sunk its teeth in. "Damn dogs."

Húlí shook himself off, his tails swooshing as he moved. *Good, they're retracting.* The sound of his pursuers was getting closer, but he wasn't as worried anymore. In a few more seconds, his scent would be back to human only and the hounds would lose his track. He lifted his gaze to the other man and was surprised to meet a pair of intense lavender eyes studying him.

"Who are you?" the man asked, crossing his arms over his chest. He cocked his head to the side. "Why are you being chased by the hounds?" There was sharp intelligence in those beautifully shaped eyes; they were finely cut jewels that glinted in the dim light of the fire.

Not jewels. Petals of a lotus flower. Exquisite.

"It's a long story," Húlí muttered, one last swoosh telling him his tails were finally fully hidden. "I don't want to bore you with it."

The stranger anchored his feet solidly on the ground and twisted his full lips into a half smile. "I have all day and nothing interesting to do."

Damn, he's no chump.

Húlí hesitated. For once he was lost for excuses. What could he possibly say? There weren't that many reasons why someone would be chased by the hounds.

"I may have stepped on someone's toes," he offered weakly, still unable to look away from the stranger's eyes. "Someone rather important." That much was true. The prince he had tried to seduce was a favorite of the emperor. His first mistake in a row of many.

"How?" When Húlí cocked his head in confusion, the stranger added, "How did you step on their toes?"

Húlí looked down and grinned, wiggling his toes inside his black leather boots. "I have big feet, really big feet," he quipped before looking up at the other man again. "You know what they say about the size of a man's feet, don't you?"

The stranger was not amused. He stood still with his powerful arms crossed over his chest. "Stop making jokes and tell me the truth or I will throw you to the hounds." Húlí didn't doubt he would do it.

"I tried to seduce one of the minor princes," he confessed, his retracted tails twitching in response. "He didn't like it a bit."

"How did he know you're a nine-tailed fox?"

He might as well have thrown a table at Húlí's head. How did the man know that?

"I saw your tails and ears when you came in." That both explained it and totally muddled things even more.

"How can you...?" No one could see his tails unless he chose to let them.

"I have my ways." The cryptic answer didn't explain anything. "How did the princeling find out?"

Still bewildered, Húlí licked his lips and tilted his head the way foxes did. "Someone I used to trust ratted me out." It still stung. He had fully trusted this friend—no, obviously not a friend. Betrayal tasted bitter, but the fact that Húlí had been stupid and innocent enough to trust Xu Ming tasted even worse. Innocent was never a term anyone had ever used to describe Húlí, not even himself. He knew better than to trust anyone. The world was full of rats, and he refused to be their prey.

The barking was so close now, it vibrated through the wooden house. A moment of panic seized Húlí. Was the tall stranger going to throw him to the wolves—well, the hounds? He stole a desperate glance at the other man, trying to decipher his expression without much success. This was someone who didn't wear his feelings for others to see but kept them hidden deeply inside instead. The perfect poker face.

After a moment of silence, the man strode to the door and opened it wide.

Shit! He's going to give me up.

The hounds stopped a few feet shy of the house, and the guards who followed them stared curiously at the guy whose body completely filled the door frame. "Why are you here?" he asked the guards, a subtle note of displeasure coloring his voice.

One of the guards called the hounds closer to him before responding. "We're looking for a demon," he said. Húlí cringed at the term. Why did people insist on calling his kind demons? It sounded so evil. "Have you seen it?"

Húlí's heart stopped for a second. Was the man going to give him away? Instinctively, he got ready to run. It would be a mad chase, but at least he had the advantage of no longer having a fox scent now.

"Not a soul."

Húlí exhaled a loud breath of relief.

The guard cocked his head, his gaze focusing inside the cabin. "Who's that, then?" he asked, pointing at Húlí, whose heart fell to his feet again.

The man turned halfway toward him. "That?" he asked as if there were more than one person inside the house. "That's my lover. He's been here since yesterday."

If the hungry hounds weren't salivating over the pebbles of the path outside, Húlí would have hugged his savior. As it was, all he could do was smile at him, a silent thank you in the upturn of his lips.

The guard snorted at the word lover as if it was filthy. "Are you certain you didn't see a fox dash through here?"

"You asked me about a demon," the stranger said, no change in his tone. "Not a fox."

"Semantics," the guard exclaimed, disapproval plastered on his face. "Well, did you?"

The man who had saved his hide nodded to the right. "A fox went that way just a few minutes ago. But no demon."

Húlí was both impressed and a bit in love with that man who had the balls to challenge the popular belief that foxes were demons in such an open way. Not to mention he was also not afraid of provoking the disdain of the guards by declaring himself queer. The men who were picked for the special royal guard were trained to hate anyone who was different from the accepted norm. After all, hate could always be used as a weapon.

"Let's go." The guard gestured to the other three guards to follow him before mumbling a slur under his breath. "Let's catch the fox."

They both stood watching as the guards and their hounds filed away from the cabin and into the thickest part of the woods, where the stranger had lied about seeing a fox. Húlí stepped outside as soon as they vanished between the trees and stood beside his savior.

"Thank you for helping me," he said. "But why did you do it?"

"I don't like the guards and their hounds," he declared in the same tone of voice he had been using all along. There was a finality to his statement that didn't invite any more questions. Húlí let it go. "Are you hungry?"

Was he ever! The race through the Shadow Forest had him famished. He nodded, hoping the man wouldn't change his mind about feeding him.

"I have a rabbit in the hearth," he said. "You're welcome to join me if you'd like."

He didn't have to invite him twice. Fox followed him inside, mouth watering at the aroma of the rabbit cooking over the fire. How could he have missed it when he first arrived?

"It smells heavenly," Húlí said, rubbing his hands together. "Thank you for the invite."

"Don't thank me yet," he said. "You might still regret having accepted it."

Now, what exactly did he mean by that?

Xiāo Yıng was the stranger's name. The tall, impressive man sat across from Húlí at a small wooden table made for two. The cabin could barely be called a house, consisting of one small room, a bathroom, and a separate outdoor kitchen. It was comfortable though, heated by the roaring fire in the hearth, a small bed hidden in a niche by translucent curtains, and floor cushions scattered around. Húlí had to wonder whether the space was as small as it felt or if it had something to do with the size of his table companion, a giant of a man who, even sitting down, towered over him.

"Thank you again for covering my butt out there," Húlí said for the third or fourth time. He was never at a loss for words, but in the presence of this handsome taciturn giant, his tongue—or his brain—refused to work properly. When Xiǎo Ying nodded and grunted his assent, Húlí sighed. "You're not much of a conversationalist, are you?"

The man did look up at him then, a ghost of a smile on his well-defined lips. "I don't get many visitors," he said, surprising Húlí. "Forgive me."

Xiǎo Ying was very handsome. Hot, really! Even though he had a lovely face with fine bones and high cheeks, he was all male, which pleased Fox to no end. His long ink-black hair was tied in a high pony-tail that swayed back and forth every time he moved, making Húlí's fingers itch to touch it.

Stuffing a piece of meat in his mouth, Húlí mumbled, "And the food is delicious. I was very hungry after running for a couple of miles."

"Why did you seduce someone who was close to the emperor?" The question came out of nowhere and threw Húlí into a coughing fit. "It seems like a rather stupid thing to do."

This guy didn't believe in beating around the bush. Húlí liked that. "It *was* stupid," he admitted. "But sometimes my need to replenish my energy takes over my brain."

Xiǎo Ying blinked twice. "So you think with your dick, then?"

Another coughing attack assailed Fox, laughter mixing with it. "You can say that, I guess," he said, once he was able to. "I prefer to think about it as my reckless side. It sounds a lot sexier, don't you think?"

The other man swallowed a bite and said, "Reckless is just another word for stupid."

Húlí flattened his palm on his chest. "That is very hurtful, Xiǎo *shàoyé*," he said, feigning outrage. "I'm a fox, and that's how foxes are: smart but reckless."

The giant continued eating while he studied Fox for a moment, his face devoid of expression.

A question had been nagging Húlí for a while. "How come you could see my tails? I had them glamoured." He was the first human ever to see through his magic. It both intrigued and worried him.

"I have a gift," the giant said. "Glamours don't quite work on me. Not fully anyway."

Interesting. I wonder why.

"So you let me stay and chose to protect me even though you knew I was a demon." The word stumbled out of his mouth, coated in acid. There was nothing he hated more than being categorized as a demon, a *yāomó*.

"Foxes are not demons. I can't in good conscience help someone who thinks that," Xiǎo Ying said, his eyes on his food. Húlí smiled. This man might claim he's immune to glamours, but Húlí's charm seemed to work anyway. "Don't flatter yourself. It had nothing to do with you personally." Could this guy read minds too? "And no, I can't read minds. I'm just really good at reading facial expressions."

Húlí wouldn't point out that Xiǎo Ying wasn't even looking at his face. How could he read it? "Well, I'm still grateful. The prince I had my eye on had been warned by someone I considered a friend, and he had the demon guard waiting for me when I showed up at his palace." Why did he suddenly feel the need to explain things to this stranger? Húlí had never felt compelled to reveal anything about his life or behavior to anyone before. "It wasn't a good day for me."

"Maybe if you stopped seducing people and allowed them to get to know you first, this wouldn't happen." The suggestion was made so casually, Húlí wasn't even sure he had heard correctly. The man lifted his gaze to him. "Ever heard of courtship?"

After a moment of stunned paralysis, Húlí burst out laughing. "Courtship? What courtship?" he exclaimed. "I'm a fox. Once they know who I am, they all run for the hills. I'm a demon. I'm evil and lowly." Even though he said the words in jest, they still burned in his tongue, bitterness closing a tight fist around his heart. It didn't matter that he was nobility; all people remembered and cared about was his demon ancestry.

"If you believe that yourself, why would others think otherwise?" the stranger said with maddening logic.

What business was of his anyway? Húlí was happy with his life. Most of the time. He enjoyed living a life of wild abandon. The danger that always lurked at the corners only enhanced the excitement, the thrill of the hunt, so to speak. He was not interested in real relationships, in the feeling of belonging somewhere. He was a free agent, roaming wherever he pleased whenever he wanted.

Húlí stood up a bit too fast, sending the chair skittering a few inches over the wooden floor behind him. "Anyway, thank you for your help, but I have to go." He bowed briefly. "*Bǎozhòng.*"

He turned to leave, but the other man stood up and blocked his way to the door. "I noticed you using the old language. Are you a Xi?"

The comment froze Fox. How did he know about the Xi? Not many remembered his family roots, the Xi dynasty that had spawned many *yāomó* like him during a time when being a demon was not considered a bad thing, when magic was appreciated, not reviled.

"How do you know about the Xi?"

Traces of a smile, however wan, curved the man's full lips. "I read a lot." Like that explained everything. Húlí almost snorted. "You should try it."

What did this Xiǎo Ying person know about what he did? He might be a free spirit, wild and unrestrained, but he was also a reader. In fact, his waist pouch cradled his current read, a forbidden literary work that only a few were able to get their hands on. Good thing he had skills that included being able to stealthily enter private and well-guarded libraries.

Before he could protest, the giant moved aside. "Well met, *shàoyé*. I'm sure we'll meet again."

Húlí stole a glance at the other man and smirked.

Not if I can help it.

CHAPTER 2
R☾TLESS
HÚLÍ

"I'm not carrying your drunken, sorry ass up the stairs, Húlí," Ling Ling exclaimed, crossing her arms over her breasts, the silky cloth of her dress gathering closer to her neck. "Will you just stop drinking?" When Húlí did nothing but wave a dismissal, she stuck her lower lip out in a pout. "Come on, Fox, be a good friend for once and don't make me have to drag you up the steps. After the last time, my back was thrown out for days."

Ling Ling may look weak, but she had the strength of a warrior, and she had often kicked his butt in fights. Húlí was not really drunk yet, but it was convenient that everyone else thought he was. It prevented people from expecting too much from him, especially his female friend who asked too many questions and had too high of an opinion about his abilities and wisdom. He preferred to be thought of as a screwup. It made things so much easier.

"Shut up and sit," he said, raising his ceramic glass. "Be a good friend and pour me another drink." When she didn't make a move to do so, he grabbed the round bottle and poured it himself. "Drink with me." She shook her head. "Please, just one more, and then I promise I'll go to bed."

She hesitated then, her pout turning into a thin smile. "Promise? For real?"

She was right to doubt his word. Húlí wouldn't trust himself either. But he really meant it this time. He just wanted to be boozed enough to forget the emptiness inside of him, the yearning for replenishment, and how unwise it would be to go looking for a lover right after what had happened with the prince. Surely all the locals were now alarmed about the *yāomó* in Taihu, and Húlí definitely couldn't hunt in Suhou where he currently lived.

Ling Ling dropped onto the floor cushion and poured herself a glass of wine, scowling as the strong drink slid down her throat. "Shit. What kind of wine is this? It tastes like straight alcohol."

Húlí chuckled. When he had first moved into the inn, the innkeeper had tried to sell him watered-down wine that wouldn't make you drunk unless you drank a shitload of bottles. After a lively discussion that involved some well-placed threats and punches, the innkeeper enlisted another local wine merchant to supply him with strong, full-bodied drink. It took a lot to get Fox drunk, but he was never above pretending.

"Can you stop sulking and be a man?" his friend said, spitting out whatever leftover wine she still had in her mouth.

"But I am not a man, according to the authorities," Húlí said. "I'm a *yāomó,* hardly worthy of being alive." Realizing he had spoken too loud, he lowered his voice to a whisper. "How can I be a man?"

"Don't be stupid," Ling Ling said, leaning in. "You're more man than most. But act like it, damn it! So what if the stupid prince sicced his hounds on you? His loss. Who wouldn't want the pleasure of your, ehm, company?"

He chuckled again. "Are you volunteering for the job?"

Ling Ling barked out a boisterous laugh. "Hell no! You don't like my kind, and I don't like being second choice." Yes, the female kind was not his preference. And even if it was, Ling Ling was a friend, the only one he had left after the princeling debacle, and he was not about to lose her just to replenish his energy.

A commotion in the street made them both look up and out the door. Húlí jumped to his feet, suddenly more than sober. Was that barking he heard? Ling Ling also stood, gesturing for him to stay still while she checked it out. She stuck her head out the door and laughed.

Húlí tried to peek around her, but her body pretty much filled the narrow doorway. "What is it? Is it the hounds?"

She turned around to face him. "No, only a dog chasing a butcher."

He crossed the space between them and joined her to watch the hilarious scene outside. The local butcher, a man in his early forties, dashed through the busy, merchant-packed street with a large chunk of meat cradled in his arms and a mangy black dog chasing close behind him. Both shoppers and merchants lined up the street, watching the mad chase, some applauding as if watching a grand performance, others laughing. Some of the children had taken after them, screeching and trailing bubbles of laughter behind them.

Ling Ling laughed. "The poor dog is hungry," she said, pointing at the running pair. "Why doesn't the man just give it a piece of the meat?"

"*Xiǎoqì*," Húlí exclaimed. "Stingy little man, as if a piece of meat would bankrupt him." It made him angry that this petty man would rather be humiliated in front of a whole town than offer the poor dog the proverbial bone. Wasn't there any compassion left in the world?

Just as he was turning away from the spectacle, the wild pursuit came to an abrupt halt. Silence fell on the street as the crowd turned their eyes to what had caused it. A tall figure, all dressed in white, was blocking the path. Even the dog had stopped, as if the man's raised hand held some kind of magic.

"Why would you not feed this creature?" The voice of the mystery man sounded oddly familiar to Húlí.

He zoomed in on the white blur at the end of the street, squinting and turning on the power of his fox eyes. "Holy shit!" he exclaimed. Ling Ling turned to him, surprised. "That's Xiǎo Ying, my savior from the other day."

Ling Ling pressed her lips together. "You mean the guy who lied to the guards to help you?" she asked after a moment.

Húlí nodded. "One and the same." You had to admire a guy who, by the simple action of standing in the middle of the street, managed to stop the town. Even the dog had halted its progress, licking its chops and sitting on its haunches. "He's impressive, isn't he?"

His friend made an appreciative click of the tongue. "You didn't tell me how handsome he was." She crossed her arms and leaned against the door frame. "Were you afraid I'd be competition?"

The memory of what he had told the guards, presumably to give Húlí a solid alibi, came rushing back and heat crawled up his neck. "You can have him. Not interested." Was that a lie? He couldn't be sure. Xiǎo Ying hadn't popped into his mind since that fateful day almost two weeks ago, but the fact remained that as he watched the giant stand out in the street, something in him stirred, and it wasn't the strong wine in his gut.

"This is my meat," the skinny butcher said, finally finding his voice. "I have a family to feed." Whispers undulated through the gathered crowd. "I can't be feeding every stray in town, now, can I?"

"This poor *gǒu* is hardly every stray in town, don't you think?" Xiǎo Ying retorted, pointing at the dog that seemed to listen attentively to the conversation, his head cocked. "How much do you want for a chunk of that meat? I will buy it from you."

The butcher tilted his head in a comically similar way to the dog behind him. "You want to buy the meat for the dog? Is it yours?"

The tall man shook his head. "It is obviously hungry," he said. "Why not give him what he needs? Didn't Confucius say that compassion is one of the three universally recognized moral qualities of men?"

The quote from the ancient philosopher both surprised and pleased Húlí. The old wisdom had long been forgotten by the population at large, remembered only by scholars and historians. Or those few left in the Xi family. Could this man be one of his relatives? No, it couldn't be. He was no *yāomó* like the Xi, so maybe he was a scholar.

"I don't know anything about a Confusion," the butcher said, mangling the name. "But I will sell you the meat if you pay well."

Xiǎo Ying stepped forward, digging inside his sleeve pocket for something. "Will ten *jīnzi* be enough?" He extended an open palm to the butcher, who stretched his neck to inspect its contents. Húlí couldn't see the man's face from where he was standing, but the enthusiastic nod of his head told him he was pleased with the price.

Ling Ling whistled. "Ten *jīnzi* for a piece of meat? Wow, this guy must be loaded." She half turned to her friend. "I will definitely go for him if you don't want him."

Húlí chuckled softly. "You speak as if he has no will of his own." Interesting that he, a nine-tailed fox, would say something like that. Wasn't that what he did? Take what was not freely given? He shook his head, annoyed with himself. No, that wasn't true. Everything he did was consensual. He would never, ever force anyone no matter how desperate he might be for the burst of *qi*. He may use his special gifts to seduce and speed up the process but not to change anyone's mind.

"Look!" Ling Ling exclaimed, pushing away from the door frame and straightening.

Húlí followed her gaze. Xiǎo Ying was crouching by the almost skeletal dog and hand-feeding it the meat he had just bought for far more than what it was worth. The dog took small bites of the meat, surprisingly gentle and cautious of the hand that fed him. The giant's free hand caressed the canine's midnight-black head, and his lips moved. Húlí sharpened his fox ears to listen in, curious and strangely touched by the stranger's gentleness and compassion.

"Good boy," Xiǎo Yíng whispered to the dog. "If you want, you can be my family from now on. I can't give you much but good food, a warm bed, and lots of belly rubs. What do you say?" The dog seemed to understand his words, stopping its chewing to bark softly in response and wag its tail. Xiǎo Yíng smiled. "Good, that's settled then. You need a name." The gentle giant thought for a moment, lost inside himself. "I know. How do you feel about Yè Yǐng?"

He was giving the dog an old language name, Night Shade, which was perfect for it considering the dog's coloring. Húlí's respect for the guy went up a few more points, however reluctantly.

The dog barked again before it resumed eating. "Glad you like it, Yè Yǐng. Let's go home."

Húlí watched as man and dog walked side by side like old friends while life returned to normal in the busy street. "Why are you smiling?" Ling Ling asked, squinting at him.

"I'm not." But he knew he was. He could feel the stretch of his lips across his face, the crinkling of the skin at the corners of his eyes, and the sparkling of something unfamiliar, uncomfortable in its warmth and strength, inside him.

Was that the blooming of hope he was feeling?

Húlí stomped on the floor and regretted it immediately. He was so weak, even that small show of anger made his whole body vibrate in pain. "Not going," he managed to say, wincing.

"Don't be so stubborn, Fox," Ling Ling tapped her foot on the wooden floor, a sure sign she wasn't happy with his reluctance to accept her offer. "Look at you: you're miserable and can barely get out of bed these days. What other choice do you have? That idiot prince is still after your tail—pardon the pun—and you need to replenish your *qi*."

Painfully slowly, he hoisted his right leg over the other knee and tried to massage the pain away. It wasn't working. Every muscle in his body was sore and cold. Despite the winter clothing he had on, Húlí still shivered in the spring-warm morning.

"How do I know this guy is trustworthy?" he asked, rubbing a particularly sore spot on his calf. "What if he steals whatever energy I have instead of restoring it? What if he's another hater who's only looking for an excuse to get rid of a *yāomó*?"

The look on his friend's face froze the remainder

of his body heat. "Do you really have such little faith in me that you think I didn't investigate this guy properly before even considering talking to you about it?" Making Ling Ling mad at him was always a great distraction from his own woes. It kept life interesting and his mind occupied. "I researched him, and he has an immaculate record. He is a spiritual healer who went into seclusion a long time ago. He hasn't taken a patient in years."

That drew his attention. He lifted his gaze to her. "Are you telling me that you want me to go beg this hermit for a service he has not provided in years? What makes you think he'll consider it? Money won't sway someone who has forgone worldly possessions, and however charming I can be, I'm so weak right now, I couldn't charm an ant."

"You do realize that I am now exponentially stronger than you, and that I can easily carry you to this guy's house without your consent, right?" She would do it too. There was a familiar glint of determination in her dark eyes. "So, choose wisely, my friend. It would be pretty humiliating to be carried over a woman's shoulders across the busy streets of town, wouldn't it?"

Mortifying was closer to the truth. Despite everything else, he had a reputation to uphold. He was viewed as a charming, strong, and handsome nobleman whom people respected and looked up to in town. At least, that's what he hoped.

"Okay, I'll go." Might as well wave the white flag. Ling Ling was nothing if not persistent, and he wasn't looking for a whole day of constant nagging. "Where is this miracle man you speak of? Do I need to wear my formal clothes?"

Ling Ling took a few steps forward and stared him down. He was still wearing his nightclothes, red curls loose over the white silk of his shirt as he sat on the edge of his bed. Lately he barely had the energy to get up, much less get dressed and washed.

"You look like a ghost, Fox," she concluded after a moment or two. "I'll help you get dressed." Not waiting for the protest she undoubtedly knew was coming, she opened the wardrobe and began shuffling through his clothes. After finding something that pleased her, she threw the clothes at him.

Húlí pulled the clothes that had fallen on his head down onto the bed with him. "You almost took my eye out, woman." She had picked one of his many black tunics. He wore them often when out at night, prowling. He was a fox after all, and hunting was in his blood. When he tried to slip into his tunic, each of his arms weighed a ton, making each tiny movement feel like a colossal effort.

Ling Ling watched him, her lower lip caught in her teeth. "Shit, Fox, you can't even get dressed," she exclaimed, taking a seat next to him and holding on to the edge of the bed. "Never mind. You lay down, and I will go convince the healer to come here." He opened his mouth to protest, but she stopped him by raising her open palm. "No arguments. I'm officially worried about you. I would get you a male whore, but I know how picky you are about your men. Fuck, I would bed you myself if I thought it would help."

He couldn't help but laugh. "No whore in this town would bed a *yāomó*." That was the reason he always hunted outside his village, the farther away, the better. "And women don't work for me, my friend. Thank you for the offer though."

Pulling herself up, Ling Ling moved quickly and grabbed her sword. "I'll be back as soon as I can. You sleep and sip on that tea I brought you." When he didn't respond, she added, "Promise me you'll do it."

He waved a hand and plopped onto his pillow, stretching his long legs on the bed. "I promise. I won't budge until you come back." It wasn't as if he could anyway. With his legs full of lead and his heart beating at such a slow pace, movement was virtually impossible. He really had done it this time.

With his friend gone, Húlí allowed his eyes to close and his mind to drift away into the land of dreams where everything was warm and safe most of the time. The noise of a door opening snapped him awake, and for a moment, he was confused, not sure where he was. His eyelids were as heavy as his head, and it took him some time to be able to open them and focus on who had just walked into his room.

Húlí's voice recovered before his eyes did. "*Nǐ shì shéi?*" He saw the silhouette of a tall person approach his bed, the whiteness of robes resembling a cluster of clouds in his muddled brain. Realizing he had fallen into the old language, Húlí rephrased his question, "Who are you?"

"Stop fretting, Fox." The familiar voice of his friend, Ling Ling, immediately calmed him down. "It's just me and the healer."

Húlí felt rather than saw a body sit on the edge of his bed and take his hand. The man's hand was cool and calloused, not the typical skin of a healer, a fact that made him jittery. He tried to pull his hand away, but the healer held it fast, wrapping his fingers around Húlí's wrist to take his pulse.

"Stay calm," the male voice admonished. There was a familiar tone in his voice, but Húlí didn't know any healers. "If you don't calm yourself down, you will only expend more of the little *qi* you have left."

The man's fingers pressed gently on the inside of his wrist and remained there for a minute or so. Húlí tried to relax into the touch, but his lack of strength and energy rattled him to no end.

"Can you see?" the healer asked, dropping Húlí's hand carefully onto the sheets. When he shook his head, the man added, "Why did you wait so long to replenish your energy?"

Ling Ling answered, "Prince Wu Ying is after him. The royal guard has been alerted, and Fox can't leave town to find the right partner." Húlí would be mortified by her revelation if he had the energy to do so. Sometimes Ling Ling's filter was not completely in place. If he always seemed proud of his powers of seduction, deep inside it was humiliating to know he needed to use them in order to survive.

"There are other ways to do it, you know?" the healer said. "Ways that don't involve risking the wrath of powerful people."

Húlí had much to say about that, but his tongue wasn't working. When strong arms slipped under his armpits to pull him into a sitting position, his heart jumped inside his chest however feebly.

"Help me keep him sitting up," the healer told Ling Ling. "And take off his shirt."

Warm hands worked on the ties of his shirt and quickly but gently divested him of it. Ling Ling sat across from him, her crossed legs touching his while her hands supported his upper body.

He was not sure what to expect from this treatment, but this was not it.

When the healer's palms met the bare skin of his shoulder blades, a surge of power went through him, straightening his back and throwing his head backward. Húlí couldn't help it; he yelped. The sensation was one of pain mixed with pleasure and power as pins and needles covered the surface of his body, digging through his skin into his muscle and sinew, running through his veins into every organ inside him.

It was glorious.

It was terrifying.

Heat transferred from the stranger's hands into his body, burning and soothing at the same time, filling him with life. Húlí had heard of this legendary technique, one he had always thought to be nothing but a myth, or at least a thing of the distant past. As he felt his *qi* refresh and strengthen, he could breathe easier, his legs and arms suddenly light, his mind relaxed.

After a few minutes, the healer removed his hands with a gasp, and Húlí opened his eyes, feeling new and vibrant. Ling Ling was staring at him with an expectant expression, her head cocked to the side. He smiled at her, and she let out a sigh of relief.

Húlí turned around to thank his benefactor and almost fell off the bed. Sitting behind him, looking appallingly pale and shaky, was no one other than Xiǎo Ying.

"You're the healer?" It was more an expression of shock than a question. Húlí opened his mouth to thank him, but he didn't have the chance as he watched his second-time savior close his eyes and collapse unconscious on top of his bed.

CHAPTER 3
THE HEALER
HÚLÍ

Húlí stared at the unconscious healer, too shocked to react. The giant body of Xiǎo Ying, his savior not once but twice, lay on his bed, too pale to be alive.

"Fuck!" Ling Ling exclaimed. "Did you suck up all his *qi*?"

He shook his head in denial. He was not sure what happened, but if he did indeed deprive the healer of all his energy, it had not been a conscious act. After the first moment of paralysis, Húlí jumped into action, checking for signs of life. However shallowly, the man was still breathing, and his heartbeat was weak but definitely audible when Fox placed an ear over his chest. But Xiǎo Ying's skin was cold and clammy, beads of sweat gathering on his forehead.

"Quick, get me extra blankets," Húlí told Ling Ling, who ran to the closet. She came back with a pile of linen just as he began rubbing the man's hands, hoping to create heat. "Pile them up over him."

Together they covered the healer in a collection of blankets, and then Húlí uncovered the man's feet and removed his shoes.

"I'll warm up some water," Ling Ling said, dashing to the tea station in the room.

Húlí began rubbing the giant's feet one at a time. He couldn't let his savior die. How would he be able to live with himself if the man who rescued him lost his life because of him? The new *qi* in his veins gave him the energy he needed to keep his ministrations going when normally his arms would have been starting to hurt. As Ling Ling came back with a cup of warm water, Xiǎo Yīng's toes twitched.

"He's coming to," Húlí said with a sigh of relief.

The small movement was followed by a stronger one, and soon the man's whole body was awakening. Húlí watched in awe as Xiǎo Yīng returned to a state of consciousness one muscle, one joint at a time. His beautifully shaped eyes were the last part of him to twitch and open, the dark pupils adjusting to the light and its surroundings.

"Hello there, stranger," Húlí quipped, unreasonably happy to see the man was all right. "Remember me?"

Xiǎo Ying blinked a few times, flopped gently to his side, and then homed in on Fox's eyes. "You again," he muttered. "Can't seem to get rid of you."

Húlí chuckled. "Well, that's not very friendly, is it? Besides, if you dislike me so much, why did you agree to save my life?" He paused for dramatic effect, raising two fingers in front of his face. "Twice, I should add."

The man coughed and tried to sit up against the head of the bed. Ling Ling rushed to his help, supporting his back and shoulders. "I am a healer. That kind of comes with the job," he said, his raspy voice betraying his weakened state. "Thou shall heal even your enemy."

Fox laughed heartily, throwing his head back. "You're so full of shit," he said, once he managed to control the laughter. "I'm not your enemy, and you probably love the fact that I owe you big, Healer."

Was that a tiny smile on the healer's lips? "Don't flatter yourself," he said. "I didn't realize it was you at first." He took a big breath, as if in need of more oxygen than his regular breathing was providing him. He glanced at Ling Ling who had sat down beside him. "Could you bring me some strengthening tea, please?"

"Ginger?" Ling Ling asked, sliding to her feet.

"That'd be great, thank you," he said. His eyes immediately turned to Húlí. "How are you feeling?"

A little startled by the question, Fox checked his arms and wiggled his fingers. "Much better," he admitted. "My *qi* has been fully recovered." He cocked his head and squinted. "How did you do that? And why did you pass out afterward?"

Xiǎo Ying closed his eyes momentarily. "You were so depleted, I used most of my own to restore it." Guilt filled Húlí. That man had risked his own life to save him. Healer seemed to read his mind. "I just need some time to recover, but I'll be fine."

Ling Ling returned with a tray heavy with a teapot and teacups. She set it down on the small table at the side of the bed and proceeded to pour everyone a cup of tea. "You were amazing, Healer," she said, handing him a small cup. "I have never seen anything like it. I could actually see rainbows of light coming from you into my friend's body."

When she put it like that, it sounded very intimate. Heat rose to Fox's cheeks. What was happening to him? When had he become so bashful?

Mortified, he watched as his friend bowed down

to the healer in thankful submission. "Thank you so much, Healer. Name a price, and I will pay it."

"Are you fucking crazy, woman?" Húlí exclaimed, his eyes widening in horror. "What if he asks for sex? Are you going to debase yourself for me?"

Ling Ling stared him down as if he were the insane one. "You're so stupid, Old Fox," she said with a shake of her head. "Don't you think I discussed it with him before heading here?"

Húlí breathed another sigh of relief. "Thank all the ghosts in heaven," he exclaimed, pressing an open hand to his chest. "For a moment there, I was worried."

She turned to the healer and pinched her lips together. "My friend is not always very smart, obviously. Please, forgive him." She threw Fox another disgusted glance. "I'm sure he's very grateful even though he has not yet said so."

Shit. She was right. He hadn't yet thanked the giant for his help. "I'm eternally grateful, Xiǎo Ying. Truly grateful." He was, but did his sincerity come across in his voice? He couldn't be sure after a lifetime of being disappointed into cynicism. "What can I do to repay you? Anything." Quickly he added, "Within reason, of course."

Xiǎo Ying didn't hesitate. "Take care of my dog."

"What?" Húlí knew he sounded like an idiot, but he couldn't help it. He had just offered to repay a life debt, and Xiǎo Ying wanted him to take care of a dog?

"My dog's alone, and I can't feed him. I won't be able to go anywhere for a while," Xiǎo Ying said. "Will you do that for me?"

Healer's house was in enemy territory, smack in the middle of Taihu. Xiǎo Ying's request was not as risk free as it sounded at first. It gave Húlí pause.

"I can teach you the back way to my place so you can avoid trouble." Again, the man seemed to be able to read Fox's mind. It was a bit off-putting.

In his fox state, Húlí could be in Taihu in about an hour and a half as long as the hounds didn't get a whiff of him. "Will that keep me away from the royal guards?" The other man nodded. He sighed. "All right, I'll do it. I'll go feed Yè Yǐng."

Healer furrowed his brow. "How do you know his name?" he asked.

Ling Ling answered, "We saw the whole scene in town a few weeks ago."

"By the way," Húlí said. "What were you doing so far from home that day?"

"Not that's any of your business, but I needed

some special herbs for my practice, and there's a good merchant in town who carries them." He leaned back onto the pillows, looking as relaxed as if he was only taking an afternoon nap. "Well? Are you going? It will be dark soon."

Giving in, Húlí nodded and sat next to the man to receive instructions on how to reach his house while evading the hounds' notice. He couldn't help inhaling the healer's scent, a mixture of rosemary and lavender, as he sat close to him. Húlí also couldn't stop his heart from doing a crazed tip-tap dance in his chest or avoid the sudden yearning their closeness had triggered.

Neither did he want to.

It was almost dark by the time he spied the healer's house. Húlí was winded, and not because of the run, which was nothing to him, but because of the fear of being spotted by the hounds. He approached the house slowly, one paw after the other as if he was stalking a particularly crafty chicken. In the growing dark, the house loomed in front of his fox-self like an ominous monster, and when a shadow separated from the backdrop of its dark walls and moved toward him, Húlí just about had a heart attack—if foxes could even have one of those.

A low warning growl reached his keen pointy ears. Yè Yǐng advanced toward him, aggressive and cautious at the same time. That dog was no dummy. Húlí tried to call the dog's name, but realized he was still in his fox shape with lips that were not made for words. He breathed deeply and focused on calming his heartbeat down so he could change into human-shape—hopefully before the dog attacked him with the sharp fangs that glittered in the moonlight.

With a shake of his tail, Húlí was able to morph into his human body, the reddish fur he had been sporting just seconds ago now turned into the soft cotton of his red tunic. It was a trick he had learned from his long-gone master when he was still a child. Instead of running around naked after the change, he learned that if he wore simple clothing made of organic materials, he could fuse it into his fox shape and turn to a fully dressed man again.

"Down, Yè Yǐng, down," Húlí whispered, his hand stretched in the dog's direction. "Your master, Xiǎo Ying, sent me to feed you."

At the sound of Xiǎo Ying's name, the canine paused and let out a louder growl that sounded a lot like a question. He whimpered a little and then sat on his hind legs, tongue lolling out of his mouth. He seemed to be studying Fox, deciding whether or not to trust him. Húlí was sure the dog could still smell the remains of his fox scent.

"You must be hungry," Húlí said, keeping his voice soft and nonthreatening. "Where does your master keep the food?"

Yè Yǐng stood up again, barked once, and then turned to walk toward the house. Húlí followed him.

Even though the house had been empty for almost two days, it was still warm and cozy. Memories of his first encounter with the big man came flooding in. It had not been the best of occasions, but then again, in Húlí's life those seemed to be either far and between or involve a lot of alcohol. He chuckled softly, and the dog stopped to stare at him, head cocked to the side.

"Don't mind me," Húlí said. "Just had a funny thought." If the feeling of emptiness could ever be funny.

The canine lost interest in him and led him to a corner of the main room where a large wooden container stood. He opened the lid and got hit by a poof of cold air. *Strange.* The large chunks of meat inside were frosted as if they had been standing out in the snow. *What kind of magic is this?* Shaking his head, Fox scooped up a chunk and threw it at Yè Yǐng. The dog didn't waste any time and chomped down on the meaty treat.

"*Qǐng xiǎngyòng*," Húlí said, falling into the old language as he often did when alone. "Enjoy!" he added, and then laughed at himself. Was he really afraid the dog didn't understand?

While the dog ate, he locked the door and began exploring the place. It was a small house with a main room where Xiǎo Ying ate and slept and a couple smaller rooms reserved for a bathhouse and storage. Looking out through the window, he surveyed the kitchen in the courtyard, a simple structure comprised of a canvas canopy over a couple of counters with two firepits and some kitchen tools. He wondered where the man cooked when the weather was bad.

Finished with his meal, Yè Yǐng sat on his haunches, licking his muzzle and staring at Húlí. The dog had filled out since he had last seen him. Gone were the ribs that poked through the dog's black coat. His matted hair was now clean with a healthy shine to it.

Húlí smiled. "You've been treated like a king, haven't you?" he said, crouching by the animal and petting his head. The creature leaned into his touch, trusting and demanding. "It's nice that you have someone who loves you like that. I'm happy for you." The dog made a funny gurgling noise and rubbed his head on Fox's outer thigh. "Everyone should have someone in their lives who trusts and takes care of them, right?"

The dog barked softly, and Húlí stood up, looking for a place to sleep. Carved into one of the walls was a niche with a simple wooden bed. Húlí took off his outer tunic and shoes, and after pulling the translucent curtains out to the side, he lay down on the bed. The mattress was soft and warm, and in no time, Fox slipped into sleep. Half in dreamland already, he pulled a cover over himself and had the faint feeling something or someone had crawled in bed with him, but he was too tired to care.

The sun woke him up. Through the windows he had forgotten to shutter the night before, the bright rays of the large star teased his eyes open like a playful lover after a long night. He opened them slowly, reluctantly. The bed was cozy, and a soft body stretched along his backside, warming his skin and muscles.

A warm body? Who had he gone to bed with the night before?

He sat up straight. Next to him, a black bundle of fur lay still, peacefully asleep against his side.

"Yè Yǐng, you son of a bitch," Húlí exclaimed with a sigh of relief. "You scared the shit out of me. I don't need to be bringing any Taihu natives into my bed right now."

The dog didn't budge, safe in the knowledge he had a master who loved and protected him. How wonderful would that feel, having someone who loves you so much you don't have to worry about your safety? Not a feeling he was familiar with. His own family was dead and gone when he was but a pup, and he had been brought up by his master whose identity was to this day still a bit of a mystery. Húlí had always called him uncle, but he couldn't be sure they were actually related by blood or even marriage.

Shūshu was not a fox, but he definitely had knowledge far beyond that of a normal human. In his preteen years, Húlí had fancied his uncle to be an immortal, a god of some sort, and his sudden and unexplained disappearance when Húlí was sixteen did nothing but reinforce that idea. Everyone knew that immortals had to go through trials that included a stint in the mortal world. As Húlí grew up into a man and tasted every disappointment and hurt known to humans, he didn't believe that anymore. *Shūshu* had simply left like everyone else in his life had. No big mystery, no grand explanation. Húlí was simply a *yāomó*, a demon who no one cared to have around.

Yè Yǐng was sleeping so soundly, Húlí didn't have the heart to wake him up. "You sleep in while I go scrape together something to eat," he told him, pulling the covers away. "How do you feel about going back with me? Your master has a few days of recovery ahead, and I really don't like being in enemy territory."

The dog didn't answer, but Fox had made up his mind; after breakfast they would set out back home.

CHAPTER 4
HEALING
HÚLÍ

Yè Yǐng was a quiet companion, the pads of his paws soft on the ground behind Húlí as they both ran the path Xiǎo Ying had drawn for him before he left. The dog had been a bit skittish when Húlí first changed into his fox shape, but then he quickly adapted and had no qualms about following him back to his master. The dog was better than most humans.

At first, Húlí had thought of waiting it out until the cover of darkness but, as unwise at it might be, his restlessness and fear of being in Taihu won, and they had set out as soon as they finished the last bite of their makeshift breakfast. Against all odds they made great time, and no danger came to haunt their progress. Húlí stopped temporarily on the outskirts of town to change back into his human form, and they walked together that last mile through the busy streets.

It was market day, and the town was bustling with activity. Even the air was crowded with the sounds of talking, the merchants' calls, children's laughter, and the cacophony of animal sounds as chickens, ducks, and other creatures were gathered for sale.

Ling Ling was seated on the stoop in front of the inn where they both lived, her sword lying beside her and her lips wrapped around the biggest steamed bun he had ever seen.

"I feel oddly turned on by this sight," he said when he was close enough for her to hear. "I need a cleansing now."

Her shiny dark eyes honed in on him. "You're back, Old Fox!" Jumping to her feet, bun forgotten, she crossed the space between them and hugged him.

He grunted. "Don't get your hopes up, woman. I'm still very gay." Húlí tried to disengage her arms from his neck, but her grip only tightened. "You're going to kill me."

That's when she noticed the black dog looking at them with its head cocked to the side like a spectator watching a show. "That's the dog from the other day," she explained unnecessarily. "Yè Yǐng, right?"

The dog barked in response, and she chuckled.

"Gods, give me patience. The dog likes her." Húlí shook his head in disbelief, but deep inside, he knew it was almost impossible to not like his friend. She might be a bit rough around the edges, but she had a heart of gold, and he loved her to death. "Where's Healer?"

She nodded toward the inn. "In your room. He is a bit stronger but still has trouble moving around."

Lovely.

He now had a permanent tenant in his own bed. A good looking one for sure, but his room was off limits for lovers. It was, after all, his private haven. Sure, it was but a room in an inn, and not even a great one at that, but it was his, the only place he could call his own. The one place where he could be himself with no fear of judgment.

"When will he be moving out?" He had to ask. As grateful as he was for Healer's help in restoring his *qi*, he still didn't want a long-term guest in his room.

"As soon as he is strong enough," Ling Ling said. "Let's go see your master, Yè Yǐng." Dog and female took to the stairs, rushing up to where Healer was blissfully occupying a space that didn't belong to him.

Húlí sighed, half resigned. "My life just gets better and better." He followed the female warrior up the stairs into the inn.

The place was still mostly empty, the bustle of the midday meal not quite started yet. A few scattered patrons sat at tables inside, sleepily enjoying their breakfasts in silence. In another couple hours, and against all odds, the place would be busting at the seams as the inn's chef's dubious cooking attracted masses of locals and travelers.

Húlí glanced ahead of him, searching for his friend and the dog who had already vanished around the corner. He let out another sigh and picked up the pace, his legs sore from the run. He could use a long hot bath. Maybe he could convince Ling Ling to wrangle him one. His friend had a gift for coaxing the often reluctant and grumpy innkeeper to do her bidding. He suspected the older man was irrevocably in love with beautiful Ling Ling, and who could blame him? Húlí himself lived in awe of her. He often thought that if his preferences didn't steer completely to other males, he would also be in love with her. Smart, pretty, skilled, and fun. What more could anyone ask from another human being?

"You move like a slug," she said as soon as he walked into the room. "I thought foxes were supposed to be fast."

The so-called fox bent over, supporting his upper body on his knees and breathing hard. "This fox just ran the equivalent of a two-day horse ride twice within a couple of days. So give me the grace of a break."

She chuckled. "That rhymes." Leave it to her to notice silly stuff like that.

After a couple of deep breaths, Húlí straightened his back and froze. Xiǎo Yīng was sitting on the edge of his bed, dressed in immaculate white flowing robes, his long ebony hair spilling over his shoulders in a silky cascade. The man was beautiful. How had Húlí not noticed it before? Healer raised his intense gaze to Húlí, the sharp slope of his nose contrasting the softness and grace of his petal-shaped eyes. Húlí swallowed hard, steering his eyes to Healer's lips, a masterpiece of fullness and deep color.

Control yourself! The man saved your butt.

"How are you feeling?" Húlí squeaked out. He cleared his throat before adding, "Are you recovered?"

The man's delicious mouth stretched into a sarcastic smile. "In a hurry to get rid of me?"

He was. His fox nature would make it very difficult to resist his sexual attraction toward this giant of a man. The man had saved his skin twice. Húlí didn't want to repay him by using his magical powers of seduction on him. Fox wouldn't be able to live with himself if he did.

"I am feeling better," Xiǎo Ying said, running his hand over the top of the dog's head. "A few more days and I should be able to return home. Don't worry, I won't overstay my welcome."

"*Bù, bù,*" Húlí rushed to assure him, shaking his hands in front of him. "I mean, no. You saved my life. You can stay as long as you want."

Maybe forever.

Fox tried to shake that thought out of his head. What the hell was he thinking? Why would he want that stranger to stay forever? They had just met and —well, he was a *yāomó*. No one would ever want a real relationship with a demon. Prejudice against his kind was prevalent and insidious. He had been told so many times he was trash that he had started believing it himself at some point.

Yè Yǐng, in obvious rapture under the tender ministrations of his master, whined softly. "Good boy," Xiǎo Ying cooed. Not bothering to look up, he added, "No need for thanks. It was the right thing to do. But you must learn different ways to replenish your *qi* or you'll be constantly in danger."

What other ways were there? The only way he knew how was by seducing and absorbing sexual energy from others. His master had never mentioned anything else. Of course, he had disappeared too soon from Húlí's life. Who knew how much more he would have learned from him if he had been around longer?

"I'm open to suggestions," he said, an edge of resentment in his voice. "Even though the way I do it is pleasant and exciting." And often degrading. But he wouldn't mention that.

Healer lifted the corners of his lips higher. "You have a lot to learn, Húlí *shàoyé*." The man's use of the old language made his heart beat faster and brought heat to his cheeks. "I'll be glad to teach you."

And, despite his oversensitive defense instincts, he was very willing to learn.

"REMIND me why I let you talk me into this?" Húlí asked, placing his hands on his waist and frowning at the wooden chessboard. On the other side of the board, Healer sat placidly, watching his opponent steam over the fact that he was losing the game. "This is an impossible game. No matter what move I make, I'll lose."

"You're such a fucking sore loser, Fox," Ling Ling yelled from the other side of the room. "Grow up and take it like a man."

Húlí turned his head to her and blinked a few times. "Says the woman who throws a tantrum every time I beat her at archery."

"That's because you cheat, Old Fox."

It was true. He did cheat often. Not when he was the one doing the shooting, but when his friend did. He always managed to find a way to distract her just enough to skew her aim. Nevertheless, he wouldn't give her the satisfaction.

"Healer is a lot better at chess than you. Admit it and move on."

He would do no such thing. He would beat the handsome Xiǎo Ying yet. He just had to practice more. And maybe cheat a little.

"Losing is part of winning," Healer said, not bothering to move his gaze from the disgruntled fox.

He could be so annoying sometimes. Not to mention cryptic. He had been Húlí's guest now for over a week, and even though he was so quiet, it would be easy to forget he was there, he'd been sleeping in Húlí's bed, which meant one thing: Fox had to sleep curled up on the floor with the dog. Even his inner fox disliked that, craving for the softness of the mattress and the warmth of the bedclothes.

"Very deep, but losing is losing no matter how you dress it," he said, dropping his hands alongside his body and his head down until his forehead touched the edge of the table. "I surrender." It came out like a whimper, and he was immediately embarrassed by it.

He heard Ling Ling snort across the room, but no sound came from his opponent. He turned his face up just enough to steal a glance at him. The man was still sitting up, straight like a rod, not a hint of a smile on his lips. As their eyes met, Xiǎo Ying raised one single eyebrow.

"How do you do that?" Húlí asked. He wagged a finger in his direction. "The eyebrow thing? It's kind of creepy."

"It's a gift." Didn't his spine bend like everybody else's? How could he sit so still and so straight? "Are you going to make a move, or should I take a nap while I wait?"

Another snort from the female warrior reached Fox's sensitive ears. "If you think it's that funny, woman, you should come and play with this guy."

"*Hǎo*," she exclaimed, striding toward them with wide, determined steps. "Move aside and I'll show you how it's done." She pulled up a nearby stool and sat next to him, pushing him roughly out of the way. "Watch me."

"This I've got to see," he said, leaning over and resting his chin on his hand.

Ling Ling studied the board for a few seconds before making her move. Why was she moving that piece there? Too risky. The icicle across the table made another move, trapping her game piece just like Húlì thought he would. Ling Ling moved another one. Yet again, a risky, foolhardy choice, because Healer immediately seized it. Another move and another, all of them foolish and poorly thought through. Ling Ling was normally not that careless. What was going on?

"First rule of the game of war: take them by surprise and you up your chances of winning," the female warrior said, her lips twisted into a sardonic smile. She leaned over to push another game piece across the board. "I win, my friend."

"What the hell?" Húlì jumped off his stool,

sending it skittering along the wooden floor. "How did you do that?"

Much to his surprise, Healer barked out a laugh. "Smart warrior. She lulled the opponent into thinking he was winning, and then, boom, she made her winning move," he said, clapping his hands a couple times. "*Zuò dé hǎo*. Well done."

A smug smile erupted on Ling Ling's lips. "I told you I was a master in strategy," she said, raising her eyebrows. "But I think our friend here was onto me and just let it happen." She turned to Xiǎo Ying. "Right?"

Healer nodded once. "You're right. I wanted to see if you could do it," he said. "And you certainly can. Ming Xin *shàoyé*, you're lucky to have someone like her by your side."

Húlí's eyes rounded. "How do you know my real name?" In this world, only Ling Ling knew his name, Xi Ming Xin. Not a lot of his kind had survived the centuries of persecution, much less those who were Xi like him. It was better to keep it under wraps and not stir up memories better left in the distant past.

Ling Ling's mouth had fallen open. "Yes, how do you know that?" she asked, her brows knitted together.

Xiǎo Ying opened his mouth to answer, but Húlí

stopped him. "And don't say it's a gift," he said. "That's getting old. I want the truth."

Healer waited for a moment as if weighing his choices. What kind of cockamamie excuse was he going to give them now?

"*Hǎo*," he started. "If it's the truth you want, the truth you will get."

CHAPTER 5
TRUTH
HÚLÍ

Ling Ling had pulled the stool even closer to them and leaned over the chessboard, propping her elbow on the table and her chin on her hand. Húlí couldn't blame her curiosity. He himself was tingling in anticipation—for what, he wasn't sure. The truth could be a good thing or maybe something disastrous to his survival.

"Well, let's have it," he said, his voice trembling a little.

Healer didn't even blink, staring at him with emotionless eyes. No! Maybe impassive, but not without emotion. Húlí thought he detected a twinge of—what? Regret? Pity? Compassion? The man was impossible to read.

"Remember *shūshu*?" Xiǎo Ying asked unexpectedly.

Fox straightened on his stool. His uncle? "Of course I remember him. He was my master." And his only family really. "How do you know about him?"

"He's my master too."

Shūshu had other students? Húlí always thought he was the only one, since his master had never spoken of anyone else. Shock paralyzed him for a moment. Then that usual distrust he had so carefully cultivated throughout his adult life came back with a vengeance. "Not possible. I was his only student."

"Did he tell you that?" What kind of question was that? His master didn't have to tell him. He just knew. "Weren't there times when he disappeared for a few weeks and didn't tell you where he was?"

Shit. How did he know that? "He was in seclusion, renewing his *qi*." Or so he had assumed at the time.

Xiǎo Ying shook his head slowly. "*Bù.* He was with me."

"Wait!" Ling Ling exclaimed, slapping the top of the table and almost tipping over the chessboard. "Are you saying you guys have the same master?"

Xiǎo Ying nodded. "How do you know about this Old Fox, but he doesn't know about you?"

"*Shūshu* was my master before he was Ming Xin's." Which, in a crazy sort of way, actually made sense. Healer was older than Húlí. "*Shūshu* found out about Ming Xin's existence and decided to take him under his protection and tutelage. By then I had achieved mastery and could defend myself."

Húlí was quiet for a moment, trying to digest all that new information. "Will you stop calling me Ming Xin?" he burst out. "My name is Húlí." Both Healer and Ling Ling stared at him as if he had grown two heads. "What? I don't like being called that."

His friend was the first to speak. "You're shitting me, right? Your savior just told you he has the same master as you and you're worried about your name?" Her eyes had gone from mere slits to huge orbs of disbelief. "You're crazy, my friend. All-out bonkers."

Xiǎo Ying's lips curved up in the corners. It was subtle, but Húlí knew it was a smile. "What about I call you Xin Xin?" Healer suggested with barely disguised amusement.

Fox bristled, but even he could not quite

pinpoint why. "What about you call me Húlí like everyone else?"

"But I'm not everyone else," he said with maddening calm. "I am me, the one who was trained to train you."

Húlí covered his head with his arms and grunted. "Ugh, what in the names of all gods in heaven does that mean?" He peeked at Healer from underneath an arm. "You said you were trained before I was and before the master knew about me, so how could you possibly be my trainer?"

"Let's just say our master had great insight into the future," Healer said. "He was not like others, you know."

And what is that supposed to mean?

Húlí buried his head in his folded arms again. "I'm taking a nap," he said, voice muffled by his sleeves. "My head hurts."

A chair dragged on the floor with a loud creak, and a warm hand covered the top of his head, comforting and sympathetic. The hand belonged to Ling Ling, his best friend and the only person in the world who understood his pain to some extent. Except it couldn't be hers. This hand was heavy and masculine, large enough to cover the whole crown of his head. Húlí chanced a peek and startled at the sight of Healer's large body standing next to him.

"I can give you a massage or acupuncture for the headache," the man offered, his voice as emotionless as always and in sharp contrast with his caring gesture. "I know it's a lot to process, but look at it from the bright side: you're not alone anymore, and I can teach you safer ways to replenish your *qi*."

Can you also teach me how to take revenge on those who decimated my kind, my family?

Húlí grunted. He didn't like those thoughts. They conveyed the anger he felt when he remembered the past, the way his kind had been persecuted for being different, and how he had been bullied and on the run for most of his life. He had managed to control that rising wrath in his heart even as a pup, but there were times when the anger came out unchecked. At times like that, his usual kind heart was overtaken by murderous thoughts that made him cringe and filled him with guilt.

He shook off the warm hand, then regretted it immediately. Xiǎo Yīng's palm had felt right, and now that it was gone, it had left an emptiness, a coldness Húlí didn't quite understand. The man was a stranger, one who claimed to know things about him and his kind like no one else did.

Fox stood up suddenly. "I'm going for a walk," he said, whirling on his heels and dashing out of the room. He needed to clear his mind, calm down his heart, and shake off the weird effect Healer's touch had on him.

On his way down the stairs, Húlí rubbed his chest with the palm of his hand, trying to erase the ache that had taken residence there. His poor heart had taken a beating lately with Xu Ming's betrayal and now this, something that felt a lot like a betrayal in its own way. Why hadn't his master told him about his other student? Why the big secret? Hadn't he trusted Húlí? Was he another person who thought him worthless and untrustworthy because he was a *yāomó*? His heart missed a beat and he coughed, still holding on to his aching chest. How much betrayal could a man take before crumbling into a pile of human dust?

He was halfway down the street when he realized Yè Yǐng was following him, the pads of his paws leaving a track of prints in the packed dirt. Every time Húlí slowed down, the dog did the same. When he stopped for a moment so did the dog. "Why are you following me?" he asked, making a 180-degree turn on his heels to face the animal. "I'm not your master." Húlí shooed the dog with a hand. "*Qù!* Go to Healer."

Yè Yǐng whined, sitting back on his haunches and lowering his head before letting out a bark of protest. Dogs were not that different from foxes, so Húlí could understand the body language all too well.

"I need some fresh air," he said, looking around to make sure no one could hear him talking to the dog. "I'll be fine. Go to your master." The dog barked again, insistent, and Fox rolled his eyes. "Oh, for all the gods above, even the dog thinks he can tell me what to do."

Resigned, Húlí walked back to the inn, the dog ambling beside him, his snout up in the air as he looked at Fox. Was Húlí going crazy or was the animal watching him? "I'm fine, Yè Yǐng," he assured the dog. "I'm totally fine."

But fine wasn't the word he would pick to describe how crushed he really felt inside.

HOWEVER RELUCTANTLY, Húlí had to admit that life had fallen into a comfortable, oddly domestic rhythm—even with an unwanted roommate who was so large, there was no room left in the bed for him. Not that he wanted to share his bed with Healer. But the floor was not a comfortable spot to sleep, even for a fox. No matter if he sometimes changed into his animal form and curled up by the hearth, the cold still seeped through the thin wooden floors of the inn and into his bones.

He rubbed a particularly sore spot on his backside before sitting down to eat the less than lavish meal set on the table by one of the inn's employees. "Why can't they have noodles instead?" he grumbled, gathering his thick red hair away from his face and into a bun. He glared at the meager spread in front of him. Sad, pale greens and an unidentifiable meat he suspected to be lizard barely filled the dishes. "Noodles are cheap and so much more filling than this shit." He pointed at the dishes, a disgusted frown carved on his lips.

A low rumble of laughter made him look up at the approaching Healer. "I'll take you out to eat today," Xiǎo Yīng said in his low, soft voice as he pulled out the chair across from Húlí's and snapped a pair of chopsticks from the container on the table. "But this is not so bad." He sniffed the food before sitting down. "Lizard meat is quite nutritious, you know."

Húlí crossed his arms over his chest and huffed. "I'm a fox. Lizard meat is not in my diet."

The healer laughed again. "Just eat, and I will buy you noodles and dumplings later."

Húlí watched the man from underneath his eyelashes. When Xiǎo Ying laughed, his usually somber, emotionless demeanor changed into something quite beautiful, soft, and soothing. Something inside Fox always shimmered in response, tingling and covering his skin in goose bumps.

"You promise? Are you even recovered enough to go out?" Húlí couldn't help worrying about the man. After all, Xiǎo Ying was not only his savior, but also a disciple of his uncle and master. It would be inconsiderate of him to treat him any other way, wouldn't it?

"My *qi* is now strong enough that I can go out, yes." You would think the fare before them was delicious, judging by the enthusiastic way Healer attacked the food. "I know a good noodle shack not far from here, but they only open in the evenings." A strand of the soggy greens hung from the corner of his mouth, and Húlí had the insane urge to wipe it with a finger. Thankfully the man took care of it himself before Fox lost all sense of propriety. "And we should wait for your friend." He picked up a big chunk of the meat and offered it to the dog, who was sitting on the floor next to him. "Here, Yè Yǐng, this is for you."

Belying his scruffy looks, the dog delicately closed his jaws around the piece of meat and began chewing on it. Húlí often wondered whether the canine was a *yāomó* himself. Maybe one who hadn't as yet learned how to transform into human form. In his own case, Húli had always been able to do it as if he had been born knowing how, but he remembered his master telling him that many *yāomó* had to work hard and for many years to learn it. Which was probably just as well. At least in their animal form they were not chased by the humans who hated them.

Realizing he was staring a bit too intently at his tablemate, Húlí lowered his gaze to the pathetic food on his plate. "You're not a *yāomó*, right?" It was not quite a question, just something that he had been ruminating on in his mind for a while now. The other man shook his head. "Then, why did you need my master's guidance?"

Healer didn't miss a beat, continuing to chew his food as if he were eating a delicacy. "I'm from a long line of *shényī*. My father trusted me to *shūshu* when I was about six years old. He was to train me in martial arts and help me develop my natural medical abilities, since my family was always too busy with their practice."

"You're a divine doctor?" Húlí had heard about them, but he had always thought the divine doctors of popular legend were just that: a story to tell your kids by the fire. When Ling Ling had told him about the healer, he had not made the connection. "Those are real? You're a fucking Hua Tuo?" Hua Tuo was a legendary doctor who had lived thousands of years ago in what they called Zhōngguó back then and was the father of ancient medical practices. Fox remembered reading about him in the history books he often spirited away from the palace's library. When he still lived in the palace, a lifetime ago.

"Hardly," Xiǎo Ying answered. "Very loosely related to the same family branch though."

Húli mused for a moment. He didn't realize that the *shényī* actually existed, and here he was, sharing a horrible meal with a living and breathing legend. "What happened to your family?"

"Dead," Xiǎo Ying answered simply, that distant expression back in his eyes. "All of them."

His head was reeling with questions, but Húlí knew firsthand how painful some subjects were, so he didn't ask anything else, allowing a companion-able silence to fall over them.

In the end, it was Healer who broke the silence, stunning Fox into paralysis.

"Very much like yours, Ming Xin, my whole family was slaughtered. I was the only survivor."

LING LING HADN'T STOPPED TALKING YET. In fact, she was the only one talking during the early dinner Healer had treated her and Húlí to. Fox was still stunned by what Xiǎo Ying had revealed to him. He had carried the pain alone for so long, he had tricked himself into believing he was the only victim of a corrupt and biased government. Turns out Healer was as much of a victim as he was, and he must have carried that wound for at least as long as Fox had.

"You guys are freaking me out," Ling Ling said, chopsticks suspended between the bowl and her mouth. "Why are you so quiet? Did something happen?" Húlí avoided her eyes, which in hindsight was a mistake. "Oh my gods in heaven! You guys did it."

Húlí's head snapped up. "What? No, that's not it," he rushed to point out, stealing a worried glance at the healer. "I'm just thinking about something Xiǎo Ying said earlier, that's all."

Ling Ling threw a hopeful peek at Xiǎo Ying. "What did you say that managed to shut him up for the first time in his life?" Húlí scrunched his eyebrows and opened his mouth to protest, but she didn't give him the chance. "Is it a secret?"

Xiǎo Ying chuckled softly. "No, not a secret. Just something I don't often talk about." She waited, her eyebrows raised. He smiled and lowered his voice. "Not a conversation to have in public. I will tell you when we're back in the room."

For once, Húlí's friend looked confused and unsure of herself, but she nodded and turned her attention back to the noodles in her bowl. "Thank you for dinner, by the way," she said, confusion quickly shifting into a smile. "It's been a while since we ate a decent meal. The food in the inn is far from glorious."

"Or edible," Húlí added under his breath, slurping a large dumpling into his mouth, juices dripping from his lower lip to his chin. "Don't understand why the place is always so crowded."

Healer leaned forward and ran his thumb over Fox's chin, startling him. "You had food dripping down your chin," Xiǎo Ying explained, wiping his hand on a napkin.

With the dumpling dangerously dangling halfway out of his mouth, Fox blinked a few times, wondering at the tingling left on his skin by the track of the other man's finger.

Ling Ling laughed. "Close your mouth, idiot, or that dumpling will make a run for it."

Húlí made a big show of playing it cool, but he knew he was not fooling anyone—not even himself. He knew that the way the healer's touch affected him was as clear as crystal. His cheeks burned, an unfortunate disadvantage of being red haired and pale. He was not the bashful type and rarely felt embarrassed, but this had been happening at an alarming frequency since meeting the big man who sat across from him. What kind of power did this man hold over him? Maybe he did have magic after all.

Their meal continued without any further incident, the awkward silence between the two men filled by the female warrior's chatter. By the time they finished, the mantle of darkness was already falling, covering everything in a translucent bluish veil, muting every color and blurring every edge. It was a beautiful evening, cold but crisp like a brand-new piece of paper, one Húlí was longing to write on.

"Let's go to the river," Fox suggested, turning around and walking backward so he could face his companions. "I bet the fireflies are out."

True to herself, Ling Ling bounced on her tiptoes and clapped her hands. "Yes, let's. I'll race you there." Without further warning, the slim woman took off running in the direction of the river, her black-and-red overdress flowing behind her like wings.

Xiǎo Ying exchanged a glance with Fox, face expressionless as always, before dashing after her. "Hey, not fair," Húlí exclaimed, pointing at the two of them. "That's cheating."

Ling Ling turned around momentarily to yell out, "Then start running, stupid Old Fox. What are you waiting for? You're the fastest of all of us."

That was true enough. After a moment of hesitation, Fox started his mad dash to the river, tails unfurled as his powerful vulpine leg muscles gave him the advantage over his friends. Soon he had left them way behind.

The river sparkled with the reflection of stars and the bright light of the almost full moon. With his companions still far behind, he crouched by the water's edge and picked up a handful of pebbles. He ran a thumb over them, relishing the silkiness the gentle might of the rushing waters had smoothed onto the stones. If only the turbulent flow of life could have smoothed his person as well. Instead, it had left him with sharp edges and rugged surfaces, someone hard to love and impossible to live with.

"What are you doing here, *yāomó*?"

Damn, forgot to retract my tails.

Húlí sprung to his feet, his instincts kicking in, and turned toward the unfriendly voice behind him. A beefy nobleman dressed in black and gold stood a few feet away, his legs spread apart and arms crossed over his chest.

"You're not welcome here," the man said.

He had no idea who this noble was, but one thing was clear enough: he didn't like Húlí's kind.

"I didn't realize the river belonged to you," Fox said, a wry smile twisting his lips.

"It doesn't," the other man said, taking a step forward. "But my family holds a lot of power around here, and I am my father's only heir. So I get what I want every time. And what I want right now is you out of my sight."

Húlí swallowed the knot in his throat, torn between anger and fear. He could fight as well as any other man, but he had left his sword in the room, and this guy was at least twice his size with muscles that defied reasonable explanation. He wouldn't last long in a brawl with this man.

As always, the fear that was crawling up his limbs and making his skin shiver and burn at the same time also came out of his mouth in the form of bravado. "Well, my good man, I live here, so I am totally entitled to this corner of the river," he said, his voice steady despite the shaking of his hands. "I won't bother you if you don't bother me."

The other man barked out a loud laugh. "But I *will* bother you, *yāomó*. I'll be glad to make you leave." The man flexed his fingers in front of him, cocking his head to one side as if waiting to see what Húlí would do.

"Don't make me use my magic on you, sir," Fox said, knowing all too well that he had no magic to speak of. Or at least none that would be of any use in a situation like this. The magic of seduction only worked on people who were already attracted to him in some way. This guy was not.

The burly man feigned a shiver. "Ooh, I'm so scared, demon," he said, mocking Húlí. He took a step toward Fox, all bulk and hate. "Let's see if it works against the power of my fists."

He lifted a hand, and before Húlí could even react, he slammed it against Fox's mouth with such force, he was propelled backward and almost fell. Strangely enough, he felt no pain, only red-hot anger toward this man who hated him for no other reason than for what he was.

Húlí straightened, not willing to give the other man the satisfaction of seeing him cower. "Is that all you got?" he asked, a smirk on his lips. "You sure don't have a lot of might in those tree-trunk arms." He knew it was dumb to provoke someone who could easily kill him with his hands, but he wouldn't run this time.

"You fucking filthy demon," the man spat, closing both hands into fists. "I'm going to kill you slowly and painfully."

Just as the man took another few steps toward Húlí, a low, dangerously quiet voice said, "No, you're not."

Both the man and Fox turned halfway to see who the voice belonged to. Healer and Ling Ling stood just a few feet away from them, a vision as their robes floated around them, giving them the appearance of gods from heaven.

"Who the hell are you?" the man asked.

Xiǎo Ying didn't raise his voice. "Who I am

doesn't matter. Who you are doesn't either. What matters here is that you are attacking a friend of mine for no reason at all."

"I do have a reason," the man protested, temporarily distracted from his target. "He's a *yāomó*. What better excuse do I need?"

"Him being what he is does not justify your hate," Healer counterargued. "Has he hurt you in any way?"

"No, not personally," the man replied, stealing a glance in Húlí's direction. "But I'm sure he has hurt many before. He's a demon."

Xiǎo Yīng opened his mouth to argue, but Ling Ling stepped forward and said, "Enough! Talking is not going to work with this fool." She unsheathed her sword, a delicate piece of silver metal with a dainty amethyst-encrusted pommel that belied its power. "Let me show you why you shouldn't touch my friend."

Faster than should be possible, Ling Ling pounced on the man with her sword. Her target, almost twice her size in every direction, managed to dodge the blade despite his obvious surprise. The female warrior attacked again, holding her weapon tightly in front of her as if it was a mere extension of her arm. This time, she hit the target, though lightly.

The guy would have a large scratch on his arm which would most likely not leave a scar, but the scream that escaped his lips and the look of horror in his eyes would make anyone believe he had been stabbed to death.

An amused smile stretched across Ling Ling's lips. "You better run to Mummy before you bleed to death," she taunted with a feigned pout. "And when your friends find out a tiny girl kicked your ass, I can only imagine the embarrassment."

The big guy's beady gaze bounced between her and Xiǎo Ying before he took off at a trot, covering the bleeding wound with his other hand. He wouldn't trouble them ever again.

"Why don't you just pour vinegar over it and kill me once and for all?" The cut on Húlí's lip burned as if on fire, and the coppery taste of blood coated his tongue.

Ling Ling clicked her tongue and patted extra ointment onto the wound with her finger. "You're such a baby," she chided as he cringed away from her touch. "If you don't let me do this, you'll have a puffed, purple lip by tomorrow."

On the scale of every wound he had ever received—physical or emotional—that fat lip didn't score very high in terms of pain. But discomfort was always a distraction when his mind and heart couldn't let go of the anger. If he focused on the physical ache, he could fool himself into not thinking about what had caused his rage.

"Let her take care of it, Húlí," Healer interceded. "Why don't I distract you with my story?"

Fox's ears perked up, and Ling Ling stopped what she was doing to turn halfway toward the man.

"I so want to hear this," the warrior said, ointment dripping from her extended finger and falling onto the bed linens. "Shit. I'm making a mess."

"All over my bed," Húlí said helpfully. He stared at Xiǎo Ying. "I'm not going to lie. I'm all ears, my giant friend."

The big man crossed the distance to the bed and handed a cup of tea to Fox and another to Ling Ling before sitting on a nearby stool. The way Healer always looked like the waters of a large lake on a windless day, peaceful and unruffled, sometimes irritated Fox, who was the total opposite of composed. At least on the inside. He sure hoped he projected a very different image, that of a cool and collected individual with not a worry in the world. It'd been his armor since he could remember.

"I was born to a family of *shényī*," Xiǎo Yīng started after a long sip of his tea. "My father and mother had worked for the royal family since they were teenagers, and so did their parents before them. My siblings and I were being polished to follow on their footsteps."

"You were royal healers?" Ling Ling was leaning forward, totally enraptured by the story, Húlí's wound forgotten. "Wow. Did you live in the palace?"

Húlí doubted that. He couldn't remember a single healer who lived within the confines of the royal compound. He would know, curious child that he had been, always sneaking around and snooping.

"No, my parents preferred the freedom and privacy of living among commoners," Healer replied, confirming Fox's guess. "We lived in a small compound just outside the city limits, a lovely place in the woods. We had a large enclosed courtyard where we grew herbs and vegetables that we used both for medicine and sustenance. It was quiet and perfect for us kids to run around like wild chickens."

It sounded idyllic. Sort of like Healer's house, except that his current place was in what Húlí considered enemy territory.

"How many siblings do you have?" Ling Ling asked, absentmindedly setting the pot of ointment on the small table by the bed.

Healer was silent for a moment, and Húlí could have sworn a cloud darkened his eyes. "I had two, a brother and a sister." His use of past tense didn't go unnoticed. Ling Ling gasped, and Fox lowered his eyes. Wrapped up in his own grief, he sometimes forgot he wasn't the only one who had lost loved ones. "Both older than me."

Húlí could tell by the way his friend bit her lip that she was dying to ask how they had died, but even Ling Ling knew not to cross certain lines. If Healer wanted them to know, he would tell them when ready.

"One day the emperor got sick."

Húlí remembered a time when the old emperor had fallen prey to a mysterious disease. It had been a time of chaos and fear. The crown prince had died in battle. The emperor had many sons, all aiming to become the next monarch, but none of them had great reputations; some were womanizers and gamblers who would steal from a pauper, others were conniving and cruel. Not one of them was right for the crown, and rumor had it that the emperor had been looking at one of his own brothers to name as his heir. Húlí couldn't remember anything in detail or even keep the timeline of events straight, since he had been so little at the time.

"I was only eight, but I remember it clearly," Healer said. So they were not so far apart in age. Húlí had been only four or five when this happened. "My father believed the emperor had been poisoned, but whatever they used was rare enough that my father didn't know how to treat it. He needed time to study it and come up with an antidote. Time was not on his side though. The poison in the emperor's body was quickly destroying his organs, and he wouldn't last long if my father couldn't come up with a cure quickly."

The old emperor had died a few short months after getting sick, which meant only one thing. "He didn't find the antidote, did he?"

Healer lifted his dark eyes to Húlí. "No, he did find a cure." That was not the answer Fox expected. It made no sense. If Xiǎo Ying's father had found a way to heal the emperor, why did he die shortly after? "But unfortunately, the princes found out before my father could give it to the emperor. They did not want their father to survive."

Húlí's heart skipped a beat. Could it be? Could those princes be so cruel as to destroy a whole family just to protect their chances at the crown? Ling Ling released a little gasp as if she too could guess what was coming.

Healer looked down at his own hands that were closed into loose fists on his lap.

"My father was waiting for the arrival of a vital ingredient for the antidote when he was killed," he said in an oddly steady voice. "The assassins made a visit to our compound and massacred my whole family."

"How did you survive?" Ling Ling asked quietly.

"My father had asked me to go gather some wild herbs in the woods," he explained. "When I returned, I found the courtyard littered with the bodies of those I loved and all our servants. It took me and *shūshu* two days to bury them all."

Speechless, Húlí reached out to touch the other man's shoulder. Their stories were not that different, then. He had also walked in one day, not long before the emperor's death, to find his mother left dying in their home in the palace. He was little enough that he couldn't remember everything, but the memory of his mother's blood covering his clothes as he was wrenched away from her still haunted his dreams. The next thing he remembered was being with his *shūshu*.

83

"That must have been so awful," the female warrior whispered, covering her forehead with her hand. "What did you do? You were so little."

A ghost of a sad smile popped onto Healer's lips. "I was lucky. My master showed up the next day and helped me bury the dead. Then he took me with him."

Húlí squeezed the man's shoulder. "So sorry," he said. "I know how it feels."

He did. He knew exactly how your heart could hurt so much, you wanted to dig it up from your chest and throw it away. How your eyes burned so badly from crying that the world blurred around you. He knew all too well how it felt to be unable to muster the energy or the will to do anything or be able to envision a future without your family. Without the only world you knew and loved.

But somehow, they had both made it.

CHAPTER 6
COMMON GROUND
HÚLÍ

Húlí had never learned how to comfort someone. Nobody had been there for him when his mom died. Now, faced with Xiǎo Ying's revelations, he felt he should be doing something.

Anything.

Thankfully, Ling Ling was a lot better at it than he was. Before Fox could even come up with a pathetic effort to show sympathy, the female warrior slid an arm over Healer's shoulders in a friendly one-armed hug.

"That must have been so traumatic for you, Xiǎo Ying," she cooed in that oddly soothing tone she sometimes used on Húlí to calm him down. "I can only imagine how it felt."

Healer turned his face up to her and smiled. "Thank you, Ling Ling," he said, patting the hand she had rested on his shoulder. "It was a long time ago. It still hurts, of course, but life goes on."

Húlí's voice chose to make a comeback at that moment. "How can you say that? How can you stay so calm and not want to avenge your family? To show those bastards how it feels to lose everything?"

The volume of his voice and the hate behind each word shocked even him. He was well aware of his feelings of anger, but he mostly kept them in check. His master had taught him tolerance and how to love despite the hate that had been a constant in his life. How could he say what he had just spouted out? How could he even think it? *Shūshu* would be ashamed of him.

He hung his head. "Sorry, not sure where that came from," he whispered, shame and anger mixed up inside him.

Ling Ling made a move toward him, but Xiǎo Ying was faster. Before he could even blink, Húlí was wrapped in two strong arms, his face squashed against an equally strong and warm chest.

"Don't apologize," the man said from above

Fox's head. "Anger is natural. But you don't want to think about revenge, which is poison for your heart and soul. You want to seek justice."

The anger inside Húlí was quickly dissipating, and the other man's warmth overwhelmed all Fox's senses. This, being cuddled against Healer's body, was paradise—somewhere all the pain and hate did not exist and where he felt protected and free to be himself.

Wait! What am I thinking?

Such thoughts startled him. Xiǎo Ying was little more than a stranger. Yes, he had saved his butt a couple times, but he was still someone Húlí barely knew. For all he knew, Healer might be harboring ill intentions toward him like most people did. Even Xu Ming, who he had thought of as a blood brother, had betrayed him. He couldn't trust anyone, couldn't allow himself to be lulled into a false—and dangerous—sense of security.

Húlí pushed Healer away. "Thanks, Xiǎo Ying," he said, avoiding the other man's gaze. "You're right. I should be thinking about justice, not revenge." His master had taught him so, after all. Still, he couldn't help but ask, "Have you done so? Have you found justice for your family?"

Healer's expression was back to its unreadable status. "Not yet," he said, his hands hanging awkwardly for a moment before he lowered them down to his lap. "But one day...."

"I feel like we've had enough sadness for the day, don't you?" Ling Ling asked. Húlí couldn't be more grateful for his friend's interruption. He had so many questions, but most of them would most likely stir up bad memories for him and the other man. "Let's play some chess, shall we?"

"You think you can win again?" Fox asked, happy to be back to comfortable, mundane territory. "Healer is onto you now, woman."

The female warrior twisted her nose and squinted in a great imitation of a mischievous cat. "Oh, I don't know. I think I can still beat him."

Húlí barked out a laugh. "That, I want to see."

Anger and pain forgotten for the moment, they all pulled chairs closer to the table where the board still lay and prepared for a match, all three reaching out to set the pieces on the board. Húlí's fingers brushed against Xiǎo Ying's, and their eyes met for an intense moment as heat rushed from the point of contact all the way up Fox's arm and through his whole body, stirring feelings and sensations he was not ready for.

He pulled his hand away, but Healer held it steady in his as his gaze burrowed into Húlí's soul.

"What are you afraid of, Ming Xin?" the man whispered.

There was so much Húlí was afraid of, but mostly he was terrified of his own heart and what would happen if he ever fell in love again.

ONE MORE TIME.

He tossed himself onto his other side one more time, the hardwood floor unyielding as usual. With a grunt and a mix of discomfort and annoyance, Húlí gathered the pillow beneath his head into a ball in hopes that it would better support his aching neck.

"You know you can sleep in your bed, right?" Xiǎo Yíng's voice surprised him. He thought Healer had fallen asleep a long time ago.

"I can't make a sick man who saved my ass sleep on the floor," Fox said, not bothering to turn in the other man's direction. He might be a lot of things, but he knew how gratitude worked, and he was very grateful to that giant of a man for saving his life.

Healer chuckled softly, and Húlí heard the rustling of bed linens being pulled aside. He twisted his neck to chance a glance and was rewarded with a sharp stabbing pain.

"See? You're uncomfortable when you have a perfectly good bed here." Húlí thought he detected a note of amusement in Healer's usual emotionless voice. "It will be a little cramped, but there's room enough for both of us."

If Fox hadn't been laying down already, he would have been floored. Healer was suggesting they shared a bed?

Húlí sprang upright, every bone in his body complaining about the sudden move. "Sleep together?" For all the gods in heaven, he had lost his eloquence again.

Xiǎo Ying had the nerve to laugh, his deadpan face open and friendly for once. "Yes, together," he said. "What are you afraid will happen? That I will ravish you in your sleep?"

No. Húlí was more worried about himself and what he would do. He was a nine-tailed fox, after all. Seduction was in his nature. Normally he wouldn't hesitate, but this man was different. Húlí didn't quite understand why he thought of Xiǎo Ying in such different terms, why the thought of seducing him felt wrong. Was it because they shared the same master? Was it because he owed Healer a life debt? Or was it simply because Xiǎo Yīng elicited feelings inside him that Húlí had not felt in a long time?

"If you're worried your fox's wiles will take over," the man said, sitting on the edge of the bed, a vision all in white, "I'm immune to your charms." He said that last word with a hint of sarcasm. The icicle had a sense of humor after all.

Húlí did find his voice then. "What do you mean?"

Healer, his long hair falling over the whiteness of his nightshirt like an ebony waterfall, smiled again. "I am literally immune to your fox's seduction powers. I'm pretty much immune to any magic. Something to do with my *shényī* blood." That was unheard of. Fox had never met anyone, man or woman, who was immune to his magic. "So there's no danger of us getting hot and heavy in this bed. We can share."

Húlí totally disagreed with that conclusion. He may not be able to use his powers even if he wanted to, but there was no denying he was attracted to this man. It was almost as Healer was the one with the magic and Fox a poor helpless devil with no strength to resist him.

"It will be uncomfortably crowded in that bed,"

Húlí protested feebly. "We're both big guys, and that bed is on the small side."

Xiǎo Yīng stretched out on the bed, resting the back of his head on his folded arm. "Do as you please," he said, closing his eyes. "But it can't be any more uncomfortable than sleeping on the hard floor, can it?"

Maybe not for his bones, but would Húlí ever be able to fall asleep with the heat of Xiǎo Yīng's body against his? He lay back, fixing the pillow behind his neck and pulling the flimsy covers over himself. "Thank you, but I think I prefer the floor," he said, stealing a glance at Healer.

Xiǎo Yīng made a noncommittal sound and turned onto his side, his handsome face fully visible to Fox, who swallowed the knot that had suddenly formed in his throat. The man was gorgeous, strong but with perfect soft features, his closed eyes two black crescents against the ivory of his skin, dark strands of hair draped over his neck and the pillow. He had neglected to cover himself. The white night-clothes he wore molded to the contour of his long, strong body.

Húlí sighed, a shiver of yearning running through him. It was going to be a long night.

He couldn't and wouldn't give in to what his fox

instincts were begging him to do. Healer had risked his own life to save him. How could he even consider wrapping himself around him? *Bù*, that was too low even for a nine-tailed fox like him. He owed the man respect, maybe even a little reverence.

Besides, it turned out that Xiǎo Ying was also a brother of sorts, connected to him by his Shūshu. As he lay on that hard floor, trying to think of anything that didn't involve stripping the healer of his clothes, Húlí couldn't stop wondering how strange life could be, that after all these years he would cross ways with someone Shūshu had trained to guide him, someone who had an eerily similar and tragic history to his.

Except, instead of moaning about the past and dreaming of revenge like Húlí often did, Healer was set on finding justice for himself and his family. Fox wondered if he would ever find it and if it would indeed bring on much-needed and wanted closure. Healer had not expanded on how exactly he was doing that—seeking justice for his family—and Húlí had been so angry at the time, he didn't think of asking. But now the thought clung at the edges of his mind, pecking at it like a nestling trying to break free from its egg. Was it possible? Could he get the justice his mother deserved? That he deserved?

Now that the possibility had hatched, he was wide awake, brain flooded with questions and what-ifs.

Damn you, Healer! First you fill me with desire and now with curiosity.

There wouldn't be any sleep for him tonight.

CHAPTER 7
UNWANTED TRAINING
HÚLÍ

"Tell me again. What exactly are we doing here?"

Húlí stretched his arms above his head while taking a good look at the surrounding area. They were in the middle of the woods, a place he knew well from when he felt the need to hunt—which thankfully was not that often. He hated to kill his own food. But he couldn't understand why Healer had brought him here on a rather chilly day. The breeze lifted every lingering leaf off the ground and sent them flying like small icy cold blades against his skin.

"Training." The man still insisted on cryptic one-word answers most of the time.

Fox watched the taller man walk around in wide

95

circles while staring at the ground as if searching for treasure. "What in all gods' names are you doing?" he asked. "Did you lose something?" Like his sanity?

Xiǎo Ying didn't crack a smile. "The right spot."

Húlí shook his head, his hands now at his waist. What did he mean by that? The right spot for what? A place to hide a body, maybe? Was Healer having murderous thoughts toward him?

As usual, the man could read Fox's thoughts. "Don't worry. I'm not going to kill you."

Not really convinced, Húlí stuck his hands inside his tunic to try to warm them up. "Well, I will die anyway if we stand here in the cold for much longer," he said, stomping his booted feet on the packed dirt.

Healer stopped and lifted his chin to look at his companion. "Are you always this whiney?"

Ling Ling would have immediately said yes, but thankfully she had a job to do and had left town for a few days.

"I'm cold." His voice had gone down an octave. He didn't want his handsome companion to think of him as weak. He wasn't, really, but he had worked long and hard at building this mask of shallowness so not to attract unwanted attention. No one paid any attention to a weak, superficial man. It gave him a great cover most of the time.

"Where's Ling Ling?"

A little punch of jealousy made his cheeks burn. "She's escorting cargo to Bailing," he answered, hiding his reaction with his hand. Bailing was the nearest town to the south, a busy merchant hub where everyone in the area went for supplies. Ling Ling, with her background as a soldier, often made a living as a bodyguard for the merchants carrying expensive cargo back and forth from the town's markets. "She'll be back in a few days. Why? Do you miss her?" He bit his tongue, mad at himself for being so transparent.

"I'm not interested in her," the other man replied, his eyes back on the ground. "Not romantically."

"I don't care," Húlí rushed to say. "I'm just looking out for my friend, that's all."

A rumbling sound reached Fox's ears, and he quickly realized it was coming from Healer. Was he laughing at him? Húlí's cheeks burned hotter.

He was about to say something, but Healer spoke first, "Here, this is a good spot." He pointed at an innocuous spot on the ground that looked exactly like every other square inch around them. "Perfect vibes."

Húlí raised his eyebrows in doubt, staring at the spot Healer was pointing at. "What's so special about that piece of dirt?" Was he missing something?

Xiǎo Ying waved him closer. "Sit here and you'll find out."

More than a little suspicious, Húlí sat down as requested, settling cross-legged as his companion did the same across from him. Their knees touched and another wave of uncomfortable heat ran through Fox's body.

"Clear your mind," Healer commanded, his eyes closing as he took a long deep breath. "Feel it."

Feel what? The cold wind that was freezing Húlí's neck? The hardness of the dirt beneath him? What was he supposed to be feeling?

"I don't feel anything," he complained.

Xiǎo Ying opened his eyes and scowled. "Close your eyes. Open your mind," he said. When Fox had no reaction, he reached over and grabbed Húlí's hands in his, squeezing them. "Close your freaking eyes, Ming Xin," he snapped.

As soon as he did, Húlí felt it—a wave of cold heat emitting from the ground right into his body.

As the energy traveled through him, he got stronger. He was not sure how he knew this, but every muscle in his body felt renewed. If he had to describe the sensation to anyone, he would say he felt as if he were shimmering.

He was so surprised by it that he dropped the other man's hands and opened his eyes. "Holy fuck!" he exclaimed. "What the hell was that?"

Xiǎo Ying's lips curved into a tiny, almost invisible, smile. "That was the earth's energy recharging you."

"*Bù kěnéng*. Impossible." He had never heard of anything like that.

"Our master must have told you about it at some point," Xiǎo Ying said. "All living creatures, humans and *yāomó*, get their life energy from the earth. It's a question of learning how to harness it."

Húlí took a moment to think about it. "Are you saying I can use this energy to replenish my *qì*?" That would mean no more need for him to risk his life by seducing the wrong men.

"Once you learn how to control it, yes." Healer's face had gone back to its icicle mask. "Right now, you felt it through me. You're not trained enough to do it on your own yet."

A thought percolated in his mind. "Why didn't the master ever teach me that?"

"I'm guessing you weren't ready," Xiǎo Ying said, brushing a long lock of hair behind his back. "The trick is to be able to clear your mind of thoughts, fears, and doubts and trust your nature implicitly in order to open up to Mother Earth."

It all sounded like a lot of nonsense—the kind of gibberish fortune tellers often spewed to their audience. But Húlí had felt it. Whatever that was, he had sensed the strength, the power of that energy. There was no denying it.

Might as well surrender. He had nothing to lose. "So how do I learn it?"

"You begin by trusting me," Healer said simply.

Well, that could be a problem. Húlí had not been raised to trust anyone.

"Why should I bother learning this? After all, the seduction game can be a lot of fun." And dangerous, not to mention degrading, at times.

Xiǎo Ying smiled then. An honest to gods open smile.

"Well, you can always practice your seduction skills on me."

Húli couldn't be sure but he could have sworn

Healer was laughing as he walked away, leaving Fox behind in a fit of coughing.

THE MARKET WAS FLOODED with people. The weather had taken pity on the town dwellers and the sun shone bright, lending everything and everyone a layer of comfortable warmth. Húlí stopped at a candy seller and checked out the deliciously colorful selection the man had on display inside small wooden crates in front of him. The smell of sugar made him a little lightheaded. He needed meat first before he could indulge in sugary treats. Not that he had a lot of coin to spend, but he knew the little stall in the corner of main street sold amazing dumpling soup for very little money.

"I'll come back later," he promised the candy vendor and dashed across the street, dodging people and animals along the way.

It was still early for lunch, so there were a few tables available in front of the shop. He sat down, ordered a bowl of pork dumplings, and settled down to watch as a river of humanity flowed by him. It was no accident he could wander the streets of town without raising any suspicion. He had made sure he kept a pretty anonymous life, not sticking out in any way. Most people saw him as another idle nobleman with nothing to do and way too much time on his hands. The only people in town who recognized him on sight were the street cherubs, a group of orphans who roamed the market every day, looking for scraps.

"Get out from there," Húlí murmured, waving at a hidden silhouette. "Come here."

The little boy, face smudged with dirt, cleared the corner of the large basket he was hiding behind and came to stand sheepishly before Fox.

"Are you hungry?" Fox asked him as the boy stood, hands clasped in front of his belly and eyes lowered to the ground. The child nodded, and Húlí sighed. "Sit. I'll get you something to eat."

The urchin obeyed and rewarded Fox with a huge smile. "Thank you, Mr. Fox," he said, his hands flat on the table as he followed Húlí with his eyes.

Fox ordered another bowl of dumplings and handed the boy some chopsticks. "What have I told you before, Chen Ni?"

The boy feigned coyness. "To come and see you at the inn if I'm hungry." With a toothy smile he added, "But the food at the inn stinks. This place is better."

Húlí laughed, throwing his head back. "You *xiǎozi*," Fox exclaimed. "You're a brat." The boy laughed, his eyes rounding as the server approached with two steaming bowls. "Fill your belly, then."

In quiet companionship, the two enjoyed their food, slurping broth over their chins and the table and laughing about it. Chen Ni was one of a handful of children who had been orphaned and left to fend for themselves in the streets of town. It was the same old story; the rich prospered and the poor suffered. The emperor was not a good man and uninterested in keeping his people healthy and safe. It was no wonder the old emperor had been so reluctant to name any of his many sons to replace the crown prince. In the end, he died before he could make a choice, and it became a survival of the fittest on the way to the throne. Or the most ruthless.

"Where's Ling Ling?" the boy asked, accustomed to seeing the female warrior partaking in Húlí's meals.

"Out of town," Fox answered, sucking a dumpling between his lips and splashing a droplet of broth on his face. "She should be back by tomorrow. Why does everybody ask about her? Am I not enough?" The outrage act had a bit of truth to it. He knew it wasn't safe to stand out, but a part of him wanted to be noticed, to be missed, to be wanted.

"That's because she's a lot nicer than you," Healer said as he appeared from behind the stall, his face expressionless as usual, and sat next to the boy. "Hi, my name is Xiǎo Ying. What's yours?"

The boy, his cheeks puffed up with food, cocked his head to the side, studying the big man who had just plopped himself next to him. He swallowed the food before saying, "Chen Ni."

"Well met, my friend," Xiǎo Ying said with a nod before yelling out, "Server, bring me a bowl please."

"Who are you?" the boy asked, curiosity sparkling in his brown eyes.

Xiǎo Ying, dressed in his usual white robes, had tied his long hair into a top bun that instead of detracting from his male beauty made it ever so more intense, the sharp lines of his jaw and cheeks in perfect contrast with the softness of his lips and eyes. Húlí swallowed hard. The man was too handsome to be real.

"I'm just a healer," he said. "I have been staying with Húlí for a while, until I am recovered."

"You were sick?" the boy asked, taking another large dumpling into his mouth. "You don't look sick."

Truth be told, there was no way the man was not completely recovered, but he didn't seem anxious to leave, and Húlí had reluctantly admitted to himself that he enjoyed having him around.

"I'm almost completely mended," Xiǎo Ying said. "I should be fine in a few more days."

Húlí's heart cracked a little. Would he be leaving then? It shocked Fox to realize how sad that thought made him. Was it possible he had gotten that attached to the man who had commandeered his bed for weeks now? Wasn't he wishing to get his comfortable mattress back? What was wrong with him?

Again, Healer seemed to guess what he was thinking. "I won't leave yet, Húlí," he said, a tiny smile lifting the corners of his luscious lips. "I still have to train you, remember?"

Fox could have sworn he heard an actual whoosh of relief rush through him. "Fuck! But I want my bed back," he quipped, the burning on his face belying his words.

The young boy squinted curiously at them. "You took his bed?"

Húlí barked out a laugh, relieved he had something to joke about. "Well, he's an old man and he was sick, so I let him have it, being the generous soul that I am." Chen Ni nodded. Fox turned to Healer and said, "See? Even the urchin agrees."

When the meal was over and the boy had skipped his way back to the hovel he called home, Húlí and Xiǎo Ying walked in silence side by side back to the inn through the throngs of people in the market. Healer stopped at one of the last stalls to buy a bag of candy that he promptly handed to his companion.

"I saw you eying the candy earlier," the tall man explained, pushing the small paper bag into Fox's hands. "Enjoy."

A gift? The man who had saved his life was buying him a gift? Húlí couldn't remember the last time he had received a gift of any kind. Ling Ling sometimes brought home things she shared with him but never really a gift, something he coveted. Xiǎo Ying must have been following him earlier to notice how he was drooling over all the candy in the market.

"Were you stalking me?" he asked, opening the bag to take a peek inside. A whiff of sugary goodness hit his nostrils. He sighed.

Healer resumed his walking, staring ahead with not a hint of a smile on his face. "Protecting you," he corrected. "Doing the job Master charged me with."

"Doing your job? Is that all?" Did he sound as disappointed as he felt?

"Well, that and the fact that you are quite easy on the eye. It makes my job so much more pleasant."

Xiǎo Yīng continued walking forward, not realizing that Húlí had stopped and was staring at him like a fool. Had Healer just flirted with him?

CHAPTER 8
MAGIC
HÚLÍ

Húlí opened one eye, made sure Xiǎo Ying was not watching him, and scratched his nose. He wiggled a bit on his bottom, his crossed legs starting to tingle and his toes losing all feeling. How long was Healer going to make him stay in that position? He was supposed to be communing with the earth, opening his mind to what was within. Instead, all he got was itchiness. His butt was numb, his hands longed for movement, and his thoughts didn't stop on one thing for longer than a couple seconds. This meditation thing was not working for him. Either that or Mother Earth really didn't care to talk to him at all. Not surprising, considering there weren't too many creatures in the world who wanted anything to do with him.

"Stop fidgeting," Xiǎo Ying snapped, and Húlí closed his one eye, trying not to twist his scratchy nose. "You need to learn to be still, to be quiet. Otherwise, how will you ever be able to listen to what the universe is trying to teach you?"

The universe seemed to be otherwise engaged at the moment. "My legs and ass are falling asleep, Xiǎo Ying," he whined, not daring to open his eyes yet. "Can I have a rest? I need to stretch my legs."

His inner fox couldn't be still that long. Foxes were nervous creatures that needed to be in almost constant motion in order to survive. This freezing of all movement was killing him.

He heard a long-suffering sigh and opened his eyes. Healer was glaring at him with a mixture of exasperation and pity. "For all gods' sakes, just go run for a bit," he said, slouching over his own crossed legs. "I need a break from you too."

Húlí jumped to his feet, regretting it immediately as his legs almost gave out under his weight. "See, I can barely stand on my own two feet now."

Another sigh escaped Healer. He waved Fox away with one hand. "Go! Run, jump, do whatever you need to get rid of your nervous energy. Then we'll try it again."

Not wanting to tempt the devil—should Healer change his mind—Húli raced away, zipping around trees and bushes of the forest, relishing the cold air on his face and the strain in his muscles. This was how he communed with the earth, not the quiet stillness of meditation which only made him itchy.

When he came back to where his trainer was, he was met with a scowl. "What? You told me I could go do it."

"You've been gone for almost an hour, Ming Xin," Healer growled through his clenched teeth.

Húlí shrugged. "So what? I'm a fox. I need the exercise." It made total sense, didn't it? Why would the other man not understand it? "And why do you keep calling me that? I haven't been Ming Xin since I was a kid."

Xiǎo Ying's eyes softened. "You don't just quit being somebody," he replied. "You're still Ming Xin, no matter how many times you deny it."

"I'm Húli the fox and have been for many years," he argued. Being Húlí, however hard, was a hell lot easier than being that scared little kid who had been left alone in the world.

"Why do you refuse to accept who you are?"

He did. Would he have taken such a name if he didn't fully accept the fact that he was a nine-tailed fox? Ming Xin was a more human name, and yet he had elected to keep the one that branded him a *yāomó*. "I am a fox." He crossed his arms over his chest with a stubborn twist of his lips.

"But you're also human," Healer said, his voice soft and gentle. "You're more than an animal."

Húlí huffed. "Let's just agree to disagree. I don't think any of my past lovers would agree with you though. As soon as they found out what I was, they were out of my life before I could blink." Shit. He hated that he had just revealed one of his main hurts to the other man. Since his mother had died, he had yet to be loved by anyone other than Ling Ling, and despite his bravado, he so wanted to be.

Xiǎo Ying's eyes softened even further, his usual coolness turning into something Húlí hoped wasn't pity. "Are you ready to focus on being quiet?" Healer asked softly.

Fox nodded, not sure he'd be able to but willing to give it another chance. He dropped onto his bottom, crossed his legs, and opened his palms over his knees. "Mother Earth, speak to me," he mumbled, shutting his eyes and taking a deep breath.

It came immediately. A low rumble at first that quickly turned into an explosion of sound inside his head, vibrating through his body and sending waves of heat to his extremities. He tried to open his eyes, but whatever that was wouldn't let him. It held him captive as effectively as a chain. Húlí's heart had taken off at a trot, stealing his breath.

Don't be stupid, Fox. Breathe. Calm yourself down.

He inhaled deeply a few times, and his heart slowed enough that he could catch his breath. The sound continued, blasting inside of him as if it had taken over every cell of his body. What in gods' name was that? Was that the earth talking to him? If so, it was seriously pissed off at him.

"Listen," he heard Healer say as if from very far away. "Listen and calm down."

He took a few more calming breaths, and the volume softened as his heartbeat eased. After a while, the noise had reached a level he could easily handle, and the sounds within it were coming out clear. There were no words, yet he could understand what they were saying, seeming at first frustrated and then soothing, like a mother chiding her child.

"*Mǔqīn,*" he whispered. "Mother."

He wasn't sure why he had said that. But the feeling that sound left inside him reminded him of his mother's voice. Was it possible his mom was talking to him through the earth? They were both *yāomó,* so who knew what was possible.

It only lasted a few seconds, but it left him breathless. He opened his eyes and slouched over, trying to process what he had just experienced without much success. Xiǎo Ying's hand on his shoulder brought him out of the weird trance he had gone under.

"Are you all right?" Healer asked, crouched beside him. "Did you hear it?"

Húlí had heard something, but he couldn't be sure it was the "it" Healer referred to. "I heard my mother," he blurted out, his eyes unfocused by the glare of the sun. "I mean, it felt as if it was my mother."

"Nature talks to us in many languages and in many voices," Healer said, his voice so quiet, it was barely audible. "Earth chooses the voices we most want to hear, I suppose."

No, that wasn't it. He couldn't be sure why he knew that, but Húlí knew it; that was his mother's voice. Had she ascended to a different level of existence? Was her spirit still alive and well somewhere in the universe? If animals could evolve into humans, could humans maybe evolve into something else as well?

"*Bù*, it was my mother's voice," he insisted, running the palm of his hand over his face.

Xiǎo Ying dropped to the ground next to him, crossing his stretched-out long legs at the ankles. "How can you be so sure? Voices can be faked."

Húlí shook his head. "It wasn't the voice as much as what she said," he whispered, still lost inside of himself. He lifted his gaze to Healer. "She told me to find my father."

The other man tilted his head to the side, his eyebrows knitted together. "I thought your father was killed."

"He was," Húlí admitted, confusion clouding his thoughts. "What does it mean, then?"

"GO EASY WITH THAT, OLD FOX," Ling Ling yelled as Húlí drank the whole glass of wine in one go. "That stuff goes straight to your head."

That's exactly what he wanted. Something that would erase the thoughts swimming around in his mind. It had been so long, why bring up his family now? And who exactly was doing that? That voice was his mother's, he was sure of that. But how was that possible? And what was that cryptic order all about? *Find my father?* His father had long been dead way before all hell broke loose in the palace. Long before the old emperor had died.

He poured himself another glass. "I can hold my liquor," he boasted with a chuckle. Despite the alcohol running through his system, he wasn't drunk yet, but he would be, even if he had to drink all three bottles Ling Ling had brought from her travels. He took another swig.

"Stop." Xiǎo Ying wrapped his long fingers around Fox's wrist, preventing him from drinking again. "You're being stupid. Drinking yourself into oblivion is not going to solve anything."

As true as that was, Húlí didn't care. His head hurt with difficult and sad memories stirred up by that voice. Why now? Why ever? His life was far from perfect, but he had managed a sort of rhythm independent from his past, from those who had hurt his family and still wished him ill. He had managed to leave Ming Xin behind, and now it all came storming back like a tidal wave of unwanted thoughts and feelings.

"Let me drink," he said, fighting the other man's hold. It didn't work. Xiǎo Ying held fast to his wrist, his eyes intense on Húlí's. "For fuck's sake, Healer, let me go or...."

"Or what? You'll kill me with your bad boozed breath?"

Fox jumped to his feet, his wrist still inside the other man's hand, and looked up into Healer's dark eyes. "Or I will seduce you right here, right now."

Healer laughed. "I told you, your magic won't work on me."

The sudden upward move had managed to do what the wine hadn't: it made him swoon, the whole world tilting away from him. He reached out with his free hand and held on to the other man's tunic, afraid he would fall. "That's what you say." His voice was becoming slurred, and he smiled, happy he was finally drunk.

Xiǎo Ying growled softly. "Try me."

Húlí studied the big man in front of him and wished he would stop swaying. He closed his fingers around his collar, steadying himself. "Stop moving." Healer let loose a chuckle but didn't stop wavering. Or was it the floor that moved? Húlí tightened his grip on the other man's shirt and pulled himself closer and up onto his tiptoes until his face was almost level with Healer's. "Stop. Moving."

"Is that how you work your magic charm on

your partners?" Xiǎo Ying taunted, his words a blast of warm air on Húlí's face. "It doesn't seem very effective."

Trying to steady the movement, Húlí braced himself on the other man's chest. "*Nǐ kàn*, Healer!" He licked his lips, his mouth suddenly very dry. "Look, you haven't seen anything yet." Was he slurring his speech?

"I'm waiting," the tall man said, a tiny smile dancing in his eyes.

Everything swam before Húlí's eyes, and he closed them for a moment, trying to get his bearings. A moment later his lips were covered by another pair of soft, warm lips that prodded his gently open. The kiss was butterfly light, more tease than actual kiss, hot skin fluttering over his aching lips, a barely there touch of tongues.

It was deliriously exciting.

His nine tails fanned behind him as yearning took over, and he began to lose control of his fox. He leaned closer to Xiǎo Ying, seeking and craving further contact. He let out a groan against the other man's mouth, his hands still firmly attached to the edges of Healer's shirt.

Just as suddenly as it started, the kiss ended. Húlí was left fighting for balance, bereft of the steady support of Xiǎo Ying's body. He may have sobbed a little, his arms hanging out awkwardly in front of him. It took him a minute to breathe again and be able to open his eyes.

Xiǎo Ying stood, his legs anchored slightly apart, arms crossed over his powerful chest, an ice sculpture instead of the warm human who had just locked lips with Fox. "Well?" he said, incomprehensibly.

"Well what?" Húlí managed to say, eyes still unfocused and head swimming from the wine and the headiness of the kiss.

"Is that all you've got?" Healer asked, not betraying any emotion. "That was a rather pathetic demo of your powers of seduction, wasn't it?"

Wait! *He* had kissed Healer? Húlí could have sworn it had been the opposite, that in this case, *he* had been the one seduced and not the other way around.

"I didn't even try...." He knew he sounded pitiful, desire still thickening his voice. "*You* kissed me." He was so confused. The wine had totally muddled his brain. Had he tried to seduce Healer and that's why he kissed Húlí? Why didn't he feel like that was the case? "I tried to seduce you." It was more of a question than a statement of fact.

Had he really though?

Xiǎo Ying dropped his arms alongside his body and raised his eyebrows. "Well, I guess that's for me to know and you to find out, isn't it?" he said right before walking away.

What the fuck had just happened?

WITH THE SHARP end of the sword pointed at him, Húlí brushed a hand over his face in frustration but didn't back out.

"If you mention that again, I swear I will skewer you with my sword," Ling Ling threatened, shaking the weapon for emphasis. "I don't know the answer to that question and really don't care one way or the other."

"But I'm so confused, Ling Ling," Húlí whined again, fully aware he sounded like a child. "Did he kiss me because I seduced him or because he wanted to?"

The female warrior dropped the sword, growling and slouching until her chin touched her chest. "Why is that so important?"

Fox dropped into a chair. "Because I don't want

to seduce him. I want him to do it because he wants to."

There, the truth was out in the open. Like it or not, he was totally infatuated with Healer, and Húlí didn't like it a bit. The last time he had developed feelings for somebody, it didn't end well for him.

Ling Ling sighed. "Ask him," she suggested, sitting down beside him and placing her sword on the table. "He's the only one who can answer."

Húlí hung his head. "He won't tell me," he admitted. "I think he likes to see me squirm."

His companion laughed. "Who doesn't? You make it very entertaining."

"And you call yourself my friend."

Healer had left on an errand he didn't seem keen to elaborate on a few hours ago. Húlí was still broke and lacking a way to earn any income, so he had stayed at the inn, feeling sorry for himself and annoying his only friend, something he both felt guilty about and enjoyed immensely.

"Where do you think he went?" Ling Ling asked, scavenging through the peanut shells on the table, hoping to find a few still uneaten. "It's the first time he's shown any interest in going out by himself."

Fox shrugged. "He said he needed to buy some herbs, since he can't get the ones he has at his place." He had offered to go with Healer, bored and full of restless energy, but he had been unceremoniously turned down. "He didn't want me to go with him."

Ling Ling laughed again, her top bun wobbling as she did. "You have it so bad," she said with a click of her tongue.

He was going to protest, but the door suddenly opened, and a very familiar tall figure walked in. "Have you even moved since I left?" Xiǎo Yīng remarked, dropping a few packages on a shelf by the door.

"He missed you," Ling Ling quipped, much to Fox's mortification. "Where did you go, anyway?"

"I needed some materials for medicine," he said. "I also met with someone."

Húlí's ears perked up. "Who did you meet?" Was it a friend, a lover? Something acid begun burning in Fox's stomach. "And why?"

A tiny smile curled Healer's well-shaped lips. "Jealous?" Could the man be any more irritating? He might be taciturn most of the time, but gods in heaven, he could tease! "I got a message this morning to go meet with this old acquaintance. He had information I needed."

A man—he had met with another man. Hot

liquid fire burned Húlí's cheeks. "A long-lost lover, maybe?" He bit his tongue, but it was too late; the words had already left his lips. "Not that I care, but I'm curious."

The teasing glance Xiǎo Yīng threw at him told Fox he didn't buy his excuse. "Not a friend. An informant," he explained. "I've been searching for information about what happened to my family for years now." He had told them as much before. "I need to have proof of who did it so I can get justice for my kin."

Whatever whirlwind of emotions was stirring inside Húlí, Xiǎo Yīng's words sobered him in seconds. He, too, wanted justice for what it was done to his mother, his only family, but he had never been able to find any information about what'd occurred. He had his suspicions, of course, but he had been so young when it happened, he couldn't trust his memory of the events. Not completely anyway. Xiǎo Yīng hadn't been that much older than he was at that time, so how was he able to make contact with people who may know more about what happened?

"What kind of informant?" Ling Ling asked before Húlí could.

Healer sat on the edge of the bed, removing his

soiled boots. "Someone who, due to his job, was at the right place at the right time back then to hear certain private conversations." A servant, then. Húlí had witnessed it time and time again during his night forays into the houses of his wealthy lovers. The nobles had a ridiculous blindness about their staff. Since the servants were quiet and unobtrusive, members of the higher classes tended to forget they were there. Húlí often wondered whether they even forgot they were humans with ears and eyes. "He might have heard some important details about what went down back then and who was behind it."

"Isn't that dangerous for you?" Fox asked, oddly worried about Healer's safety. "What if the people who did it realize that they missed one of the family members? They will come after you."

Healer shrugged. "Not much danger there. No one except the master—and now you two—ever knew there was a survivor of the massacre. They were in such a hurry to hide the evidence, they didn't do a full inventory of the dead, and my parents often had patients stay in the compound. Too many wild cards for them to sort through. As far as they are concerned, I am very dead."

Ling Ling stood up, smoothing her long black

outer garment. "You keep saying *they*. You have an idea of who did it?" she asked.

Xiǎo Ying bit his lips, lost somewhere deep inside him. "I have a very good idea of who it was, yes. But until I have the proof, there's not much I can do."

"You could make sure they never see another day," Húlí said with an anger that surprised even him. "You can get revenge for your family. Eye for an eye and all that."

Healer shook his head almost absentmindedly. "*Bù*. Not a good choice." His voice was so quiet, even Fox with his great hearing had to strain to hear him. "Revenge doesn't solve anything. All it does is cause more hate, more anger, more sadness and heart-break. No. No revenge. Justice. That's what I want."

For Húlí, justice and revenge sounded the same. Wasn't killing those who killed your family the perfect sort of justice?

"I'm going for a walk with Yè Yǐng," Ling Ling said, grabbing her sword from the table where she had left it. "Don't do anything stupid while I'm gone." She threw Fox a pointed look before leaving with the dog.

What could he possibly do? Then again, he had

just been talking about revenge despite everything his master had taught him.

"I have to go north," Healer said suddenly. "Do you want to come with me?"

If the invitation came as a shock, Húlí recovered quickly, and his answer was out of his mouth before he could think about it. "Yes, I will go with you."

In truth, at this point in the game, he would follow Xiǎo Yíng to the edges of hell if Healer asked him to. Which in Húlí's book was a very scary thing.

CHAPTER 9
BEGINNING
HÚLÍ

He most definitely should have asked Healer where exactly he was going before volunteering to go along. What if Xiǎo Yíng was heading to Taihu? Was Húlí really willing to venture into enemy territory just to be close to the man? How pathetic was that? When had he suddenly become this enamored that he would be more than willing to risk his safety just to be with Xiǎo Yíng? The one thing Fox was proud of was of his independence from all others. Even Ling Ling, for whom he would be willing to die, understood that and had never asked him to do something that would require him to choose between her and his safety.

"You did what?" Ling Ling had already asked the

same question twice. She was having as much trouble believing it as he was. Húlí wasn't usually this impulsive. Not in matters that involved his own skin. "Without asking where he's going? Are you nuts? I mean, he lives in Taihu territory, so there's a very good chance that's where he's heading." She petted Yè Yǐng's head. The dog hadn't left her side since she arrived at the inn, just as infatuated with her as Fox was with Healer. "May I remind you of who else lives in Taihu?"

She didn't have to remind him. Xu Ming still lived in the capital, two steps away from the palace where they both had grown up. The boys had been friends since birth, the only two males in the all-female courtyard, and Húlí had been foolish enough to think their friendship would last forever. Xu Ming had been the only remainder from his past life who had followed him when he moved in with his master. The boy had kept silent about who Húlí was, and as years passed, Fox had fallen irrevocably in love with his friend. Betrayal had tasted all the more bitter coming from someone Fox had loved and whom he thought loved him back.

"I'm not going to Taihu." In his customary stealthy way, Healer had walked into the room. They both gasped and lifted their eyes to him, mouths falling open. "I told you I'm heading north. We're going to Xīwàng." Yè Yǐng rushed to his master, tail wagging enthusiastically. Xiǎo Ying bent down to greet the dog with an ear scratch and one of his rare smiles.

Xīwàng was north of Suhou but on the other side of river Lán. It was a city as large as the capital, sheltered by the Yǎnlèi Forest on one side and the Duǎnde Mountains on the other.

"Why there?" Ling Ling asked, always one step ahead of her friend who was still digesting the news. "They have had very poor relations with the capital for years. What makes you think you can get any information about what happened in Taihu all those years ago?"

Xiǎo Ying opened a small package and pulled out a piece of raw meat. The dog wagged his tail even more fervently and opened his mouth in anticipation. Healer didn't make him wait, and the animal gently grabbed it out of his hand before swallowing it whole.

"I have it on good authority that someone in Xīwàng will have intelligence about what happened with my family," Healer said, taking another small chunk of meat from the package.

"How can you be sure your informant is reliable?" Húlí asked, still not sold on the idea.

"He is." The simple statement carried more weight than Fox would have thought possible. Somehow those two words and the way Healer said it made it all make sense. They were going to Xīwàng.

Ling Ling, who had been quietly watching Healer feed the dog, stood up suddenly. "I'm going with you," she announced, her red lips set in a firm line. "You'll need protection."

Anyone else would have burst out laughing. Húlí was not a small man, and Healer was a giant. In fact, both were giants compared to the female's tiny frame. But Fox knew his friend to be a fierce warrior with skills and strength that belied her size. She had fought in the Border Wars before they met, and she took no prisoners. She would be an awesome asset to them, even if they were both well trained in martial arts.

"You'll pay me, of course," the female added, crossing her arms over her small breasts.

Húlí let out a chuckle. "That's my girl," he exclaimed, slapping his knee. "A mercenary through and through."

Healer barely smiled, but there was amusement

in his voice. "Of course you'll be paid. We'll be honored to have you along, Ling-*gūniáng*."

Ling Ling waved her hand and shook her head. "No need for formalities, Xiǎo Ying. Just call me Ling Ling." Healer bowed his head slightly. "And now for the important stuff. When are we leaving?"

Yè Yǐng, who often acted more like a human than an animal, sat on his haunches and looked up at them, long tongue lolling out and an expectant glint in his black eyes. Healer petted his head once more.

"We're leaving tomorrow," he said, his gaze wandering off to look at Fox, who had slipped out of his seat and crashed to the floor. "After all there's no time like the present."

Húlí agreed, but did the present have to come so soon?

It was a rather sad commentary on his life how quickly Húlí was able to pack all his belongings. Thirty-five years of living all jammed up inside a bag. He left a few pieces of clothing behind and some old, broken crockery that was not his to start with. He shook those thoughts out of his mind, threw the bag over his shoulder, and turned his back to the room that had been his home for the past few years. There was no telling if he would ever come back.

Healer had nothing but a small bag with a change of clothes and some toiletries, but at least he had the excuse of being away from home in what had turned out to be an unexpectedly long stay. The female warrior, used to traveling as a soldier first and then a security escort, had even less in her blue bag that was made of what looked like a blanket that she wrapped around her chest like a sling.

They had left town almost an hour ago and followed the main road northward. The plan was to veer off the well-traveled route after they crossed the bridge and came closer to their destination. Neither of them wanted to attract any undue attention from the locals. Once within city limits, they could easily blend in with the local population. Not that they would be arriving any time soon. The city was a good three-day walk at a decent pace with nothing to impede their progress. Since they'd already had to stop a couple times—once because Yè Yǐng had taken off at a trot after a rabbit and another time when a couple of beggars turned out to be wannabe bandits—they were already considerably behind schedule.

Nothing seemed to upset Healer. "That move against the bandit was impressive," he was telling Ling Ling, who had taught the misguided criminals a lesson they would never forget. "Was that a Bèndàn Stopping Palm?" he asked, the dog following him closely along the dirt road, his maw still stained with the poor rabbit's blood.

Ling Ling chuckled, her sword still in her hand even though the confrontation had long ended. "Why dignify it with the old language?" she said. "Let's call it what it is: the idiot-stopping palm. Perfect for those pathetic excuses for thieves."

Húlí, walking a couple steps behind them, rolled his eyes, vaguely sorry for the two devils who had so unwisely tried to rob his warrior friend. The fight had taken one whole minute and left the pair stretched out on the road, black-and-blue and crying for their mommies. There wasn't a day that went by that he didn't thank the gods in heaven for giving him such an amazing woman as a friend. He was not a bad fighter himself—growing up a *yāomó* in an intolerant world made sure of that—but compared to her, he was like a helpless baby.

"How did you two ever meet?" Xiǎo Ying asked, throwing him a backward glance. "You're so different."

Wait! Was Healer calling him a weakling or something? He opened his mouth to protest the veiled offense, but Ling Ling interrupted him.

"We met in Dǎo," she began, not bothering to even look at him, "I was training with the Hǎiyáng monks and he—" She turned her head around to peek at him, an eyebrow raised. "—he was running, as usual."

He grumbled under his breath. Running indeed. Xu Ming had alerted the authorities as to his whereabouts and offered a reward for his arrest—dead or alive. There were whole gangs of mercenaries after his neck, and in his exhaustion, Húlí made the unwise decision of corralling himself between his enemies and the ocean.

"He was lucky I was doing my morning prayers at the beach, or he would have ended up dead, either at the hands of those mercenaries or drowning in the ocean." Why was Ling Ling always so blunt in her statements?

A mixture of shame and pain infused his face with heat. "I'm a good swimmer," he protested feebly. "I'd survive."

"Not in those waters," the female warrior said. "If the cold water didn't kill you, the beasts would." She did have a point, but she was making him look like a wimp. He dropped a few steps further behind them, but his friend backstepped and slipped an arm over his shoulders. "Those bastards had sent almost ten men to catch one person. And one who had ran across two cantons already with no food or drink. How cowardly is that? It made me so mad," she continued. "If you're going to fight someone, at least give them a chance to defend themselves. That's the right way to do it."

Embarrassment forgotten, Húlí gave Ling Ling a one-armed hug. "So she became my knight in shining armor and single-handedly fought them off."

Ling Ling laughed. "With the help of my fellow monks," she corrected him. "Even I couldn't handle ten men by myself."

Xiǎo Yīng cocked his hand to one side, watching them with interest in his deep dark eyes. "If you met in Dǎo, how did you both end up north?"

"Once they had a whiff of where I was at, there would be no peace for me there," Fox explained, falling in step with the other two. "I stayed for a few days to recover my strength and then decided to go somewhere no one knew who I was. My friend here decided to go with me."

"To fight for the oppressed of this world," she

added with such ferocity, neither of them would have had the guts to doubt it. "My training was at an end anyway, and I was getting tired of eating fish, so it wasn't a hard decision."

She had neglected to tell Healer how she had left all her worldly possessions and human connections behind—including her beloved master—to follow a *yāomó* she had just met. He couldn't deny there was an instant connection between them as if they were fated in some way, and their friendship had quickly blossomed into a kind of kinship. She was not just his friend. She was his sister, someone he would do anything to protect. Not that she needed that, of course.

"I never had siblings," she continued, finally sheathing her sword. "But I do have a big brother now."

Húlí hid a smile behind his hand. And *he* had a little sister. He was a lucky demon.

CHAPTER 10
MONSTER
HÚLÍ

Find your father.

Húlí sat up, his head swimming from the sudden movement, and rubbed sleep from his eyes. Why did he keep hearing that voice? That strange request. Even his dreams were infiltrated by his mother's voice asking him to do something that was impossible. His father was dead. He had died when Fox was only a cub. Húlí's mother had never told him how or when exactly, just that he had long been gone from their lives. He might have been a *yāomó* too, since both Mom and Húlí were, but other than that, his father's origins and ending were a complete mystery. He was sure his mother would have revealed the whole story to him once he was older, but she never got the chance. The truth about his father had been buried along with her and the old emperor.

"Are you okay?" Healer's voice, slightly slurred by sleep, rose from the mound of blankets a few feet away from Húlí. "You were mumbling in your sleep."

They had stopped for the night in a small grove of bamboo trees, the only sheltered area in the vast prairie that stretched from the northern bank of the river to the Yǎnlèi Forest, which was still some ten miles or more away. Ling Ling was curled up by the fire, ever in need of light, and Healer had stretched his bedroll between her and Fox. It was cold, and his inner fox was begging him to either go closer to the roaring fire or swallow his pride and inch closer to Xiǎo Yíng's warm body. Neither were good choices. The first meant he had to face one of his biggest fears, and the second meant he'd have to face his own desires and this growing yearning for the other man.

But the dream had chased the chill air away, replacing it with cold sweats and the uncomfortable feeling something was not right. "I'm fine," he lied. "Just had a bad dream."

The rustling told him Xiǎo Yíng had turned

around to face him. "Why don't you get closer to the fire with Ling Ling? It'd be warmer."

"I'm not cold," he protested, a hint of a headache developing behind his eyes.

"He's afraid of the fire." *Damn you, Ling Ling.* Healer, who was now sitting up with a blanket over his shoulders, tilted his head in question. "He once fell asleep too close to the fire, and his tails almost burned. I think he'd rather freeze than go near it."

It wasn't as simple as that, but Húlí was grateful she didn't disclose the entire rather embarrassing story. She knew that he had been too intoxicated by a man who had replenished his *qi* and grown careless, barely escaping death. But there was a deeper reason why he refused to sleep close to the fire—he just didn't know what it was. The fear came from deep inside his blurred memories, something Húlí almost remembered. Almost.

All was quiet for a while, the crackling of the fire the only sound in the thankfully windless night. Then Healer whispered something in Yè Yǐng's ear, and the dog jumped up and rushed to Fox's side to curl up against him. "He'll keep you warm," Healer said before lying back down and turning his back on Fox.

The relief was immediate. The black dog exuded heat from every pore and was very willing to share it. Húlí smiled, petted the unruly fur on the dog's back, and pulled the blankets over both of them. He was asleep in no time.

The tantalizing smell of roasting meat woke him up. Yè Yǐng had also perked up his ears as he sniffed the air. What was that heavenly scent?

"Morning, sleeping beauties." Ling Lang's sing-song voice brought a smile to Húlí's face every time. "I caught a couple rabbits for breakfast," she chimed.

In seconds both Fox and the dog were sitting by Ling Ling, mouths watering as they watched the warrior roast the two rabbits over the fire.

"I thought you were scared of fire, Ming Xin." Xiǎo Yíng, stealthy as always, had appeared and was now crouching by their sides, hands stretched out toward the heat of the flames.

"I am." There was no point in denying it. "But only when I can't give it my full attention. I don't go close to it when I'm asleep." The other man looked confused. "When I am awake, I can prevent it from burning out of control, but when I'm asleep how would I know what the flames are up to?"

Healer thought for a moment and then nodded. "Makes sense," he said even though the expression on his face conveyed something totally different. "Better the devil you know than the devil you don't, right?"

Something like that. At some deep level, Healer really understood Húlí, and for some reason, that knowledge gave Fox endless—and irrational—satisfaction. A wide smile broke the straight line of his lips, and he immediately tucked his chin to his chest to hide it.

Yè Yǐng barked once and ran a big wet tongue over Húlí's cheek. "Stop that," Húlí demanded without much conviction. "So sloppy, so very sloppy." Inside, he beamed. For someone who had grown up without much love, he sure was fortunate to have the care of such a great friend and now that mangy canine. His heart swelled with pride.

"Hurry up and eat," Ling Ling said, ever the practical one. "At this speed we'll get to Xīwàng by next year."

Soon, they were on their way again. They had left the main road some miles back and followed a much less beaten path toward the forest. From where they stood, nothing but empty land and patches of dry grass could be seen, but Húlí knew there was a thick evergreen forest beyond. They hoped to reach it before nightfall so they wouldn't have to spend the night so exposed. There were plenty of stories about bandits in this part of the world. Whether they were true or not, Húlí preferred not to find out and would make sure they spent a quiet night.

What they could see of the sun from behind the dark contours of faraway mountains to the west was just beginning to tip over the horizon when they finally reached the edges of the Yǎnlèi Forest. One minute they were out in the open, the next they were completely sheltered by tall, powerful trees.

"Why do they call this forest the Forest of Tears?" Ling Ling asked. Even though not one to use the old language often, the female warrior was well versed in it.

"It is said that there are many untold dangers among these trees and that anyone who ventures in will certainly end up in tears," Healer explained, moving a low-hanging branch out of their way. Both Ling Ling and Húlí glanced up at him. "Don't worry. Nothing but old superstitions."

As if on cue, branches around them began rustling, moved by something or someone they could not see. Yè Yǐng began barking, baring his fangs, and Ling Ling unsheathed her sword.

Húlí gasped. "*Bù hǎo!*" he exclaimed, shaking his head. From between the trees, something dark and sinister swarmed closer. "Not good at all."

Húlí had seen a lot of strange things in his life, but this was new and terrifying. Whatever this creature was, it held no fixed shape, its contours moving and fluidly changing. It resembled a black cloud of smoke more than anything solid, dipping and rising, curling around trees and bushes, and had no discernible features. It made no sound either, even though the leaves and branches groaned at its passing.

"What the hell is that?" Húlí yelled, his hand flying to the hilt of his sword. "A ghost?"

Xiǎo Ying had taken a defensive stance, his strangely gnarled sword at the ready. "Evil spirit," he answered, not taking his eyes from the flying darkness.

"Is there a difference?" Fox asked, setting his back against Ling Ling's to cover all angles. Yè Yǐng stuck close to their legs, a low growl making him vibrate like a string in a *pipa*.

"A ghost is not necessarily wicked," Healer explained as calmly as if he were lecturing in a school. "An evil spirit, on the other hand, is basically all the hate, resentment, envy, and every other negative feeling that person had in life made flesh—well, not flesh, but that smoky thing we're looking at." That did not sound good at all. It was bad enough to face hate from humans, but to deal with the same from an incorporeal being took it to a whole new level.

"What do we do?" Ling Ling asked, her whole body stiff, a coiled mass of lean muscle ready to spring. "Our swords won't do much against it, I'm guessing."

"Yours won't," Healer admitted. "But mine will."

Both Húlí and the warrior were so surprised by his statement that they both momentarily took their eyes away from the danger. "What do you mean yours will?" Fox asked, returning his focus to the moving shadow. "What's so special about it?"

Healer took a couple steps toward the darkness that now hovered almost motionless as if waiting to strike. "It's a spirit sword," he said just as plainly as if he was saying his sword was made of metal. "Every *shényī* has one."

Húlí had heard the stories, of course. What child growing up in the kingdom hadn't? Every storyteller in the land was known to have at least one tale about the spirit swords of the *shényī* that chose their owners instead of the opposite. Legend had it that sword and master were connected by blood and that these weapons could cut a lot more than just flesh. But Xiǎo Ying's sword didn't look powerful or special in any way. In fact, it looked barely functional, made of unpolished metal that seemed rusted in places, with a twisted blade that might very well be blunt. How was that a mighty spiritual sword?

They never had the chance to ask the question because the evil entity attacked. It was intelligent, and instead of aiming at Healer or the warrior, it went for Húlí, the weakest link in the group. Fox let out an embarrassing squeal before jumping into action. Sword raised, Húlí braced for impact. How could you fight something that had no solid body? He was a dead man for sure.

Just as the creature was mere inches away, Fox closed his eyes, holding his sword in front of his face, a string of irrational pleas escaping his lips,

"Not the face. Whatever you do to me, leave my face alone."

The strike never came.

After a few seconds, Húlí opened his eyes one at a time. Healer was engaged in a brawl with the creature just a few steps away from him. Unlike most of the fights Fox had ever witnessed and been part of, this one was oddly silent. In fact, the whole forest seemed to have gone quiet. Even the cicadas had stopped their chirping. Xiǎo Ying swung his sword in arcs before him, slicing through the smoky body of the spirit who disintegrated into wisps of darkness only to gather together again seconds later. Healer moved gracefully back and forth, his long hair swaying behind him, a choreographed battle dance that Húlí couldn't take his eyes away from.

"Not the face?" Ling Ling whispered by his side. "What the hell, Old Fox? Not the face?"

Húlí, eyes still glued to the battle ahead, shrugged. "My pretty face is important to me," he said. "How can I seduce anyone if my face is damaged? Might as well cut off one of my limbs."

He couldn't see it, but he could imagine the eye-rolling as the female warrior mumbled, "What you need is some other part of your body cut off."

Feigning outrage, Húlí replied, "And you call

yourself a friend." He tsked, never once prying his gaze from the mesmerizing scene unfolding in front of him.

Xiǎo Yīng lunged, thrusting his sword forward and hitting his target every time. The spirit broke apart and then reorganized itself into its fluid shape, but its color was fading into a dark gray. Did that mean Healer's strikes were weakening it? Húlí watched how the man spun on his own heels, his long robes twirling around him, a mixture of strength and grace. Compared to him, Húlí looked like a nine-year-old fighting the bullies in the schoolyard. Fox's chest filled with a mixture of awe and envy, but he soon discarded the latter; he was not one to hang on to negative thoughts for long.

Yè Yǐng whimpered when Healer lunged and sliced one last time, scattering what was left of the spirit into the air and oblivion. Húlí could barely contain his admiration. "Holy fuck, *ge*, that was awesome!" Fox rushed to Xiǎo Yīng's side, closely followed by the dog, dropping his sword on his way before squeezing the man's upper arms with his hands. "I feel I should carry you on my back for the rest of the way."

Xiǎo Yīng, emotionless as usual, raised an eyebrow and stared at his companion who held on enthusiastically to his arms. "You? Carry me?" He ran a skeptical glance over Fox. "Really?"

Húlí chuckled, dropping his hands. "Well, if you weren't as big as a freaking tree, I would," he corrected himself. "I have trouble carrying tiny Ling Ling." That was not true. He had, on more than one occasion, carried his best friend on his back with no difficulty. He was so used to his mask, this deceitful appearance of weakness, he had started to believe it himself. In fact, Húlí was much stronger than his lithe body led anyone to believe. He had the smarts and agility of a fox combined with the strength of a body used to fighting for survival at every corner. But pretending to be daft and weak served his purposes well enough, keeping him in the background, unnoticed or forgotten.

"Don't let him fool you," Ling Ling said, picking up Fox's sword from the ground and handing it to him. "He might be a fox, but he is strong as an ox." Húlí glared at her, and she scowled. "Don't give me crap, Old Fox. You could easily carry him if you wanted to."

Húli was about to protest but was interrupted by Healer, who raised a hand to stop him. "Forget it," he said, turning his back on them and resuming his walk into the dark forest. "We make better time if I walk on my two legs. Save it for a day when I might not be able to."

Fox's heart skipped a beat. What did he mean? Was he expecting worse trouble ahead? Were they all heading into a giant pot of deadly situations? Whatever happened, Húlí needed to make sure nothing bad came to Xiǎo Ying. He wasn't quite sure when it'd happened, but he knew now that should he ever lose Healer, he would also lose his heart.

CHAPTER 11

LAVENDER POWER

HÚLÍ

The journey through the forest seemed to take an eternity. More than once they had to fight their way against wicked creatures from another realm, and one time from a fierce wild animal Húlí had only heard of but had never seen—a giant rodent-like creature appropriately called a *jù shǔ* which literally translated from the old language to big rat. This creature had colossal teeth inside its pointy maw and claws as sharp as knives, and it looked nothing like the cute-looking rats Fox used to play with when he apprenticed with his master.

"I had a pet rat once," he thought, realizing too late that he had spoken out loud. Both his companions threw him an amused glance. "Not really a pet," he corrected. "I was just trying out some of what my master was teaching me on him…. It." His face burned, and he cast his eyes down on the forest floor.

"What was his name?" Ling Ling asked in a honeyed voice, batting her eyelashes in a feigned coy expression.

Cheeks burning as if on fire, Húlí picked up his pace, trying to stay ahead of his friends. "I may have called him Xiao Xiao," he mumbled under his breath.

"What was that?" Ling Ling said. "I can't hear you."

With a great big sigh, Fox stopped in his tracks, turned around to face them, and said, "All right, I may have called him Xiao Xiao because—well, because he was small. Are you happy now?"

Ling Ling burst out laughing and slapped him gently on his shoulder as she walked past him. "That's my Old Fox."

Húlí stood there, mortified that Healer had heard him and about what he might be thinking of him at that moment. A rat for a pet? How pathetic was that? Yes, he had grown up in the palace, but once all hell had broken loose and he found himself taken in by the man who became his master, his life was anything but wealthy, anything but fun. He had no friends other than Xu Ming, no permanent home, nothing to call his own. Xiao Xiao had filled an empty space in his heart, giving him something to love. But he knew how it sounded to others.

"I think it's endearing that you took care of a rat." Xiǎo Ying's voice startled him. "It shows you have a big heart. I like it."

No one would be able to wipe that smile from his face. Ever.

Húlí threw a glance at Yè Yǐng walking beside him, his tongue lolling out of his mouth. "You're a coward, you know?" he told him. The dog's ears twitched. "Not once did you jump in to help us fight the giant rat. Aren't you supposed to be the most loyal of animals?"

Ling Ling clicked her tongue. "He's just smart," she said. "What could he do against that freakish animal? He knows how to pick his fights. Unlike you, Old Fox."

He humphed, not convinced. "Right. Smart, my ass. He's just a big hairy chicken." The dog turned his head and barked at him as if protesting the accusation. "*Hǎo ba, hǎo ba*, you're smart... ish."

"We should be close," Ling Ling said, pressing

ahead, and the dog set out at a trot after her while throwing Fox a disparaging look.

Of the three of them, she was the one with the most experience in traveling. Her jobs as a security escort had taken her to many corners of the kingdom. The journey through this forest was unfamiliar to her though, considering the only reason they were using the less beaten path was to avoid detection from people they'd prefer to stay invisible from. But she had been to Xīwàng before, traveling on the main roads with everybody else. She had been regaling her travel companions with stories about the city named Hope for a good reason. This was where all broken people went for a second chance at life. Húlí had considered moving there at one point, but he was still oddly attached to his side of the world where his few good memories had once been reality. As hard as he tried to cut himself from his past, the truth was, he couldn't forget his mother was part of that life. The old emperor whom he remembered as a caring, gentle man was part of that past just as his master was too. He could never let that go.

As soon as they cleared a bend where the trees were so thickly spaced, there was no way to squeeze between them, a valley of incredible beauty appeared before their eyes. The bright grass stretched and flowed like a green ocean from the edge of the forest all the way to where the gray shapes of buildings rose in the horizon. Purple popped here and there, floating along with the grass and lacing the air with the sweet scent of lavender. Húlí thought he heard them all sigh as if a weight had suddenly released from their chests and a great sense of peace washed over them.

"It's the lavender," Healer explained as if he had heard Húlí's thoughts. "Hépíng lavender, a special kind. As soon as it's inhaled, its leaves release a mild relaxant that soothes anxieties and muscle tension." He took a deep breath. "Legend has it that Emperor Mo Wu planted them centuries ago to welcome his guests and new residents and assure them this was a place of peace."

There was no telling whether that was true or if those lavender plants ended up there after being carried by a strong wind or a flock of birds, but Húlí didn't care. He hadn't felt this relaxed in years. He followed Xiǎo Ying's example and took a deeper breath, inhaling as much of the perfumed air as he could.

"Where do we go now?" Fox asked, reluctant to move.

Ling Ling pointed to the right. "We follow the edge of the forest until we meet the main road a mile or so that way. Then we blend in with the other travelers."

Nobody was going to argue with her. The two men followed her as she made her way to the main road, half hidden by the cover of the trees. It took them less than half an hour to get there, and as luck would have it, there wasn't a single traveler in sight. Walking along the main road was much easier than on the paths they had chosen so far. The surface was smooth, covered in shreds of tree bark for a soft tread, and Húlí once again wondered at the measures the old emperor had taken to make every visitor comfortable. Little had he known that years after his death, the city would be at odds with the south. Then again, who wasn't fighting with the capital, ruled as it was by a tyrant and a fool?

A few minutes later, they did come across other travelers, some going in the same direction they were, others leaving. A small group of farmers crossed paths with them, laughing uproariously at some joke as they carried their empty baskets. Business was good, then. A cart, heavy with farming products and containers of wine, passed them on the right. The burly farmer guiding the ox waved at them, a wide smile on his sun-reddened face. Húlí thought he might be imagining it, but it seemed as if even the air felt lighter here. He couldn't stop the smile that spread across his face any more than he could stop his heart from beating a happy tempo.

Intoxicated by the feeling of lightness and an unfamiliar joy, Húlí slipped an arm over Ling Ling's shoulders. "I feel like I've come home," he said.

Surprisingly it was Xiǎo Ying who chuckled. "Don't be fooled by this feeling," he said, throwing Fox a side-glance. "Just like the lavender fields we crossed, there are other herbs and flowers strategically planted along the road to make sure no one enters the city with ill-will in their hearts. Sometimes the best defense is to subdue the foe before they become the enemy."

How very smart—and sly—of the old emperor. He might very well have been a fox.

Xiǎo Ying slapped the back of Húlí's head a few times before they arrived at the inn. The soothing herbal scent that permeated the air in town was too distracting for Fox, who kept on veering off their path to buy sweets and talismans from street vendors.

"Stay focused, for gods' sake," Healer mumbled, his lips stretched into a tight line. How could he stay so unaffected by the calming scents? "During our next lesson, remind me to teach you how to shut out sensory distractions."

Húlí thought he should be offended to be treated like a child, but he felt too good to care. He offered the big man a foolish grin and a chuckle. "I can't wait." It was true that he enjoyed their lessons together. After that first startling one when his mother talked to him, there had been no incidents of strange events or disembodied voices in his head. But being with Healer, feeling his big hands on him when Fox's positions needed correction, his hot breath on Húlí's face when he whispered something to him—all of it was heavenly, stirring something both new and old in him.

The inn Ling Ling picked was small and cozy, with a restaurant on the ground floor and guest rooms upstairs. It was oddly reminiscent of the inn Fox had called his home for the last few years, but the decor was better. Instead of bare walls and bare windows, Heaven Bound Inn had colorful paintings hanging from every wall and pretty, bright curtains over every window. Vibrantly colored crockery pieces and small, elegant stat- uettes depicting gods and goddesses in their iconic poses were set upon wooden shelves along the walls. Like the rest of the town, the place had a bubbliness that soothed all your senses and made you feel at home.

They were shown to two spacious rooms with beds covered in brightly colored linens. A tile-topped square table squatted in a niche in one corner, while large cushions peppered the wooden floor by the opposite wall. Ling Ling sequestered herself immediately in her room, claiming she needed a long nap. Yè Yǐng followed her, always ready for naps and food.

Xiǎo Yīng and Húlí were left alone. They had been sharing a room for over a month now, and yet, sharing a room while traveling felt like a new level of intimacy. Fox stood awkwardly at the center of the room, his bag still flung over his shoulder, one hand rubbing the back of his head.

"It looks like it's just us," he said, wishing he'd bitten his tongue instead of stating the obvious. "Who's going to sleep where?" It was out of the bag, and his stomach filled with butterflies in anticipation of the answer.

Healer dropped his bag on top of the bed, stretched, and then headed for the door. "We both take the bed," he said, leaving Húlí frozen in place. "I'm off to the baths. Are you coming?"

CHAPTER 12
SOAP AND SUDS
XIĂO YING

Xiăo Ying couldn't completely suppress the bubble of mirth that climbed in his throat. For someone whose life had been a series of leaps from one bed to another with a string of lovers he thought he needed in order to survive, Húlí was acting like a teenager on his first sleepover with someone he had a crush on. Xiăo Ying found it endearing even though he would never admit it to his companion.

Fox didn't immediately follow him, but he caught up a few minutes later. Xiăo Ying had slowed his pace to a crawl to allow Fox to join him before he arrived at the bathhouse, a small building in the backyard of the inn. A twisted side of his normally serious personality enjoyed seeing Fox squirm. It

159

was no secret they were attracted to each other, but Healer was not certain Húlí knew it was mutual. Fox's fight-or-flight instincts had left him unsure of himself, timid about life in general. He didn't seem capable of trusting people or even reading others, never too sure about how people felt or what they meant. Xiǎo Ying was itching to teach him how to trust again, how to believe in himself and allow his brilliant self to be loved, but he must be patient. Thirty-odd years of running away from intolerance with no one to care for him had severely jaded Húlí. It would take time and finesse to snap him out of that.

"I really don't need a bath," Húlí rambled beside him as they turned the corner at the back of the house. "I mean, I'm a little ripe, but I can go another day or so without." Xiǎo Ying didn't comment and kept walking, his gaze focused on the path ahead. "There were times when I was on the run that I would go without a cleaning for weeks. I stank like shit, but it didn't kill me," Fox continued, his moving hands betraying his nervousness. "I didn't have any friends anyway, so it wasn't as if anyone would complain." Healer's heart shrank a bit at his words. What kind of childhood did this poor man have? "I was mostly sleeping in the forest with the other foxes—those who were tolerant enough of my presence. I was bitten by the alpha male a few times, and even once by a female who was protecting her cubs."

Xiǎo Ying knew that the uncontrollable torrent of words was a reflection of how nervous Húlí was, but he had to wonder whether Fox wouldn't later regret having offered all that information about himself. So he put a stop to it. "Why are you so nervous? You've never bathed in the same room with another man?"

A gasp escaped Húlí's lips. "Plenty of times," he claimed, sounding outraged. "I'm only tired. I talk a lot when I am exhausted."

Healer cracked a smile and stole a glance at his companion, who seemed wildly interested in the beaten-dirt floor. "That explains it, then." Not even close, but he had to allow Fox some dignity. That didn't stop him from finding Húlí adorable.

Xiǎo Ying opened the door to the bathhouse, and they walked in, Húlí slightly behind him. It was a small space with three round bathtubs at the center and a long, low shelf along the walls that held various bath-related accoutrements. At his request the staff had already filled two of the tubs with hot water, and steam filled the small space, coating their exposed skin in warm droplets. He closed the door behind them and immediately began disrobing. After days of travel, he felt grimy, and a hot bath sounded like heaven. As soon as he was down to his long underpants, he took a few steps away from the tub and grabbed a bottle of lavender oil. Turning around to sprinkle it in the water, his eyes met Húlí's. The man was still fully dressed, standing by the tub closest to the door, a haunted look on his face. For a moment, Xiǎo Ying thought he would lower his eyes, but he didn't. Instead, Fox held his gaze, a ferocity he hadn't seen before mixed with the same amount of gentleness and yearning.

It was Xiǎo Ying's turn to feel awkward.

Healer lifted the bottle in a silent offering, and Húlí nodded as if unable to speak, eyes never leaving Xiǎo Ying's. Healer rushed to the tubs and splashed a few drops of oil in each one before retracing his steps back to where he'd been. He set the bottle down, and after shimmying out of his underpants, he lowered himself into the hot water with a sigh of pleasure. Every muscle in his body relaxed, and a great calm overtook him. That oil was a mixture of plain and hépíng lavender, and even he, with a built-in resistance to drugs and poisons, couldn't fully stay unaffected. He let out another sigh, closed his eyes, and allowed himself to sink deeper into that sense of serendipity.

Xiǎo Ying must have briefly fallen asleep, because the next thing he knew, there were a couple of big warm hands on his head, massaging his scalp, running deft fingers through the strands of his long hair. He opened his eyes, startled, and turned his head around.

Húli was behind him, still fully clothed and kneeling on the tiled floor, sudsy hands partially lifted from his companion's head. He wore an expression of—what? Wonder? Surprise? Bliss?

"Sorry. I'll stop it if you want," Fox whispered, blinking. "You looked really tired, so I figured I'd wash your hair."

It took Healer a few seconds to recover his composure and voice. "It's all right," he said. "I was just surprised, that's all." He turned his head and leaned against the back of the bathtub in silent permission. Húlí dipped his hands into the water to pull the edges of Xiǎo Ying's hair out of the tub, then he ran his palms down its length.

Xiǎo Ying closed his eyes and allowed himself the pleasure of Húlí's fingers combing his dripping hair, massaging his scalp, and occasionally brushing against his jaw and his neck. Despite the fact that the air around them seemed to crackle with electricity, all was quiet.

"Can you tell me something?" Fox asked, breaking the silence. "I want the truth."

Healer nodded. "Sure." What was Húlí about to ask him?

"Am I doing this?" he asked, surprising his companion. Healer twisted around to look at him. Húlí shuffled on his knees so he was beside the bathtub and wagged a finger between them. "Am I unconsciously seducing you?"

Xiǎo Ying was tempted to tease him and allow him to believe that this whole situation was caused by his fox wiles, but Húlí looked so torn that he didn't have the heart to do it.

"What do you think?" he asked, his hair still imprisoned within Fox's hands.

Húlí blinked a few times as his Adam's apple bobbed in his throat. "I don't know," he confessed, licking his lips. "Not consciously, but I never had anyone try to seduce me, so I am confused." He ran a hand absentmindedly over Healer's long hair. He lowered his gaze. "You think I'm stupid. Don't you?"

Healer swallowed, his throat suddenly dry. "What if it is you? Haven't you done this a million times?" he asked. "Are you ashamed of who you are? Of needing to recharge this way?"

Fox hung his head. "Not ashamed. I never hurt or forced anyone, but you are different." He raised his eyes to Healer's again. "I don't want to be the one seducing you. I want you to sincerely want to be with me." He paused for a moment, color rising in his cheeks. "I'm sorry I brought it up. I will leave."

He let go of Xiǎo Ying's hair and stood up, but Healer caught his hand. "No. Stay." he begged, his voice husky with emotion. "I'm sorry. It's not you, Húlí, it's me." The other man's eyes widened. "I have been seducing you, my sweet fox. I do want to be with you. More than anything else and with my whole heart and soul."

Húlí opened and closed his mouth in a perfect imitation of the sacred carp, his red hair only emphasizing the resemblance. If Healer hadn't been so full of love and so tense from desire, he would have laughed. As it was, he was finding it hard to breathe, so he did the unthinkable: he pulled on Fox's hand, hard and suddenly, and his companion, caught by surprise, lost his balance and fell headfirst into the bathtub, his long body following it directly.

What was he doing? Was he trying to make love to this man or drown him?

The water splashed over the sides of the bathtub in furious waves as if Húlí's fall had caused a small underwater earthquake. Xiǎo Ying tried to grab a hold of his collar to pull his head out of the water, but the man was as slippery as an eel. For a few moments they both struggled in the tub, chaos getting the best of them until Fox's face finally emerged from the soapy water.

Xiǎo Ying covered his mouth to suppress a chuckle. His companion was a mess, sputtering bubbles from his lips. His handsome face was blotchy and his eyes red as he tried in vain to wipe the cascading water falling from his hair. Once he managed to balance himself on his knees, the white tunic he had on was stuck to his upper body like a second skin, which was not a bad look for him, Healer thought, considering it accentuated the well-toned muscles of his chest and arms.

"Don't you dare laugh at me," Húlí spat out once he had cleared his throat of all the bath water. "Are you trying to kill me? I thought masters were supposed to treat their disciples well."

Healer swallowed another laugh and sat straighter against the back of the tub, pulling his legs closer to him to give his companion a bit more room. "That was an accident," he managed to say, a hand still over his mouth. "You did need a bath though."

Húlí's freckled cheeks twitched. He wiped his eyes and brushed the hair away from his face before glancing back at Healer. "I mean, if you didn't want me to wash your hair, you could have just told me so." His lips curled in a tiny smile. "No need for violence."

The two men stared at each other for a few seconds before bursting out laughing. Húlí's laughter was contagious, his whole face transforming into something so beautiful, it was hard to describe. Healer hardened under the water and stopped laughing. He may play the part of a detached man, but there was no lack of emotion when it came to how he felt toward Fox. The attraction had been instantaneous that first time they had met at his cabin in the woods. It was something he couldn't explain but certainly felt—a pull so strong, it couldn't be casual or temporary. And after he had replenished Fox's *qi*, that connection grew even stronger and more intimate.

Húlí had stopped laughing too, his blue eyes fixed on Healer's. He raised a hand and brushed his fingers along Xiǎo Yīng's jaw, making him shiver in delight. He seemed to suddenly realize what he was doing and tried to pull away, but Healer caught his hand and held it in place.

"Don't stop, Ming Xin." A whisper, a prayer. "Come closer."

Fox obeyed, scooting nearer, his hand still captured by Healer's. He licked his lips, and Xiǎo Ying groaned, the desire to kiss them overwhelming him. Húlí read his mind and leaned over to take Healer's lips with his. His skin was wet and warm, soft and yielding under the pressure of Healer's demanding mouth. Xiǎo Ying cupped the back of the other man's neck and pulled his face even closer, prying his lips open with his tongue. He moaned against his mouth, delighting in Fox's sweet and spicy taste. He hardened further, desperate to close the space between them, to feel Fox's skin against his.

Reluctantly, Healer pushed his companion away. Húlí groaned in protest but complied. "Sorry, I didn't mean to—"

Xiǎo Ying interrupted. "No—no need to apologize, Ming Xin. I just want to undress you."

Húlí's eyes rounded in an almost comical way. "Oh, I s-see," he stuttered. "Sure."

He moved as if to remove his wet clothes, but Healer stopped him again. "No, I'll do it."

Fox mouthed an "Oh" but didn't utter any sound, dropping his hands back into the water. Healer began peeling Húlí's tunic off, which was not as easily done, as it stuck to every inch of his body. It was a slow, infuriating process, but it fueled Xiǎo Ying's fire to the point where he thought he would burn from the inside out. Once the top tunic was removed, Húlí stood up in the bathtub, his silky white pants glued to him, his desire painfully obvious under the wet fabric.

Xiǎo Ying kneeled before him, glanced up at his man with hunger in his eyes, and began pulling on the pants. Unlike the tunic that was made of stronger material, the silk of his underpants slipped off him easily, revealing hard abdominal muscles, an Adonis belt that made Healer's mouth water, strong, beautiful upper thighs, and.... His hands dropped from the fabric and wrapped themselves around Fox, clasping the man's firm buttocks and pulling him closer still.

Fox moaned as he realized what Healer was about to do, but he didn't move. Xiǎo Ying's lips closed around Fox's erection, and he suckled, his tongue dancing over the velvety skin as he held on tightly to the other man's backside. Húlí let out a scream that mixed his human and his vulpine side and held on to Healer's head, pressing it closer, deepening the contact. Xiǎo Ying closed his eyes and thought he saw heaven, or what he thought heaven might be, his lover's flavor in his mouth, his heart overflowing with heat and honey.

Gods in heaven, he was hopelessly in love with this fox. His mate. His beloved.

CHAPTER 13
AFTERGLOW
HÚLÍ

He was no stranger to the pleasures of sex. As a fox *yāomó,* Húlí was more than accustomed to the physical bliss that it brought him. The sensual delight mixed with the oddly exciting feeling of renewing his *qi* was a sensation that he could not possibly describe to anyone who had never felt it. But this was better. So much better. Having Xiǎo Ying's lips closed around his erection trumped any other delight he had ever experienced. His whole body had come alive, a blend of ice and fire running through his veins, making his skin pucker and tingle. If he didn't know any better, he would have sworn he was shining like a star in heaven.

He moaned, pressing himself closer to Healer's

mouth, his hand at the back of the other man's head. "Why are you doing this?" The question left his lips before he could stop it. What a stupid thing to ask at a time like this. But that kernel of doubt that he always carried inside him had somehow escaped unbidden.

Xiǎo Ying stopped his suckling and slid his warm lips off Húlí, who couldn't suppress a groan of disappointment. "What do you mean why?" Healer asked, licking his lips and glaring up at him. "Why do you think?"

He was so used to being the one doing the seducing, he couldn't wrap his head around the idea that another man would want to take the initiative. Who would want him? A *yāomó*, a fugitive with no fixed home and no wealth. He knew he was attractive, but no one had ever tried to flirt with him. Not since Xu Ming. *Fox* was always the one who took the lead.

"Why would you want me? I'm dirty, a demon," Húlí whispered, hating the words he uttered. Words he had heard so many times from others, even from his lovers when he invariably got kicked out of their bed after a night of pleasure. He could hide his true identity most of the time, but not when he was that vulnerable. At times like that, his tails and ears had a mind of their own, unfurling in all their visible glory when his pleasure reached its apex.

Xiǎo Yīng was hard to read at the best of times, and that moment was no exception. His handsome face darkened in anger, but his eyes were soft, shiny. He pulled Fox down until they were sitting face-to-face, cross-legged and chest deep in the water.

"Are you fucking daft?" Healer asked, his expression somber. "When have I given you the impression that I give a fuck about what you are? Why would I bring you along with me on this trip if I cared about that? And why—oh for all gods in heaven—would I make love to you if I cared you're a *yāomó*?"

Fox lowered his gaze to the soapy, cloudy water, embarrassed he had shown his most vulnerable and weakest side to the one man he wanted to be strong for. "It's always in the back of my mind," he confessed in a whisper. "I know you're different from all the others, but...."

Xiǎo Yīng finished the thought for him, his hands seeking Húlí's under the surface of the water. "But you always wonder whether someone can truly care for you despite what you are. You don't believe you are worthy of that."

It was true. Every word. Húlí played the role of the carefree, aloof, and self-assured bohemian to perfection after so many years of practice, but right below his skin, there was always that fractured image of himself shattered to a million pieces over years of being the target of irrational hate and intolerance. Cracked by a lifetime of accusations and ego-splintering judgments. That was the image he saw every time he looked at himself in the mirror—real or metaphorical. At vulnerable times like these, that thin layer of feigned confidence dissolved, and the broken ego surfaced.

Healer raised a hand and cupped the other man's cheek, a sweet, comforting caress. Fox leaned into it. "Why am I doing this?" Xiǎo Ying repeated, his voice a mere breath. "Because I'm attracted to you." He rubbed his thumb on the corner of Húlí's lips. "Because I like you." His lips lifted at the corners, a rare mischievous expression on Healer's face. "Because I like furry creatures," he teased.

Despite himself, Húlí laughed, his eyes watering both from joy and pain. "I can always use a good scratch behind my ear." He raised his eyes to Healer's, still smiling and feeling strangely coy all of a sudden, sitting naked in the same bathwater with the man who had saved his life twice. His usual playfulness returned, and he ventured to say, "But you probably need a good scratch somewhere else by now."

Healer's lips stretched into a wide, amused smile. He cocked his head to one side, a glint in his eyes. "I wouldn't say no if offered," he said, a low rumble in his throat. He reached out to grab Fox's hand and guide it between his legs. "As you can tell, the need is most definitely there." He winked and then groaned as Húlí wrapped his hand around him. "Just the thing," he muttered, sliding back until he was leaning against the bathtub with his head on the ledge. He spread his long legs, one on each side of Fox, wrapping them around his waist and pulling him closer. "I'm all yours."

Húlí swelled underneath the now tepid water, tightening his grip on Healer's arousal and wrapping his unfurled tails around him. Busy with making sure his man got his pleasure, Fox didn't register until much later that Xiǎo Yīng hadn't said, "Why wouldn't I fuck you?" but used the term "make love" instead. When he finally realized it, the smile that had been plastered to his face for the past few days grew even wider.

And it had nothing to do with the *héping* lavender they all had been inhaling since their arrival.

IT HAD BEEN A LONG JOURNEY, and despite their hunger for each other, both Húli and Healer had fallen asleep shortly after returning to their room, still damp from the bath and intoxicated by yearning. Húlí opened his eyes to find his lover draped over him, a long, muscled leg pinning Fox's down to the bed and an arm protectively covering his chest. He turned his head to look at Healer's just a few inches away from his, the man's warm, steady breath caressing Fox's cheeks. He was exquisite, an artful version of a male with chiseled cheeks, a straight-as-an-arrow nose, and luscious, well-shaped lips. But his eyes were the true masterpiece, now closed into dark crescents, raven eyelashes fanned over sun-kissed skin. Húlí watched him in silence, drinking him in like a parched man after a long walk in the desert. He couldn't afford to fall for anyone again. He couldn't run the risk of having his heart shattered and scattered to the wind. Once had been more than enough.

But Xiǎo Ying was not Xu Ming. He had nothing to gain from betraying Húlí. Healer had already proved himself—more than once—to be trustworthy, willing to put his own life at risk to protect

Húlí's. Fox's heart was dangerously toeing the line between attraction and falling in love. Laying there, gazing at the tall man peacefully asleep beside him, was tipping his heart over the line. Húlí was not sure he should be happy about that, but his very soul was dancing to the new feeling, nevertheless.

As he lay there, watching Healer in his slumber, Húlí was assailed by an unsettling thought: what if his partner would regret a night of abandon? What if it had all been a side effect of the powerful calming and mildly intoxicating herbs the city seemed immersed in? It would be more than just awkward if that were the case. It would be devastating to see horror in Xiǎo Ying's eyes as they met his.

No. I've got to get out of here now.

With all the stealthiness his fox-self could muster, Húlí lifted the other man's arm and leg and slid from underneath them and out of bed. He hurried to grab his clothes from where he had thrown them when they had returned to the room, still a bit damp from the wet towel he had dropped on top of them, and put his pants on, half hopping out of the room. He would go talk to Ling Ling, who by now was most likely in the dining room downstairs, having breakfast. The inn was still quiet at that early hour of the morning, and Fox slipped his black tunic on and tied it on the side as he took the stairs.

As expected, Ling Ling was already feasting on breakfast, the only patron in the dining room, Yè Yǐng by her feet. The squat table in front of her was covered by an array of platters from which she enthusiastically fished off a variety of food, dropping a chunk for the dog every so often. Húlí stopped on the last step to watch her, a smile dancing on his lips. That girl always had a big appetite. She seemed to have a special love for food and could eat large quantities without putting on a single ounce. Her job as a freight escort was physically challenging, making her sometimes walk for days on end with little rest, for even when the caravans stopped for the night, she was still in charge of keeping guard over the cargo. Húlí often felt guilty. His status as a *yāomó,* always hiding from the authorities, didn't allow him financial wealth, and during the winter when Ling Ling's jobs were far and between, they sometimes went without much to eat for days. He was a good-for-nothing who couldn't even keep his best friend fed and happy.

"Are you joining me or are you going to just stand there, staring like an idiot?" Ling Ling twisted her mouth the way she often did when she was annoyed with him.

Snapping out of his own self-defeating thoughts, Húlí stepped down and joined her at the table, bending down briefly to scratch behind the dog's ear. "Hi, Yè Yǐng," he said as the dog cocked his head to give him easier access to the back of his ear. "You're much friendlier than this female over here."

Ling Ling took a giant bite of a steamed bun and mumbled between chews, "Yè Yǐng doesn't know you like I do. Give him a few more months."

Húlí chuckled and piled a bun and an egg crepe on his plate. "You wouldn't know what to do with yourself without me." The truth was, she could do so much more without him by her side, but he was forever grateful for her friendship and loyalty. "Eat some more, grumpy warrior."

The dog let out a soft bark and placed his paws on Fox's knees, begging for more food. Húlí obliged with another chuckle.

"Where's Healer?" Ling Ling asked in between bites. Húlí poured himself a cup of steaming tea, the herbal aroma wafting to caress his nose. "He's not the type to sleep in, so I'm guessing he's out and about?" It was more of a question than a statement.

Húlí lowered his eyes to his teacup and cleared

his throat. "He's still in bed," he mumbled, bringing the cup to his lips.

The female warrior was quiet for a moment, studying her friend with half-closed eyes. "Why would he still be asleep?" she asked eventually. "He is always the first one awake and usually gone before the sun is up." She studied him closer, her eyes narrowing to slits. Húlí kept hidden behind the cup, taking short sips, never daring to raise his eyes to her. She slapped a hand on the table. "You guys fucked last night," she practically screamed.

Húlí put the cup down and gestured for her to lower her voice. "Can you be any crasser?" he said.

"It's about time," she said, not bothering to lower her voice even a bit. "You've been dancing around each other for weeks now. Glad you finally scratched that itch."

Fox ran a palm over his face with a grunt. "How can a *gūniáng* like you talk like a field soldier?"

Ling Ling licked her fingers one at a time and shrugged. "You pick up a lot of colorful language on the road," she said. "When did you become such a prude anyway?"

Good question.

Was it because what he felt for Healer was not the same basic physical need he felt for others? Was this attraction much more than that? Or was it because this time, his heart and not his libido was calling the shots?

HE'S SO HANDSOME. That little beauty mark under his lower lip is so sexy. I just want to—

"What in all heavens are you doing, Old Fox?" Ling Ling demanded, startling him out of his reverie, and his chin slipped from where it was perched on the palm of his hand. "All dreamy eyed and disgustingly in love."

Húlí bristled at that, heat climbing his neck and flaring on his cheeks. "I am not in love." *Sure, lie to yourself, why don't you?* "I just didn't sleep well."

His companion laughed, finishing her cup of tea. "Right, I forgot you spent the night banging Healer. The same one you can't take your eyes off right now."

Indeed, Xiǎo Yīng was coming down the stairs, his usual white robes flowing like water around his body. Or maybe that was all in Fox's head. Yè Yǐng leapt to his paws and ran to greet him at the bottom of the staircase, jumping on his legs and getting rewarded with a thorough petting. For a moment,

Húlí wished he was the dog. Damn it, he was so head-over-heels, there was no coming back from it.

"Good morning," Healer said, taking a seat beside Húlí, who immediately filled his cup with hot tea. "*Xièxiè*, A-Xin. Thank you."

Fox nearly spilled the tea at Healer's use of the endearment. It was the first time he had ever addressed him as A-Xin. No one had ever done it except for his mother, and even that could have been a fake memory, wishful thinking on his part. It had been so long, and he was so young back then.

"Aww, you made Fox blush," Ling Ling teased, placing her chin on her cupped hands and batting her lashes rapidly. "So cute. It almost makes me jealous I don't have someone in my life. Almost."

Xiǎo Ying barked out a laugh and brushed his fingers on Húlí's that was still wrapped around the teapot. "What's for breakfast?" he asked casually, as if he hadn't just made it abundantly clear there was something going on between them. Húlí was not sure what he'd expected—that maybe Xiǎo Ying would pretend nothing happened and go on as usual? But Healer had used an affectionate form of his name and blatantly caressed his hand for anyone to see. Was he really acknowledging a relationship and not just a one-night-stand type of thing?

Húlí couldn't remember the last time he had been quiet for that long. He was afraid that if he said something, it would break whatever spell he was under that made him believe Healer might actually care for him. He quietly watched Healer converse with Ling Ling while he ate his usually meager breakfast. Xiǎo Ying wasn't much of an eater, choosing to eat sparingly even when there was an abundance of food.

"I have an errand to run," he said, wiping his lips on a napkin. "Then we'll train, A-Xin."

Húlí's eyes rounded in surprise. They hadn't trained in a while, but then again, they had been on the road. "Where?"

"I'll come and get you," Healer said. "The innkeeper told me about this abandoned courtyard not far from here that will be perfect for it."

With the grace of a cat, Xiǎo Ying stood up, straightened his simple white robes, and left. Both Húlí and Ling Ling watched him leave in silence, awed by the aura the man always left behind. At least, that was true for Fox, so he assumed it was the same for his friend.

"I can totally see why you drool over him," Ling Ling said after a moment. "Be glad you're my best friend, or I would totally give you a run for your money."

Wrenched out of his momentary paralysis, Húlí grunted. "I give thanks to the heavens every day that I am not on the wrong side of you, my friend. Every single day."

Húlí couldn't tell how he spent the rest of the day, anxious and excited as he was for the return of Healer. It occurred to him much later that the other man hadn't said where he was going. He knew Xiǎo Ying was hoping to find clues as to who exactly was behind the massacre of his clan, but Healer had never been very clear about how he was going to do that. Was he meeting with a contact, someone with information or clues he could follow? Fox made a mental note to ask him later. Being around Healer made his power of concentration murky and twisted to the point where all he could think about was how Healer's lips had felt when fused to his. The rest of the world and all other problems faded into the background.

It was the middle of the afternoon when Healer finally returned, his white robes billowing behind him like sails on a ship as Húlí sat on the stoop outside the inn's entrance. The scent of lavender and other herbs he couldn't quite identify wafted over to him as the other man approached, soothing his restless soul. His lips stretched into a grin as the mighty figure of Healer came to stand close, shading him from the bright rays of the sun.

"Are you ready, A-Xin?" It seemed as if the intimate term was not just a passing fad. Fox's belly filled with warmth. He had never known the simple joy of being called by an affectionate name. He smiled even wider. "What are you staring at, Fox? The day runs short. Let's go."

Back to business, it seemed.

Ling Ling had gone exploring. In all her travels, she had never visited the city itself, and she was curious about how these calm and welcoming people lived their daily lives. Húlí jumped to his feet, now eager for action, and followed Healer down the street.

The courtyard Xiǎo Yīng had spoken of was spacious, with weeds growing between the cracks of the large ceramic tiles that covered the floor. The flowers that once had grown in stone-framed beds had long shriveled up and died, taken over by ivy that spread over the ground and crawled up tree trunks. Despite the daily bustle outside its crumbling high walls, the courtyard immersed in silence, as if enclosed inside a bubble. The hairs on

Húlí's arms stood on end, a strong sense of foreboding creeping through his body.

"What's this place?" he asked, hugging himself and spinning on his heels to scan the whole perimeter of the place. "So creepy."

"You're really gifted with words, A-Xin," Xiǎo Ying said, a one-sided smile on his lips. "It should be creepy like you said. After all, it is haunted by all kinds of restless spirits."

Being a fox *yāomó*, Húlí had grown up used to ghosts and all other sorts of spiritual lore. Not much surprised him anymore, but that didn't mean he wanted to be in the middle of a courtyard riddled with evil, resentful souls. "And you think this is the perfect place to train?"

Healer scoffed and turned to his companion. "What better place to practice focusing on the inside than around a bundle of noisy, attention-thirsty spirits?" he said, pointing at an empty spot right in the center of the yard. "If you can concentrate here, you can do it anywhere."

Húlí couldn't fault the logic of his statement, but he still wasn't happy about opening himself up spiritually where he could easily be attacked by an evil soul. "So what do I do, exactly?" he asked, resigned.

"Sit down, empty your mind, and let it come to

you," Healer said as if it were just as easy as ordering a steamed bun at a street vendor.

Fox sighed. Loudly. Then he dropped onto the ground, crossed his legs, and opened up the palms of his hands over his knees. With another long and noisy sigh, Húlí closed his eyes, only to reopen one of them a few seconds later. "You *are* going to watch over me, right?" he asked, his head cocked to the right. "As my master, it is your responsibility to make sure I come out of this alive and still sane."

Much to Fox's surprise and delight, Healer crouched before him, cupped his cheek with one hand, and whispered, "And as a lover, I also have the responsibility of making sure you're safe and capable enough to make love to me tonight."

Before Húlí could react, Xiǎo Yīng leaned over and kissed him. No ghost, no matter how evil and powerful, was going to wipe that smile from Húlí's face.

CHAPTER 14
WITH MALICE
XIǍO YING

The yellowed leaves lifted from the ground and swirled up in the air in three or four small funnels around Húlí, who was still sitting cross-legged in the center of the yard. The previous silence was now filled with whispers and moans as the spirits that inhabited that space fussed about their intrusion.

Xiǎo Ying leaned against a dead tree a few feet away from Fox, watching and waiting. Húlí was potentially a lot stronger than he gave himself credit for being, but he hadn't been properly trained, and his self-esteem was broken by the many years of being chased and chastised for who he was. When Healer looked at his lover, he saw a shining star as brilliant and intense as the sun, but Fox saw himself as the outcast he had always been treated like, the worthless demon the crown and its cronies told him he was. Xiǎo Ying wanted to change that. He hoped to open Húlí's eyes to the amazing human being he was and watch him bloom.

Once, he had told Fox, whose eyes were still closed and lips set into a tight line, that he would teach him a way of renewing his *qi* without having to risk his life seducing men who would run as soon as the feat was accomplished.

He had lied.

Or at least to a certain extent. Heavens' willing, his fox would never have to fuck anyone else to feed his spirit, but for a fox *yāomó*, sex energy was indeed the sole thing that worked properly. Xiǎo Ying was more than willing to be the one renewing him every time the need arose, either by making love to him or depleting himself of his own *qi* like he had done before. That day at the cabin, Fox had invaded more than just his house. He had besieged Healer's heart, and that's where he had stayed ever since. Xiǎo Ying was in love with this man of mysterious past that fate and their own master had thrown in his path, and there was no way around it.

A sudden burst of wind snapped him out of his thoughts. A quick glance in the direction of his man told him Húlí was holding his own even as spirits of all kinds assailed him from every direction. Pride filled his heart, but Xiǎo Yīng's smile was short-lived.

A large ghostly shape appeared, bright red with vestiges of purple and green. The form hovered almost stationary over Húlí, threatening and angry. Xiǎo Yīng couldn't understand what kind of spirit that could be. He had come by the courtyard earlier on his way back from meeting with an informant and established that none of the ghosts were particularly virulent or vengeful. This one, on the other hand, was all that and more. Whatever that was, it hated Húlí with the passion and bitterness of a jilted lover.

Healer put a hand to the hilt of his sword so he was at the ready. He wasn't going to let anything bad happen to his fox. A quick glance told him Húlí was unaware of this nasty spirit, his eyes still shut tight and lips set in concentration. Xiǎo Yīng hoped whatever had talked to Fox a few weeks ago with the voice of his mother would make a return. There was a message there, he just couldn't figure out what it was. Yet. Now, with this odd and malicious apparition, that didn't seem viable anymore.

The spirit wavered for a moment as if hesitating,

then pulsed like it was about to explode. It was going to attack.

Xiǎo Ying slid his sword halfway from the scabbard, ready to intervene, but Húlí suddenly opened his eyes, raised his hands chest high and palms down—a sure sign he was gathering energy to defend himself—and then pushed his hands up above his head, a ray of white light shooting from his palms, straight into the evil spirit. The shape burst into a million fragments and disappeared, tiny flecks of red smoke raining down on Fox.

"Well done, A-Xin," Healer exclaimed, his heart swelling with pride and love. He didn't expect Fox to be this strong so soon.

Húlí blinked and stared at him, a look of confusion in his eyes. "What just happened?" he asked, his voice hoarse.

Xiǎo Ying cocked his head to the side. "What do you mean? You just kicked that spirit's butt." Why did Fox look so bewildered?

"It wasn't me," Fox whispered, shaking his head. "It wasn't me."

Before Healer could do or say anything, Húlí's eyes rolled back, and he collapsed to the side in an unconscious heap.

He had never felt so helpless. Xiǎo Ying was not

the kind to panic in any situation, but at that moment as he watched his fox slump all the way to the ground as if there wasn't a bone in his body and then laid there, eyes closed, pale, and barely breathing, it filled Healer with a sense of loss he didn't know how to deal with. He fell to his knees, ignoring the sudden jabs of pain that shot to his upper thighs, to check Húlí's pulse.

Please, be alive.

He was. Despite his pallor and faint breathing, Fox was still very much alive. Xiǎo Ying exhaled a breath of relief, flattening one hand on Húlí's chest and rejoicing at the beating of Fox's heart against it.

"Thank all the heavens above, A-Xin," he murmured, slipping one arm under Fox's neck and another under his legs. "You scared me half to death, my love." Healer picked his lover up and stood in a fluid movement, as if the man he lifted weighed less than air. "Let's go to the room."

Ling Ling was sitting on the stoop of the inn with Yè Yǐng, and as soon as she laid eyes on them, she was on her feet and running toward them, her face a mask of worry. "What the hell happened?" she asked as she fell in step with Healer with the dog between them. "Were you attacked?"

Xiǎo Ying shook his head. "I'm not sure what

happened, but he lost a lot of his *qi*," Healer said, not pausing for a second in his dash up the stairs to the inn. "He needs healing."

The warrior followed Healer inside the inn and up the stairs to the room he shared with Fox. She opened the door, and Xiǎo Yīng dropped Húlí gently on the bed, covering him with the red bed linens. Yè Yǐng jumped on the bed and stretched his dark body alongside Fox's with his muzzle in the crook of Húlí's neck, and he whimpered.

Healer patted him on the head. "He'll be all right, I promise." He wasn't sure who he was trying to convince, the dog or himself, but he meant it. Húlí would be okay even if he had to move heaven and earth to make sure of it.

Ling Ling brought a small bowl of cool water to the bedside table and began wiping away the beads of sweat that were collecting on Húlí's forehead with a wet rag, cooing like a mother hen. Healer couldn't help but smile at the scene. He would have never thought the tough warrior had that kind of gentleness in her.

"Why isn't he coming to?" she asked, brushing the rag over Fox's parched lips.

He wasn't sure either. It was hard to tell, considering he had no idea what had actually happened.

Húlí claimed the sudden attack against the evil spirit hadn't come from him. So who used his body as a conduit for such a powerful surge of energy that had obviously depleted most of Húlí's *qi*?

Despite his uncertainty over what had happened, Xiǎo Yīng knew what to do.

What he had done that first time Húlí had been too weak to even leave his room wouldn't work now, since Healer couldn't afford to be bedridden for a few days; there was much he had to do. That left him with one option. But would that even work while Fox was completely unconscious?

He had to try.

"Get out," he told Ling Ling suddenly. Then, realizing how harsh he sounded, he explained, "We need privacy for what I am about to do."

The warrior eyed him suspiciously, the rag still in her hand and hovering over Húlí's face. "What the hell are you going to do?" she asked. "Get him naked and have your way with him?" Xiǎo Yīng hid his eyes. He was not the kind to blush, but he still felt the heat licking his earlobes. Ling Ling's eyes opened so wide, they looked like perfect circles. "Holy shit, you *are* going to have your way with him. He's unconscious. Isn't that just a little...." She searched for the right word. "Unconscionable?"

Healer cleared his throat. "Sexual healing is what a fox *yāomó* needs to renew his energy," he explained, uncomfortable with the idea himself. It would be a totally different thing if Húlí were awake, but seeing that he wasn't, the whole thing reeked of lack of consent. The *shényī* in him told him it wasn't a question of morals here, but a life-or-death situation that needed to be urgently addressed. The man who loved the ailing Fox was divided between the need to save his mate and the urge to protect his personal rights and dignity.

"Do it!"

The voice, weak and hoarse, caught both Healer and Ling Ling by surprise. They both snapped their heads toward the man lying on the bed. Had he really spoken? His eyes were still closed but his lips were moving. In unison, they leaned closer to Húlí.

"What did you say, A-Xin?" Xiǎo Ying asked softly.

"Do what you have to do," Húlí mumbled. "I don't want to die, but what better way to do it than in your arms?"

Ling Ling exhaled a sound that was a cross between a sob and a chuckle. "Stupid Old Fox," she said. "What the hell are you talking about? You're not going to die if I have anything to say about it. I will fuck you myself if that would help."

A strangled groan escaped the ailing man. "Gods in heaven, no. I'd never be able to look you in the face again." Ling Ling laugh-cried again, and Húlí opened his eyes for a moment to glance at Healer. "Are you going to do it or are you going to let me shrivel up and die?"

Xiǎo Ying replied with a kiss—a long, desperate kiss that left him weaker in the legs than the man he was kissing. "We'll talk about this later," he whispered, mouth hovering over Fox's.

Then he kissed him again.

CHAPTER 15
WHERE'S THE QI?
HÚLÍ

Ling Ling had left in a rush, throwing last-minute worried glances at the man lying on the bed. Húlí followed her with his eyes, fighting the need to close them but refusing to take them off his one and only friend on the off chance it was the last time he saw her. Once the door closed behind her, leaving him and Healer alone in the room, his eyes roamed to Xiǎo Yīng's. The man was sitting on the edge of the bed, eyes clouded by concern and lips swollen from the kiss he had just bestowed upon Fox.

"Again." Left with little strength, Húlí's mono-syllabic request had to be enough. He hoped his eyes did the rest of the begging.

Healer must have understood, because he leaned

over again and covered Fox's parched lips with the softness of his, sucking on his lower lip and prying them open with his tongue. "Take it, A-Xin. Take as much as you need."

Húli had always taken the sexual energy he needed without hesitation. But that had been from men he barely knew, men he was not interested in at any level. Men who would be gone before his spilled seed was cold and dry. Not that they were unwilling victims of Húlí's vulpine nature. He always repaid the favor by giving them the ride of their lives. In the end, and before the truth of his nature became too obvious to ignore, they were both satiated by the interchange. But he was still taking something from them that didn't quite belong to him. Every time he replenished his *qi*, he left a bit of an empty shell behind. He took nothing that wouldn't be recovered within a month or so—he was not a killer and would never take more than what his partners could handle—but they'd be a shadow of themselves for a while, too weak to work, too feeble to even defend themselves should the occasion arise.

He couldn't do that to Xiǎo Ying. The heavens knew he had already given him so much. Húlí wouldn't be able to live with himself if he left Healer bedridden again.

The sweetness of Healer's tongue, dancing and mingling with his own, stirred more than his *qi*-parched body. Húlí could feel life being brought back to each of his extremities as if Xiǎo Yǐng was causing the slow flow of his blood to somehow speed up toward all other parts of his body. The surge of energy from that simple touch filled him with emotion. In the past, Fox had to reach a climax in order to feel what he was feeling at that moment. This kiss carried the punch of a thousand.

Xiǎo Yǐng trailed kisses down to his chin and along the edge of his jaw. He gently nibbled on Fox's earlobe before touching it with his tongue, sending a tidal wave of shivers down his spine. A pleasant but demanding yearning tightened in his belly. It wasn't hard to keep his eyes open anymore, and he found that he could move his arms as he circled Healer's waist to pull him closer.

"You can stop at any time," Húlí whispered. "I may take too much."

"Take all you need" was the answer as Healer trailed more kisses down Fox's neck so tantalizingly slowly, Húlí thought he may die of pleasure. If this man could have this effect on him with just kisses, how would it feel if they fully consummated their relationship? A shiver ran up and down his spine at the thought.

Today was not the day for that. He wasn't fully in control of himself, and he was afraid he'd go too far. Images from a time long ago when he had been starved of *qi* came gushing in. The authorities had been on high alert, looking for him after Xu Ming sent them on his trail. He had been young and naive, unfamiliar with the world outside his hometown, so he had holed up for weeks in a small cave in the woods just outside the city walls, too scared to venture out, too brokenhearted to care. When a farmer happened to choose the same cave for an overnight resting place, he had lost control and almost sapped the life of an innocent. The incident had scared him so much, he had vowed never to allow himself to get to that point again. And here he was now, at an even lower point of his life, using the man he loved and running the risk of killing him.

Húlí pushed Xiǎo Ying away. "I have taken enough," he said in a choked voice. It was not nearly as much as his body and soul were demanding, but enough to keep him alive and going. Maybe Healer could perform a bit of his *shényī* magic to refill his store of energy afterward.

Healer closed his hands around Húlí's fists and

pinned them to the bed beside his head. "Not even close," he rasped, his face mere inches away from Fox's, his lavender eyes almost purple now. "Will you just relax and let me love you back to health? I know what I'm doing. I'll stop if it's going too far. I don't have a death wish."

An unexpected smile popped onto Húlí's lips. He blinked his eyes, still heavy with the lack of energy, and quipped, "You wouldn't die for me?"

Healer's mouth curved into a cocky smile. "I barely know you, A-Xīn. Don't want to die before I have the pleasure of tasting you fully and thoroughly, many times over."

Warmth spread inside Húlí's chest, an unfamiliar joy giving him wings. Should he allow himself to believe he could be loved? Was it wise to let hope enter his heart again? Was it worth risking another broken heart?

The answer came unbidden.

Hell yes, it is so worth it!

Recovered but not fully satisfied, Húlí turned to face the man who had yet again saved his life. Xiǎo Yīng had fallen asleep a while back, exhausted from parting with a big chunk of his *qi* and from kissing Fox to within an inch of both their lives. Húlí hoped that last part at least was pleasurable for Healer, who now lay on his side, eyes firmly closed into perfect black crescents, the sound of his quiet breathing matching the rising and lowering of his bare chest. They may not have fully consummated, but last night spent in the arms of that beautiful man had far exceeded any other time with a lover.

With his head on the pillow, Fox watched Xiǎo Ying sleep, tracing the deep arches of his eyelashes and the perfect curve of his full lips with a finger and hoping the man wouldn't wake up. Not yet. Húlí needed time to fully absorb the masterpiece that was his healer.

"How am I supposed to sleep with you staring at me like that?"

Damn!

Húlí bent his arm at the elbow and raised his upper body. "It is an admiring stare," he protested, a tiny smile twitching the corners of his lips.

"It's creepy," Healer said, flopping onto his back with an unconvincing huff. "Stop it, already."

Fox chuckled and ran his fingers over the other man's chest, sighing in satisfaction when Xiǎo Ying let out a barely audible gasp. "Thank you," Húlí whispered after a moment. "Third time you've saved my sorry ass."

"Fourth," Xiǎo Ying corrected, turning his lavender eyes to Fox, who raised his eyebrows in question. "I rescued you from the evil spirit not that long ago."

How could he forget? Watching the man fight the creature with his spiritual sword had been a highlight of Húlí's life. The graceful yet lethal moves of Healer as he sparred with the spirit had done more than just rescue Fox's soul from being eaten; they had brought Húlí's body and heart to life from an eternity of loveless entanglements.

"That doesn't count, since we were all in danger," Húlí protested, drawing lazy circles on Healer's chest.

"I think you know that thing was going for you," Xiǎo Ying said. Fox stopped his fingers. Healer was right; the evil creature had come at him, not the others. But why? He was a nobody without much spiritual power. What could have the creature been after? "Are you going to tell me what happened in that courtyard, by the way?"

Snapped out of his thoughts, Húlí met Healer's eyes. "*Duì*. Yes, of course." This beautiful strong man had made him forget the reason they were in that bed together. Part of him hated to be reminded. He preferred a different version of the truth—that Healer was lying beside him because he loved him. "I can't be sure, but it felt as if something took control of me and gathered all my energy to protect me."

"You mean almost killed you," Healer said with a frown. "It sapped you of all your *qi*."

Húlí shook his head. "No, it wasn't malicious. It really felt as if it wanted to protect me. Maybe it didn't fully realize how much it would hurt me."

Healer didn't look convinced. "That kind of power is not common even among *yāomó*," he said, turning on his side to face Fox. "Whatever did it was a very powerful entity."

Húlí couldn't help but noticing Xiǎo Ying's choice of words. "Entity? You think it was something other than a spirit?"

Healer nodded, his lavender eyes lost in thought. "I'm thinking god-level entity." Húlí let out a loud gasp. "That took a lot of power. Yes, it was partly stolen from you, but your spiritual powers are not that strong yet. Most of it came from whatever— whoever—was controlling you. Do you remember anything else?"

With Xiǎo Ying's eyes back on him, Fox closed

his, trying to recall any other details of what had happened and how it'd felt. All he could remember was that overwhelming surge of power running through him and out his palms and fingers. Instead of the panic he thought he should have felt, there had been a comforting sense of love, protection....

"Mother!" he exclaimed, his eyes flying open. Healer was still staring at him, waiting. "It was my mother."

The sudden realization had him shaking from head to toe. It could not have been anything else. He had been very young when his mother was killed, but even if memories of what she looked like were fuzzy, he would never forget how she made him feel every time she drew him into her arms, propped her chin on the top of his head, and cooed soothing words into his ear. That's exactly how he felt when the entity took over him; it felt like a warm hug, as if he had been suddenly cocooned in comfort and love.

"Your mother?" Healer arched his eyebrows. "Why would your mother hurt you?"

Húlí shook his head. "*Bù*, she wasn't trying to hurt me. She was protecting me," he said, all his doubts gone. "She just thought I was stronger...." His voice dragged and his brow furrowed. He caught his lower lip between his teeth before raising his gaze to

Healer. "Xiǎo Ying, if my master hadn't died and I had been trained all these years, would I be much stronger than what I am?"

Healer took a moment to reflect. "Yes, you would. Your latent spiritual power is great, but your lack of training hasn't allowed it to fully realize."

A smile pulled at the corners of Fox's lips. "My mother left me in the care of a master. She couldn't have guessed that he would die shortly after," he explained as much to himself as to Healer. "She would assume I am now fully trained and completely in charge of all my powers, wouldn't she?"

Xiǎo Ying cocked his head to the side. "I never thought of it that way," he said. He reached toward Húlí's head and ruffled his hair with a smile. "Look at you, being smart."

The intimate, almost childish gesture made Fox smile from ear to ear, a feeling in a way similar to the familiar comfort and warmth he experienced every time he remembered his mother. Could it be? Had he finally found his soul mate?

CHAPTER 16
DISSONANCE
XIǍO YING

Xiǎo Ying didn't know how long he had been staring at the bottom of his teacup. They had both come down for breakfast, followed shortly by Ling Ling and Yè Yǐng. The dog had curled under the table, patiently waiting for them to hand him his morning meal, and Ling Ling had immediately flooded Fox with questions about his health.

Healer had lost himself somewhere far inside his mind.

His meeting with the informant had not been as fruitful as he had hoped. The man had little information Xiǎo Ying was not already aware of, and he couldn't even be sure how trustworthy the information was. All he got from the meeting was a finger pointed in a new direction. A breadcrumb and nothing more.

A cold wetness on his hand snapped him out of his reverie. Yè Yǐng was prodding his fingers with his nose. He chuckled. "All right, no need to remind me," Healer said, petting the dog's head. "I'm awake."

His two companions stared at him. "Where have you been?" Húlí asked, stretching across the table to touch the back of Healer's other hand.

Xiǎo Ying smiled and turned his hand over to hold Húlí's. "I was just thinking of my meeting with the informant," he explained, squeezing Fox's hand. "With all that happened afterward, I had almost forgotten it."

Ling Ling snorted, her eyes firmly focused on their joined hands. "Can you be any cheesier with the public show of affection?" They ignored her. "What information did you get?"

"Not much," Healer admitted. "But I know where we're going next." Even the dog had trained his dark eyes on him and was waiting. He almost laughed at the expectant expressions on all three faces. "Duǎnde Mountains," he revealed, taking a bite of his fried dough stick. "There's a hermit there I need to talk to."

No one moved, all eyes still on him as he stopped his bread-filled hand that was halfway to his mouth again. It was as if they were petrified. He wasn't sure whether to laugh or worry.

Húlí broke the silence first. "Are you going to eat that *youtiao*? Because if not, I'll be glad to do it."

"*Bèndàn!*" Ling Ling exclaimed, slapping the back of Fox's head. "Idiot. Always fixated on food."

Fox let out an exaggerated yelp of pain and rubbed his neck. "You're one to talk," he said, lips pursed in a sulk. "Damn, you have a heavy hand, woman. I will be walking around with scrambled brains for the rest of the day."

Ling Ling chuckled. "They were already scrambled, Old Fox, and I had nothing to do with that."

Xiǎo Ying smiled, took another bite of the bread, and then handed it over to Húlí, bringing an immediate grin to his face. "I can order more if you want, A-Xin."

Fox shook his head, taking a huge bite of the *youtiao*. "*Xièxiè*, A-Ying," he uttered tentatively, as if tasting the familiarity of the term. "Is it all right if I call you that?"

Healer's lips stretched wide. His heart loved it very much indeed. There was no denying it. He nodded. "Yes, it's fine," he said, realizing what an understatement that was. He lowered his voice and leaned over the table. "I like it."

"You are going to make me throw up, you two." Ling Ling made a great show of gagging but never stopped eating. Yè Yǐng barked once as if agreeing with her, and the two men laughed.

Now that he had nothing left to do in town, there was no reason to linger, but the serenity of the place and the fact that his relationship with Fox was pleasantly progressing made him want to stay longer. There was no harm in waiting a few days. He had waited a lifetime to find out what exactly had happened to his parents and clan, so there was no reason to rush now. Whoever was responsible for the massacre was not going anywhere, safe in the belief he was none the wiser.

They spent the day strolling along the lively streets and markets of the city, enjoying the sights, smells, and tastes the place had to offer. Everyone was so friendly and calm, there were moments when even he—however immune to the wafting scents of magical herbs—found himself wanting to stay there forever. To forget the past and make a home in that wonderful place.

Something was off though. At first, he couldn't quite identify it, but the more he thought about it, the more certain he was that there had been some dissonance in the melody that was Xīwàng.

"I have it!" he exclaimed, stopping suddenly. The other two continued their path for a few more steps before realizing he wasn't with them anymore. "The attack in the courtyard."

Húlí turned around and scratched his head. "What about it?"

"It shouldn't have been possible," he said cryptically. He was still trying to make sense of it in his head. "Even the evil spirits in that courtyard were pretty subdued by the magic of the place. So how come such a powerful entity was able to gather enough strength and hostility to attack you?"

"Have you met Fox?" Ling Ling quipped unhelpfully. Húlí gave her the evil eye. "I'm just saying, hate can motivate people to do things they normally wouldn't or couldn't do. And Húlí has pissed off a lot of people in the past."

"Thank you, friend," Fox replied with a pat on her shoulder. "With friends like you, who needs enemies?"

The warrior laughed. "I love you, Old Fox—you know that. But not everyone does."

"There is only one way a spirit would be able to

break through the magical effects of the herbs," Xiǎo Ying said. "Someone was controlling it."

Both Ling Ling and Fox stopped walking to look at him, mouths half open. "What does that mean?" Ling Ling asked, cocking her head to the side. "Why would someone try to control a spirit to attack Húlí? I mean, even though I love him, he can be a little annoying at times, but he's not powerful or important enough for someone to be after him."

Xiǎo Ying disagreed, but that was a conversation for another time. There were more pressing matters right now. It seemed as if there was more to Húlí's identity and past than they were aware of. Yes, Fox would have the *yāomó* hounds after him, since he'd bedded the spoiled and powerful Prince Wu Ying, a terrible decision on his part. But even the prince would not expend the effort and the money necessary to hire someone powerful enough to summon and control a wraith with that kind of might.

"Someone wants you dead, A-Xin," Healer said, reaching for Húlí's hand again. "And I'm going to make sure they don't get what they want."

After a lifetime of chasing shadows, nothing much surprised Xiǎo Ying. The fact that someone was trying to kill his man was not shocking. Húlí had undoubtedly ruffled quite a few powerful feathers with his never-ending need to siphon *qi* from his lovers. But to summon such a mighty spiritual power was no easy task. Whoever was behind it had a much stronger motivation than just making Fox pay for an indiscretion. The question was, why? What could Húlí have done to pose such a threat to anyone?

Or maybe the right question was, who was Húli really? His past was shrouded in mystery, his broken childhood memories not enough to paint a complete picture, and with no one to turn to for answers, who knew what secrets his past held?

"We have to do more training," Healer said suddenly, the urgency of having Húlí ready to fight back a probable future attack foremost in his mind.

Fox clearly had someone's—his mother's?—spirit protecting him, but that kind of action had nearly killed him this time. What would happen the next time? Whoever, whatever was protecting him had little awareness of what Fox could or could not handle. Húlí needed to be able to call upon all his latent power to shield himself from those who would harm him, and the only way he was going to be able to do that was by training.

Hard.

Fox tilted his head in a birdlike motion. "Now?"

Ling Ling ruffled the dog's ears. "I agree with him. You need to be able to defend yourself," she said. "It's the second time you've been the target of an attack. Who the hell did you piss off this time, Old Fox?"

"*Méiyǒu rén*." Húlí's expression of surprise was almost comical. "No one. I haven't—you know—anyone in a long time." He avoided Healer's gaze. "I mean, not before you. I have been holed up at the inn for a while. You know that, Ling Ling."

"This has nothing to do with you rubbing someone the wrong way," Healer said. Ling Ling snickered at Xiǎo Yīng's choice of words. "It must have something to do with your past—maybe your family."

Húlí scratched his head. "They're all dead. Even my master. Why would anyone bother seeking me out?"

Healer shook his head, frustrated with the lack of answers. "No matter," he said, raising his arm and pushing the long sleeve of his tunic behind him. "We will train every minute we can before leaving town and then continue the lessons on our way to Duǎnde Mountains."

"I was hoping to squeeze in some naps with you," Fox whispered, eyebrows knitted together.

Xiǎo Ying smiled, warmth running through his body and pooling in his lower belly. "Training first," he said, finishing the sentence in his mind with *loving later*. There would be plenty of time for that once he could rest at ease, knowing his lover was well protected from evil.

Húlí hung his head. "No rest for the wicked," he mumbled, stirring a chuckle from his female companion. He raised his eyes to her, his lips set in a straight line. "Are you laughing? Well, you are coming with us when we train. Don't even think of relaxing while we work."

"Like you could make me, Old Fox," she said, standing up. Yè Yǐng, who had obviously fallen in love with the warrior, stood up as well, ready to follow her wherever she might go. "Think again." She stared at the dog and smiled. "Let's go have some fun, Yè Yǐng. Let these two work while we roam the streets in search of treats." The dog barked his approval, and they walked away side by side.

Fox braced his elbow on the table and leaned a cheek into his open hand. "Sometimes it sucks to be me."

The urge to laugh almost won over Xiǎo Ying's will to remain serious. "It won't be so bad," he promised, leaning in closer to Fox's ear. "There might be some kissing during breaks."

Húlí lifted his head so fast, he almost hit Healer's. "*Zhēn de*?" His eyes were round as saucers, and his mouth stretched into a wide smile.

Healer was frozen for a moment, stunned by Fox's beauty: his bright red curls gathered into an unruly man bun, ocean-blue eyes so transparent, he could almost see his soul, and the brownish freckles that covered Fox's pale skin, blending in with his sexy reddish scruff.

"You're beautiful," Xiǎo Ying muttered, reaching out to touch Fox's cheek. "I'm so glad you walked into my house that day."

And there it was—the bare-naked truth. Fox's bright eyes and large pupils fixed on him in rapt attention only confirmed it; Healer's heart was no longer his alone.

CHAPTER 17
SPIDERS
XIǍO YING

Yè Yǐng stubbornly stuck to Húlí's side, a fact that both worried and made Xiǎo Ying smile. It warmed his heart to know that his lover had another protector besides him. The gods in heaven seemed to have a special love for this fox, providing him with not one but three fierce champions. For all her joking and teasing, Ling Ling was just as ferocious as both Healer and the dog when it came to protecting her friend. Xiǎo Ying looked at her as she walked in front of them, feigning detachment while inspecting the path ahead for any danger. Healer smiled; despite all the misfortune that had befallen his lover throughout the years, Húlí was indeed a lucky man. And so was he for having had the fortune of crossing paths with Fox.

"How far do you think we still have to go?" Húlí asked, breathing hard from the ever-steepening climb. "Maybe I should morph into my fox. I'd have an easier time going up this mountain."

"No!" Ling Ling yelled in unison with Healer.

Húlí stopped the climb and stared at them in surprise.

"It will be hard to protect you if you go ahead of us," Healer explained. "Not to mention that as a fox, you will disappear against the vegetation." That was a blatant lie. Húlí's red fur would stand out like a sore thumb no matter where he roamed. But as a fox, he would be able to go a lot faster than they could and place himself in possible danger. "Besides, we'd miss your company."

Ling Ling huffed. "Speak for yourself, Healer," she said, making a face at him. "It would be nice to have a moment or two without his constant whining."

Xiǎo Ying chuckled softly. The female warrior talked tough, but she'd do just about anything to protect her friend.

"I'm not whining," Fox protested, straightening his hunched back. "I think my *qi* is dwindling again." He threw a wistful look in Healer's direction. "Maybe you can help me with that, A-Ying."

Healer smiled wider. "We may want to wait until we have some privacy," he said with a nod in the female's direction.

"Ling Ling won't mind," Fox claimed. "Right?"

The warrior stopped suddenly, turned halfway toward her friend, and placed her hands on her hips. "Are you fucking kidding me, Old Fox? Do you really think I want to witness you shagging Healer? Have you totally lost your mind?"

Húlí managed to look appropriately repentant, his chin dropping to his chest. "Sorry. My *qi* deficiency must be clouding my wits."

She huffed again, louder this time. "More like your brain deficiency, fool." She turned back around and resumed her climbing, pushing low-hanging branches and brush aside. "Sometimes I wonder how we are still friends."

Fox, having lost his feigned remorse, smiled with a twinkle in his eye. "It's because you know I'm special."

Xiǎo Yīng shook his head and resumed walking as well.

"You're special, all right," Ling Ling said. "But not the good kind of special."

"You love me, and you know it," Fox yelled out, winking at Healer.

They had just stepped into a small opening in the forest, its ground covered in ferns and moss, when Xiǎo Yīng heard a strange rustling. "Shhh." The other two stopped moving and fell silent. Healer sharpened his ears but still couldn't quite locate the origin of the sound. "A-Xin. Fox ears!"

Húlí immediately closed his eyes to turn on his vulpine hearing. It took only a few seconds before he turned around and pointed at a spot behind them. The other two swiveled on their heels in that direction and watched in horrified awe as an army of giant spiders crawled out from the bottom of a tree.

"What the hell are those?" Húlí squeaked, his pointing finger trembling. Yè Yǐng growled, baring his long sharp teeth.

"My guess would be spiders." If sarcasm was a weapon, Ling Ling would have killed her friend. "*Dàzhīzhū*," she exclaimed, voice shaking a bit.

Fox let out a sour chuckle. "*Big* spiders? They're the size of a fucking piglet and just as fat."

It was Xiǎo Yīng's turn to argue. "Piglets don't kill. These spiders are poisonous." Panic was rising in his throat as he watched the enormous arachnids dash across the forest floor toward them. "So many...."

"You can't be afraid of a few creepy crawlers, can

you?" Húlí said, his hand on the scabbard of his sword.

But he was. There weren't many things in this world that scared him enough to paralyze him. Spiders could. Any size, any kind. His chest contracted, and breathing became harder than anything else he had ever done.

Ling Ling had already released her sword and grounded her feet wide apart, preparing for the attack. "I'll show these creepers who the boss is."

"Get your sword, A-Ying," Húlí yelled, a few steps away from him. The dog barked by his side.

Xiǎo Ying couldn't move. Images of him as a child surrounded by poisonous spiders came flooding into his mind. He'd been five or six when he fell into a yellow spider's nest. Unlike most spiders, those nested in holes underground like ants, building large networks of tunnels that weakened the surface and turned perfectly innocent ground into a deadly trap. A small child like him stood no chance.

Húlí's hand, wrapping itself around Xiǎo Ying's arm, snapped him out of the nightmare. "You have to get your sword. There are only—" Fox stopped to count the spiders coming at them. "There are only about ten of them. We can beat them." Healer must have grimaced, because the other man squeezed his forearm. "Come on, big guy. I have never seen you look so terrified. Even I am not afraid of spiders."

It was Húlí's turn to be the hero because Xiǎo Ying couldn't make himself move. All his instincts told him to run the other way, but his legs wouldn't obey him. He stood there like an idiot, staring at the giant creatures scuttling toward them. "I can't. I just can't."

Fox jumped in front of him, protecting him with his own body while the female warrior defended the flank. "Don't let them get close to A-Ying," Húlí told Ling Ling.

Healer couldn't even gather wits enough to feel ashamed he had to depend on his two friends to defend him. Cold sweat beaded on his forehead and dripped down his nose as his heart threatened to escape through his mouth.

"Go for the pincers up front and between their eyes," Ling Ling said. "Without pincers they can't inject the poison, and their tiny little brains hide between their eyes. They will be disoriented and just fall."

Húlí braced himself as the spiders came close enough to touch. Just as the first one stretched its pincers toward the trio, Húlí swiped its legs with his sword, cutting off a couple of them but missing the poisonous needles. He huffed, withdrew his sword, and went for a thrust this time, burying the tip of his sword between the creature's eyes. The *dàzhīzhū* stumbled and fell onto its back, the remainder of its legs twitching in the air.

"One down!" Húlí announced unnecessarily.

Healer watched as another spider broke formation and came at his fox from the side. "A-Xin, *xiǎoxīn*!" he yelled in warning.

Fox turned halfway and stabbed the animal between the eyes like he had the first one. "Two down!" Beside him, Yè Yǐng had another spider between his strong jaws.

"Will you stop counting them, please?" Ling Ling yelled from the side. "It's annoying."

"It makes it more fun," Fox replied, cutting the pincers off the next spider.

Xiǎo Ying would have laughed if he hadn't been so scared. His childish little body had been covered in yellow spiders on that day so long ago. If it wasn't for his father's extraordinary medical skills, he would have died. But he remembered the horror and the pain the poison of dozens of spiders had caused him, how he had swelled like a balloon and almost stopped breathing. It may have happened many years ago, but it felt like it was only yesterday.

"You're an idiot," Ling Ling called out while dispatching a couple more of the spiders to their deaths.

"But a lovable one," Húlí countered, thrusting his sword at the last spider. "All done here." He slid the weapon into its scabbard and wiped his hands on his tunic. "Gross. These guys squirt when they die. This is not poison, is it?"

"Nah, just spider fluids," Ling Ling confirmed, putting her sword away as well. "Hopefully we got the whole colony, but just to make sure, let's make a fire to keep them at bay."

Yè Yǐng had made his way to Xiǎo Ying's side and was licking the spider gunk from his paws. Healer still couldn't move, his eyes roaming over the dead—or incapacitated—spiders scattered around them. "Kill them," he whispered. Húlí glanced at him. "Kill them all."

Ling Ling was the one who answered. "We'll throw them into the fire and watch them pop like chestnuts." She nodded in Healer's direction. "Hug the man, Old Fox. He needs it."

Húlí didn't have to be told twice. He threw his

long arms around his lover and drew him close. "It's okay now, A-Ying. You're safe now."

Being within those arms was heaven. His heart slowed down, his breathing normalized, and his muscles relaxed against Fox.

"I hate spiders, A-Xin," Xiǎo Ying whispered against the other man's face.

Húlí chuckled softly and rubbed his back. "I don't like them much myself."

Healer leaned in further and brushed his lips on the other man's ear. "I hate them. Hate. Them."

Fox pulled away to look in his eyes, brushed his hand on Healer's face, and smiled.

Xiǎo Ying leaned against his lover's hand. "I love you, A-Xin. I love you so much."

It came out in the heat of the moment. Panic had taken hold of Xiǎo Ying so tightly that when it let go, his confession had rolled out unbidden, fueled by relief. Not that it was a lie. Every single word was the truth. He had known now for a while that he was very much in love with Fox. He was reluctant to admit it because he didn't want to put any undue pressure on his lover. Húlí had an uneasy past and an even more complicated present. Healer had no wish to add to it and wasn't sure how wise it would be to get emotionally entangled right before finding out the truth behind his parents' killings.

Húli had been very young when it happened, but he was indeed someone who lived in the palace at the time. The emperor was a frequent visitor at his courtyard, and Fox seemed to remember him fondly. What if it turned out Húli was somehow connected to the massacre? Xiǎo Yīng had checked the timeline, and both Húlí's mother's and his own parents' deaths were mere weeks apart. Was it a coincidence, or was there more to the story? There were too many unknowns to make him feel comfortable revealing his true feelings to the red-haired man gaping at him.

"Well, I didn't see that coming," Ling Ling exclaimed, crossing her arms. "I mean, I obviously knew you felt that way—any fool can see that—but I didn't expect this sudden love confession after a spider attack."

Húlí waved a hand at her without looking. "*Bì zuǐ!* Let the man talk." He held Healer's hands in his. "What did you say, A-Yīng?"

For the first time since he was a child, Xiǎo Yīng's face burned. He wanted to hide his eyes, but he knew that wouldn't be fair to his lover or himself.

He loved this man. There was no shame in it. You could control a lot of things, but the heart was not one of them. He had always known it, but he had never fallen for anyone, having lived a rather reclusive life dedicated to cultivating his powers and strengthening his spirit.

"I love you, A-Xin. *Wǒ ài nǐ* more than anything or anyone else," he said, not worried about Ling Ling's obvious amused curiosity. "It's okay if you don't love me back. After all, we haven't known each other that long, and you—"

He was interrupted by a kiss. Húlí covered his lips with his and kissed him until even his toes tingled, their tongues dancing together as the kiss deepened.

"Okay, guys, don't make me poke my eyes out," Ling Ling yelled. "This is all very sweet, but we are still in the middle of a possible *dàzhīzhū* nest. I think we should make a fire and burn these suckers."

However reluctantly, the two lovers pulled apart. Húlí's face was flushed, his freckles standing out even more than usual. Healer smiled. His fox was so beautiful, and he was so deeply in love with Húlí, it was rather pathetic. He would literally do anything for this man. Which was rather scary for someone who had been all alone since his family was massacred.

"Ling Ling is right," he said, trying in vain to calm down his stampeding heart. "We won't be safe until we have a roaring fire going on."

Between Húlí and his best friend, the dead or dying spiders were efficiently and rapidly disposed of. Xiǎo Ying hated that he could do nothing more than watch them with a mixture of morbid fascination and terror, still paralyzed by the old trauma. Fox gently prodded him into spreading out the bedrolls while he built a couple more fires. In the end, they had a tight circle of flames protecting them from whatever danger might befall them during the night. Even in his dread, he couldn't stop admiring Húlí and Ling Ling for how quickly and skillfully they had taken care of a dangerous situation. There were so many layers to his lover's character despite his shallow exterior.

With Fox spooning him under the covers, Xiǎo Ying was finally able to doze off, his muscles relaxing, lulled by the rhythmic rise and fall of the other man's chest against his back. He couldn't tell how long he slept before he heard Fox whispering something.

"Why are you so scared of spiders?" Húlí

repeated in a quiet voice, his breath a burst of warm air against the back of his neck. "You're not afraid of anything."

Xiǎo Yīng swallowed hard. "I fell into a yellow spider nest when I was a kid," he explained, voice cracking a bit. He didn't want to talk about it, but this was his lover, the one person he wanted no secrets from. "I was bitten many times over and almost died. My father was able to detox me, but it was a long, painful process. I've been terrified of spiders ever since."

Húlí grunted in empathy. "Wow, that must have been terrifying." He wiggled even closer, his arm tightening around Healer's chest. "But you know what, my love? You've got me now. Besides being a fox, I am the spider-killing champion of the world. I will protect you."

A smile grew on Healer's lips. He didn't know what was more gratifying: that Húlí had proclaimed himself his protector or that he had just addressed him as his love.

CHAPTER 18

JOURNEY

HÚLÍ

The pounding in his head was not getting any better. The more Húlí tried to focus inward, the more his temples throbbed as if something was trying to escape his skull. Maybe he should have drunk more wine before training.

A pair of large warm hands closed on his shoulders. "Does it still hurt?" Xiǎo Ying's familiar voice soothed him instantly, his long fingers kneading Fox's tight muscles. "I'm afraid pain is to be expected, at least for a while. Your powers have been repressed for so long, they are all struggling to get out now that you're trying to access them."

"You're a healer," Húlí growled, his eyes still closed and burning. "Can't you prescribe some kind of elixir or pill for this damn headache?" Another low rumble escaped his lips as the pounding got even worse. "I swear my head will explode."

Healer kneaded some of the tightness from Fox's shoulders but not enough to fully relieve him of the pain. Sick of fighting it, Húlí opened his eyes and took a deep breath, leaning against Xiǎo Yīng's legs. Healer didn't say anything, allowing him to come out of his tumultuous meditative state and absorb some of his peace.

Yè Yǐng came bounding from around the corner as if being chased by a wolf. Ling Ling turned the corner right after him, huffing and puffing. "Fucking dog took off running for no reason at all," she said, stopping to brace herself on her knees. "What is wrong with him?"

The dark dog stopped next to Húlí, sat on his haunches, and licked Fox's face. "Yikes, Yè Yǐng— dog slobber," Húlí exclaimed with a frown. The dog didn't stop and gave him another wet lick, running his tongue from his chin to his forehead. "When did you get so affectionate, my friend?" Despite the sloppiness of the dog's attention, Húlí was amused. "I guess you love me."

Ling Ling managed to stumble the last few feet until she was beside the two men and then dropped to her knees. "What a run. Never knew he could run that fast," she said, crossing her legs beneath her. "What has gotten into him? And why aren't you guys training?" She pointed at Húlí where he still leaned against Healer's legs.

"Húlí has a terrible headache, so we stopped for a bit," Xiǎo Yīng explained, brushing his hand over Fox's hair. "Maybe you had enough for the day."

Fox had gone very quiet. "Guys," he whispered. "My headache is gone." He hesitated and then stared at the dog. "As soon as Yè Yǐng licked my forehead, the headache went away."

All three pairs of eyes turned to the dog, who was happily stretched out on the dirt floor, scratching his ear. "Is it possible?" Ling Ling's mouth had fallen open, and she blinked so fast, it made Húlí dizzy. "Can his spit heal?" The others' gazes that had momentarily moved to her returned to the dog in awe and confusion. "Is he even a real dog? You think he's a *yāomó*?"

Yè Yǐng was blissfully ignoring them, still laying on the ground and scratching himself, the perfect picture of innocence. None of them could move for a while, trying to digest what had just happened. Was it possible? Was the dog a lot more than what he seemed to be? And if so, how had he ended up with them? Was it an accident or something perfectly orchestrated by someone?

Húlí hopped to his feet, feeling like a new person. Whatever magic the dog's saliva contained was miraculous. His mind had cleared, and his body was light and energized. "Yè Yǐng, you're better than any amount of cultivation," he threw in the dog's direction, wiping the dirt from his clothes. "I hate to say this, but he is better than you, Healer."

Xiǎo Ying grunted. "Maybe he can keep you company at night then," he said, walking away in a huff.

Ling Ling didn't bother covering up her laughter as Fox took off at a trot behind Healer. "I didn't mean it that way," he said, falling into step with his lover. "There is no comparison. You must show me all your wonderful skills."

Healer waved a hand. "No, you don't need it, apparently. I'll get my own room."

"A-Ying, I really didn't mean it that way," Fox pleaded, looking like a child in trouble. "No one could match your... ehm, *qi*-renewing skills. No one."

Ling Ling crouched by the dog and gave him a good ear scratch. She shook her head and tsked. "Yè Yǐng, those two are worse than children. What do you say we go to the local butcher to get you a good chunk of meat?" The dog perked up his ears and wiggled to his feet. "Let's go."

"Remember that we're leaving," Healer said, turning around to glance at her. "Don't be too late." Not that Húlí's friend needed a lot of time to pack, but the journey to Duǎnde Mountains wouldn't be the easiest one, and they'd be better off if well rested.

The female warrior didn't bother to look back at them, waving a hand above her head with Yè Yǐng right beside her. "I won't. Have fun, lovers."

Judging by the stony expression on Xiǎo Ying's face, Fox doubted very much that fun would be had at all.

JUST AS OMINOUS and majestic as the mountains that jutted up to the heavens in front of them, Xiǎo Ying's stoic composure scared him more than any malicious spirit could. Healer had barely spoken a word to him since his offhand comment about the dog. Who would have thought that a silly little joke like that would piss off Xiǎo Ying so much, he had slept the whole night with his back turned to Fox?

Ling Ling stopped every so often to watch them, curiosity and a dose of amusement in her eyes and the curve of her lips. Húlí wanted to strangle her every time she peered at them with those dark slashes of her eyes. She smirked at his murderous glares, let out a semi-chuckle, and continued ahead, Yè Yǐng practically glued to her legs as usual. Húlí watched his friend walk ahead of them, half annoyed and half grateful for her company.

"Are you ever going to talk to me again?" he finally asked, sick of the suspense. He hated how needy he sounded, but he already missed Healer's touch, the sound of his soft breath in his ear at night, the warmth of his lips on his own.

Healer grunted quietly but didn't say anything, lavender eyes trained on the ground ahead.

"For all the gods in heaven, it was only a joke," Húlí pleaded, speeding his step to keep up with Healer's. "I fucking miss you, A-Ying." It was out before he even realized what he was going to say, but greater truth had never been spoken. It had been less than twenty-four hours, but it already felt like an eternity.

Xiǎo Ying didn't even blink, never slowing down his steps.

"A-Ying!" Húlí yelled, an irrational fear grabbing

hold of him. He ran a few steps ahead of Healer, turned on his heels, and threw his hands around the other man's arms in an awkward hug. "Stop. Talk to me please. *Duìbùqǐ*. I'm so sorry."

The soft chuckle against his temple was a balm for his soul. "I'm not mad at you, fool," Healer breathed onto his skin. "I've been thinking about what happened with the attack and the fact that Yè Yǐng was able to heal you. Trying to figure out what exactly is going on—that's all."

Húlí pulled away and squinted at the taller man. "Then why didn't you say so? Why did you let me think you were pissed off at me?"

Healer cracked a smile. "Well, I'll admit it; it was kind of fun to make you twitch."

Fox's chin dropped a couple inches. "You were enjoying my discomfort?" His outrage mixed with a hefty dose of admiration for his lover. You had to appreciate that kind of mischievousness from someone who was normally so serious. It was unexpected and strangely pleasing.

"Sorry, my sweet Húlí," Healer said, poorly hiding his glee. "You seem to bring out a side of me I haven't seen in years." That had to be a good thing, right? Húlí flushed in delight. Xiǎo Ying leaned over so his eyes were leveled with Húlí's. "I love that you do that, A-Xin." His lips fell lightly upon Fox's. Energy, hot and bright, ran through Húlí's body, rejuvenating every inch, every cell. Healer was quite literally his lifesaver, a giver of life.

Húlí walked as if floating on clouds for the rest of the day. When night fell and they stopped for the night, the smile that Healer had magicked out of him was still plastered on his face. There were no villages in this part of the world, trees as far as the eye could see all the way to the bottom of the mountain, so they would have to camp instead. Ling Ling was the first one asleep. While Xiǎo Ying fussed with the fire and Húlí with the bedrolls, she had wrapped herself tightly in a blanket and now snored softly a few feet away from the roaring fire. The dog, uncharacteristically, came to lay down close to Húlí, a fact that had Healer in an uproar.

"Why does that bother you so much?" Fox asked, smoothing out the crinkles on the bedroll. "Are you jealous? Yè Yǐng has a discerning taste, that's all."

Healer shook his head. "Don't be so cocky, A-Xin. I'm worried." About what? Yes, the forest was thick and desolate with menacing shadows lurking in every corner, but surely it wasn't any more dangerous than Yǎnlèi, and they had made it out without too much damage. "Think about it. Until now the dog has been glued to Ling Ling's side, and all of a sudden, he changes gears to stick with you instead. Right after he somehow healed you."

"You think he is possessed by some evil spirit?"

Xiǎo Ying hung his head. "No, fool. I think he can smell danger ahead and wants to be close to protect you."

Húlí did a double take. "Why would anyone want to hurt me, and why here?" he asked no one in particular. "I mean, not even I knew I'd be here."

"Is there something about your past you're not telling me?" Healer asked, stretching out on his bedroll.

Surprised by the question, Húlí dropped to the ground faster than he had planned, sending up a small cloud of dirt and leaves. "What do you mean? I'm not hiding anything from you."

"Maybe something you've forgotten or didn't think much of at the time." Xiǎo Ying turned onto his side, facing Fox, whose incredulous eyes blinked rapidly. "Don't be mad, A-Xin, I know you are not hiding anything. At least not on purpose, but our memories sometimes play tricks on us. Maybe something happened when you were a child that your mind hasn't processed as important or strange."

Húlí blinked again, trying hard to review the few childhood memories he still had, but nothing stood out. He barely remembered how life was before his mother was killed: a vague memory of the kindly emperor who came to visit often, the beautiful, gentle face of his mom, and the cherished presence of his one and only friend, Xu Ming. Fragments of things like furniture pieces, bed coverings, trees and flowers in the courtyard, and his mother's smile flashed in his mind, bringing the familiar sting of sadness and pain. He heard a whimper, and realized it came from him.

Healer patted the space next to him on the bedroll. "Come join me, A-Xin," he said. "Between Yè Yǐng and me, we'll keep you safe."

A smile stretched across Fox's lips, and he wasted no time sidling in close to Xiǎo Ying's warm body and flipping the other bedroll over both of them.

Xiǎo Ying nuzzled the crook of his neck, sending a firework of pleasure down his spine. He closed his eyes, shimmying closer to the big man, wondering at how amazing it was that their bodies fit so perfectly, his back cradled by Healer's long shape and the other man's arm draped over his side, palm opened against his chest.

"We must keep you safe, A-Xin," Healer breathed on the side of his face. "After all, you are very precious to both of us."

Had he died and gone to heaven already?

CHAPTER 19
THE ʜERMIT

HÚLÍ

Húlí loved the way Xiǎo Ying clung closer to him for the rest of their journey up the mountain. Until then, Healer had been the one protecting him, and even though Fox didn't mind at all—in fact, he liked the feeling a lot—shame sometimes gnawed at him. What kind of man was he if he couldn't even protect those he cared about? *The same kind of man who had survived when everything he cared about was ripped away from him*, the voice in his head always answered. No matter how many times he reminded himself he had been a small child at the time of the killings, the guilt was still there.

"How much longer until we get there?" he asked in a whiney voice. Healer was such a strong individual, Húlí hated to think he would feel lesser because of what had happened. To make sure that didn't happen, Fox was more than willing to continue to exude his feigned weakness for the whole world to see.

"For all the gods in the heavens, can you gag him or something, Xiǎo Ying?" Ling Ling grunted from some distance ahead.

Healer chuckled and squeezed Húlí's hand in his. "Not much longer, A-Xin," he said. "We should be cresting in the next hour or so, I think."

Húlí grunted. "My human legs are not built for this," he complained. His legs were fine, built with strong if not bulky muscle, and used to long runs. But he had an image to uphold. "If I could only change into—"

Both his companions turned to him, daggers in their eyes. "No fox!"

He lifted his free hand in appeasement. "All right, all right—I won't turn into my fox." Inside he was laughing. It was always fun to rattle Ling Ling, and now he had someone else to do it to as well. "I'll suffer a bit longer. But you'll feel really bad when I collapse."

Ling Ling humphed. "We should be so lucky."

She continued her climb without so much as a glimpse at him trailing behind.

"I will carry you if you collapse, A-Xin," Xiǎo Ying whispered, leaning closer to him. "Just say the word."

Húlí's lips turned up into a deep curve, warmth spreading inside his chest. How lucky was he to have found Healer? After a lifetime without love, this amazing gift had been thrust in his path.

Healer hadn't lied. In less than an hour, they had reached the top of the mountain, but after the first moment of elation came crushing disappointment. There was nothing there but grass that stretched all along the narrow crest and down the other side.

"Fuck! Where is this hermit you spoke of?" Ling Ling said, her hands braced on her hips. "There's nothing here and no place to hide."

With his hands cupped over his eyes to protect him from the glare of the sun, Xiǎo Ying scanned the area, calm as always. The man who had cowered before an army of spiders was gone, and Healer who feared nothing was back.

"Don't jump to conclusions," he said. "This hermit is not a regular guy. He's been cultivating for longer than we have been alive. He's here somewhere."

Húlí didn't want to be the bringer of bad news, but his mouth still opened to mutter, "He must be invisible, then."

Healer shook his head. "*Bù*, not invisible. Shielded. There's a power formation hiding him from view." Xiǎo Ying pointed at a spot in front of them, but Fox couldn't see anything at first. "Focus, empty your mind, and see."

Squinting, Fox took a deep breath and willed himself to see what he couldn't. Much to his surprise, a shape made up of shining golden lines appeared in his line of sight a few seconds later. "I see something," he yelled out, a bit too excited.

"Good, I knew you could," Healer said, squeezing his shoulder in approval. "Now, take it down."

The command threw Húlí off. He gaped at the tall man. "What? Take it down? How in the hell can I do that?"

Ling Ling, who had been exploring the perimeter, stopped and turned to them, curiosity rounding her narrow eyes. "This I want to hear."

"You can do it, A-Xin," Healer insisted. "All you have to do is focus on the formation and dismantle it with your thoughts."

Fox's mouth fell further open. "Who am I? Some god from the heavens?"

Xiǎo Ying chuckled. "No, but you certainly are a Xi—it runs in your blood, I'm sure of it."

"What runs in my veins other than very thin blood?" Blood that he had somehow managed to keep inside his veins despite all odds.

"Power, my love," Healer said, brushing his thumb along Fox's jaw. "Cultivating power runs in your veins. Believe it. You can do it."

Trying to digest what his companion and lover said, Húlí focused on the formation again and, not sure what to do, studied the intricate pattern of the gold threads woven into a filigree of sorts. He had once accidentally knotted silver embroidery thread that his master traded with women from the palace in exchange for information. It had taken him over an hour, but he had been able to disentangle it before his master found out and had his hide. This didn't look that different. Without hesitation, he began the laborious puzzling out of knots and weavings. He didn't know how long it took him, but at some point, the formation collapsed, and what was hidden became visible.

"I knew you could do it," Xiǎo Ying exclaimed, giving him a one-armed hug.

"Shit, you did it, Old Fox," Ling Ling said, drawing closer. "What do we do now?"

Still stunned by what he had just done, Fox shrugged and said, "Now we go meet the old fart that lives over there."

They began the short walk to where a crumbling shack stood, looking as if even a gentle breeze would cause it to fall. Húlí imagined the hermit who lived in such a decrepit place to be a tiny, shriveled up old man with a silly white goatee. However, the man that emerged from behind the door was nothing like that. In fact, this person was not old or shriveled up but completely the opposite. Xiǎo Ying was a giant, but this hermit towered at least a half foot over him and had shoulders to match.

This was no frail cultivator. This was a mighty warrior.

"Not sure whether to congratulate you on the brilliant way you dispersed my formation or kick your ass from here to the Southern Sea." The so-called hermit had a booming voice that carried as if he was using some sort of amplifying device. He stood with his thick, bare arms crossed over his chest, the muscles of his biceps bulging out from underneath his short, frayed sleeves. He had—by his very presence—effectively silenced Húlí and his three companions. "*Wéi*! Are you all deaf or just dumb?"

Xiăo Ying was the first one to finally react to his presence. "*Buhaiza*, Great Master." He linked his hands in front of his chest and bowed. "I'm so sorry. We're just very surprised and honored to meet you."

The big man cocked his head to one side, studying them with sharp eyes. "And who exactly are you? You've interrupted my meditation, and I don't take kindly to that sort of thing."

Healer bowed again. "I apologize for our intrusion, but this is a matter of great urgency and importance," he said. "I am Xiăo Ying." He turned slightly to point at his two companions. "This is Húlí and Ling Ling." Cued by Healer's actions, they both bowed to the man. "None of us mean you any harm."

The hermit studied them for a while longer before letting his long arms fall to his sides. "A Xi and a *shényī* together? Now that's interesting and worth being yanked from meditation."

How did he know Fox was a Xi when his lover had not disclosed his family name? And how had he guessed what Xiăo Ying was? Húlí couldn't help but gawk at the man, unable to hide his curiosity.

"Since you know who we are, it's only fair you tell us your name," Xiǎo Ying said.

"I am called Dānchún. You can call me Dān." The cultivator waved them inside the hut. "What are you waiting for? Let's go in. I have many things to ask you."

Still stunned, Fox followed Xiǎo Ying and Ling Ling inside the small shack, wondering how they were all going to fit. But a bigger surprise awaited inside. The tiny hut was not what it seemed. Inside, the space belied the outside. Magic again. The humble exterior hid a much more grandiose interior. Not that it was as sumptuous as a palace, but it was roomy and comfortable, with pillows strewn all over the floor of the main room. At least two doorways seem to hint at other rooms beyond.

"*Zuò*! Sit!" the big man ordered, pointing at the floor cushions. Húlí's legs were sore from the climb, so he didn't have to be asked twice. He dropped onto one particularly inviting one, closely followed by Ling Ling, who hadn't uttered a word yet. He threw her a glance, making sure she was still breathing, but she seemed to be all right, just a little stunned. Their host and Healer were the last ones to sit down. "Tell me, how did a Xi ended up with you, a *shényī*?" he asked, addressing Xiǎo Ying.

"It's a long story," Healer answered.

"I don't have anywhere to be any time soon," the man said, raising his open palm between them in invitation. "Go on! Enlighten me."

Húlí almost jumped out of his skin when a cup of steaming tea suddenly appeared on the table in front of him. This cultivator had strong magic.

Xiǎo Yīng leaned forward a little and cleared his throat. "When I was a kid, my whole family was massacred in our own house." Clearly, Healer wasn't about to mince words and decided to go straight to the heart of the matter. "As you already seem to have guessed, we were the only *shényī* clan in our kingdom and were working for the emperor. Yet, someone wanted us all dead. I think I know why, but I want to know who did it."

Dān was silent for a moment, stroking a nonexistent beard. Then, he turned to Húlí. "What about you, Húlí? What do you want to know?"

Shock didn't start to describe how Fox felt at that moment. They weren't there for him, so why would the cultivator think he was there to ask questions?

"Wasn't your family also slaughtered shortly after the Xiǎos?" Dān asked. Fox shrugged, utterly confused by the question. "It has never crossed your mind that the massacres of both families were connected?" Húlí saw his bewilderment reflected in his lover's face. "When I saw you two together, I assumed you had figured that out."

Healer found his voice first. "What do you mean? Our families didn't even know each other. How can their deaths be connected?"

The cultivator shook his head and clicked his tongue. "You've got to be kidding me. You never really connected the dots? Are you dumb or something?"

Húlí opened his mouth to defend Healer, but Ling Ling spoke first. "Stop belittling them and just tell them the truth, you old fart. They had never met until a few months ago, and they were both young children when it happened. Why would they think the two cases were connected?"

Fox cringed at her tone of voice, but he couldn't help a small smile anyway. His friend had always been blunt and fearless.

Dān chuckled, obviously not offended by her at all. "I like your spunk, *gūniáng*," he said. "I suppose you're right, but you would think they'd have grown suspicious of it somewhere along the way, don't you agree?"

"Tell them!" Ling Ling's eyes had rounded into

almost perfect circles, not an easy feat considering how narrow her eyes were. Húlí covered his mouth to hide a laugh.

The cultivator raised his hands in surrender. "*Hǎo*, I will, I will." He turned back to face Healer and Fox, rolling his eyes like a teenager. "How do you put up with that?" Húlí wanted to laugh. "The deaths of both families are intimately connected and happened for similar reasons."

Xiǎo Ying sought Húlí's hand across the space between them. Fox wondered whether he needed or was offering comfort. "What reasons could anyone have to kill A-Xin's family?"

The old man sighed loudly. "This is going to take some time," he said. "I suggest we grab something to eat now because you may not have much of an appetite after I tell you."

CHAPTER 20
ALL WILL BE REVEALED
XIĂO YING

The food the cultivator conjured up from nothing was simple but tasty. The grilled chicken was moist and tender, the greens just crunchy enough, and the lotus root had been cut thinly and fried to a delightful crisp. Xiăo Ying was not much of an eater, but he was grateful for the non-charred, not-dried meal. These past days while traveling up the mountain, they had made do with dried meats, stale bread, and the occasional game, invariably overcooked over the campfire. Yè Yĭng had been offered a large chunk of chicken as he rested between Fox and Ling Ling and now lay happily munching on it, his tail wagging back and forth like an upside-down pendulum.

Once most of the food was gone, they all looked

at the old man, hoping he would finally divulge what he knew about both their families' massacres. Dān didn't seem to be in any hurry. He sat on the floor cushion, rubbing his belly and alternating from belching loudly and making sounds of contentment. Healer took deep breaths and willed himself to be calm and patient. Were all cultivators this annoying?

"*Wéi,* old man!" Ling Ling finally said. "Are you ever going to get on with it or are you planning to keep us all in suspense forever?"

Xiǎo Ying threw her a sideway glance and smiled. The woman's lips were curled into a murderous grimace. A quick peep in Húlí's direction told him his lover was just as amused as he was.

"Patience is not a virtue you embrace, is it?" Dān said, giving his belly a final tap. "Don't get your undies all in a twist, woman. I'm getting to it."

Ling Ling leaned forward, crossing her arms. "No need to announce it. Just do it!"

"*Gòule!* Has anyone ever told you, you're a bully?" the old man said, not looking too concerned.

"Bully, schmully. I'm just practical and assertive."

Dān took a deep breath followed by a loud and long belch before starting. "As I'm sure you all know,

the old emperor was well loved and fair to a fault."
Everyone nodded. That was one thing that could not
be argued. Xiǎo Ying had never met the man, but he
remembered all the conversations his parents and
the rest of the adults in their enclave used to have.
Emperor Gōng Zhèng was true to his name, fair and
tolerant, generally loved by his people. "Unfortunately that same fairness made him quite a few
enemies among the noble families who were not
happy with his requirements of sharing fairly. They
didn't like the fact that they were required to give
away part of their wealth to a special royal fund that
was then distributed to the poor of the kingdom.
That alone took away part of their riches, which in
turn diluted some of their power. How could they
control the people under their authority if the
emperor himself had the backs of the poor?"

Healer remembered his father, who kept well
away from court politics, saying he heard unsettling
rumors of rebellion brewing among the upper
classes. He was very young then, but that thought
had left a bitter taste in his mouth, almost as if he
knew it would somehow come to harm him and his
family.

The cultivator turned his gaze to Húlí, who sat
transfixed and was leaning forward to listen better.

"How much do you remember Emperor Gōng Zhèng?" he asked Fox.

Fox blinked and hesitated for a moment. "Not much," he admitted. "I remember him as an old, kind man who used to visit my mom and me often. He always brought a gift, a toy or candy. My mom enjoyed his visits and even cooked for him often. Sometimes he stayed for a day or so when he seemed to be tired or sad. I was very little."

"Do you remember Gōng Hǎoxīn?" It was a strange question. The once crown prince had died young before he could truly be called an adult. Rumors had it he had been poisoned, but the truth was, he had died in battle at the border. Xiǎo Yǐng's father had attended to the young man growing up and was heartbroken to hear of his untimely death.

Húlí shook his head. "He died when I was too young to remember," he said. "My mother told me stories about him not long before she died; how he was barely twenty when he went to war and died. How he had grown up with my mother and how she missed him a lot. She told me he was kind, hand-some, and had a wonderful soul like mine." Húlí paused, the corners of his eyes crinkling. "Now that you ask, I also remember the emperor talking about him in hushed tones. I remember thinking he was crying, but even my young self knew it was understandable, since this had been his beloved son."

"Hǎoxīn was the one in line to inherit the crown," the old man continued. "But as fate would have it, he died early, leaving the emperor with a handful of other sons he preferred not to have in any position of authority. They were all bullies who did nothing but fight and scheme against one another for the position of crown prince."

Xiǎo Ying remembered the whisperings about the other princes who stopped at nothing to get a hold of the emperor's scepter, but his family had been killed before the old emperor died, and life had become a blur after that. "He picked Gōng Làn for his heir, days before he died, right?"

The disgusted snort Dān released left little to the imagination as to what he thought of that choice. "Not that Gōng Zhèng had a lot of good choices, but still." He shook his head one more time. "I can't be sure, but I am almost positive his was the hand that served the killing dose of poison."

"This is all very interesting, but what does that have to do with the deaths of both our families?" Húlí asked, pointing his finger at the cultivator.

Healer spoke up. "I know my family was murdered so that the emperor didn't get the antidote to the poison. It doesn't take much to put two and two together there. But what about A-Xin's?" Once again, he stretched across the short space between them and held on to Fox's hand. "His mother had nothing to do with that. A-Xin was just an orphaned boy who the emperor took a liking to." He gave Fox's hand a comforting squeeze.

"Young people are so impatient," the old man said, closing his eyes for a moment. "Isn't it obvious?"

They all shook their heads. Whatever the connection was, Xiǎo Ying couldn't even begin to guess.

The cultivator tsked and said, "Our young fox here is Gōng Hǎoxīn's one-and-only son and legally in line for the crown."

Xiǎo Ying felt the cushion beneath him move. Húlí's hand trembled and tensed inside his. Did he hear correctly? Could that possibly be true? Of all the theories he had concocted in his mind for weeks now, that was not one of them.

"What the fuck did you just say?" Fox asked, voice choked and strained.

The cultivator nodded and shrugged. "You heard me. You are the old emperor's descendant, born of a secret marriage between your mother and his son, and had Gōng Zhèng survived the poison, he would have surely made you crown prince."

Ling Ling lifted her hand in the old man's direction. "Wait! What is happening right now? Am I hallucinating or did you just say Old Fox is of royal blood?"

"Can't be," Húlí said, sweat beading on his forehead. "The old emperor never once mentioned that he was my grandfather. Neither did my mother."

"He was trying to protect you and your mother. And the empire as well." Dān bit his lower lip. "Think about it; all his other sons were fighting for the crown. He trusted none of them. He most likely hoped that once he was cured of his illness, he would wait a few more years before writing the edict to make you his heir. You were his favorite son's flesh and blood. With him as your father, and the kindness and smarts of your mother, he was sure he would make a much better emperor than either of his power-hungry children."

"But he never got that chance," Healer interjected, his mind finally clear. It all made sense now. "One or all of his sons killed the only people who could detoxify the emperor. The path to the throne opened up. What the emperor didn't know was that someone knew about A-Xin." He paused for a moment, a new idea brewing. "Or maybe he did, and that's why he had you removed from the courtyard that day. I bet he's the one who placed you with our master, afraid they would kill you too."

Húlí had gone ashen. Even his trembling lips were devoid of color. Xiǎo Ying held his hand tighter, hoping the gesture would be comforting. Healer had known for a long time why his clan was killed. He just needed proof so he could offer his family some kind of justice. But Húlí had no idea. He had always believed he was a nobody, the bastard son of some nobleman who didn't want him or his mom, a child that had been taken in by the emperor as a simple act of charity. After all, Gōng Zhèng was known for doing that; he had a whole courtyard filled with women and their orphaned children who had lost their husbands and fathers one way or another. Why would he have thought he was different?

Silence fell over them like a thick, heavy blanket, and for the next few minutes, no one spoke, their breathing the only sound.

Xiǎo Ying broke it first. "Which of his sons did it? And how can I get proof?" he asked in a dangerously quiet voice. "Were there any witnesses? I was told you might be one. After all, you do know a lot about what happened."

The cultivator waved a hand, dismissing the idea. "No, I wasn't a witness, and I have no idea how you can prove any of this," he admitted. "I know all of it because one of my acolytes was indeed a witness. He worked for one of the princes and was an expert at making himself invisible in the eyes of the rich and powerful. He eavesdropped on many conversations between the brothers. Yes, it was not one prince but several working as a team who are guilty. But proof? I have none."

Disappointment filled him with a mixture of sadness and rage. "There has to be a way," Healer growled, Yè Yǐng echoing him with one of his own.

"Maybe you can find my acolyte," the old man suggested. "The young man had the wisdom to lose himself before anyone suspected what he had witnessed."

Both Xiǎo Ying and Húlí glanced up at the man. "You know where he is?" Fox asked.

The cultivator confirmed it with a nod. "He is one of the monks in Mó Fēng Temple. He shouldn't be too hard to find." Smiles popped onto the couple's lips. "But don't get too excited. He might refuse to bear witness, and who can blame him? These are dangerous and powerful men."

The dog seemed to be even more thrilled than

they were and dashed around the room in full circles.

"What about proving Fox is who you say he is?" Ling Ling asked, voicing the same question Healer had held back.

The old man shrugged and belched again. "I can't guarantee it, but knowing my acolyte, I'd bet he can do that too," he said with a dry chuckle. "Before he decided to follow the rule of the gods, he had very clever fingers."

A quick glance at Húlí told Healer how stunned his man was. And who wouldn't be, finding out that he was not only of royal blood but also the rightful heir to the throne? Xiǎo Ying leaned over and touched his forearm. Fox offered him a weak smile, but it was a smile nevertheless.

"We'll be on our way, then," Healer said, anxious to get to the side of the mountain where the temple had been built.

Both Ling Ling and Fox grunted in protest. Even the dog whined and crouched by the female warrior. It had been a very long, hard journey up the mountain. Another arduous track to an even higher peak was indeed an overwhelming proposal.

"Don't be stupid," the cultivator said, slinking up to his feet a lot more gracefully than Xiǎo Ying thought possible. "You'll stay the night and be on your way when you are all rested." His tone suggested no other recourse. "You two can sleep in my room. I'll take the meditation room, and the warrior can bunk right here with the dog."

Healer thought of protesting, but the tired expressions on the faces of his friends made him change his mind. He nodded. "All right, we'll stay."

They all stood up, more than ready to spread their bedrolls and sleep for hours without fear of being attacked by strange beasts.

Dān's lip curled up in one corner. "And you two have some unfinished business to take care of, haven't you? The room is very private."

"I have no idea what you're talking about." Húlí protested. But the rapid pink hue rising up his neck to his face told Healer otherwise.

Yes, it was time they took their relationship one step further. And like their master always pointed out, there was no time like the present.

CHAPTER 21

IS THIS HEAVEN?

HÚLÍ

Not since his first time with Xu Ming a lifetime ago had Fox ever felt as awkward as he did standing in the small room with Healer. It wasn't as if they had not been intimate before, so why didn't this feel the same? Hell, Húlí had bedded more men than he could count, mostly for survival, but quite a few just for fun. Why then did the prospect of having sex with the man who had saved him multiple times feel so overwhelmingly different?

Because you love him. You didn't love the others.

Just because it was the truth didn't make it any less hard to swallow.

As Xiǎo Yīng circulated the room, dropping his bedroll in a corner, Fox thought back to the time when he and Xu Ming had first made love. Húlí was but a teenager, all long limbs and little wisdom. His childhood friend was only a couple years older than he was, but he was already much more worldly. Húli, star-eyed and intoxicated by his infatuation and need to replenish his *qi*, had thought him to be mature and experienced. Of course, Xu Ming was none of those things. Yes, Fox was not his first lover, but his supposed experience was only a notch or two above Húlí's. What Fox hadn't known then was that Xu Ming had a hidden agenda and was not in love with him enough to commit to a relationship that could bring him nothing but trouble. After all, Húlí's mom had been killed, and there were reasons to believe that her son was in danger. Húlí now realized that Xu Ming had known about his heritage. He wondered if maybe he had allowed himself to be close to the young fox because of it. And whether he had abandoned Húlí in the end because he was scared.

"It can't be the truth, can it?" Fox said, surprising even himself. Xiǎo Ying turned to him, a question in his eyes. Húlí clarified, "That I am the old emperor's grandson."

Faster than Fox could register, Healer was standing before him, his arms thrown around his sides in a tight hug. "Gods, you must be so confused right now." He was indeed confused and utterly stunned with the news. But he was even more annoyed by the fact that here he was, alone in that room with the man he loved, and yet all he could think of was what the old cultivator had said. "Do you want to talk about it, A-Xin?"

Húlí shook his head, leaning against his lover. "No. All I want is to make love to you, A-Ying," he admitted. He wanted to wipe the news from his head—at least for a while. Eventually he would have to face it, but for now, he just wanted to get lost in Xiǎo Ying's kisses.

Healer pushed them apart a few inches, seeking Fox's eyes. "I want that too, my love. I want to forget about the killings and the political scheming against us. I want to focus on you and me." He smiled, a crooked lift of his full lips that made him look years younger than he was. "Mostly I want to focus on that beautiful body of yours."

Fox let out a chuckle. "I have no objections at all." He opened up his arms wide. "Go at it. I'm all yours."

The usually stoic Xiǎo Ying didn't need to hear it twice; he dropped his arms from Fox's shoulders and began stripping him of every layer of clothing, one piece at a time. Once Húlí was finally down to his undergarments, a crisscross linen shirt and matching white loose pants, Healer slowed down, kissing every inch of skin he uncovered. He started at the hollow where Húlí's shoulder met his neck, scraping his teeth on Fox's sensitive skin before running back over it with his tongue. Húlí whimpered, heat gathering in his gut and other body parts.

"You like that." It was not a question, but a simple observation from someone who was used to diagnosing physical and spiritual ailments. Húlí would have laughed if he wasn't so busy focusing on Healer's lips that were now working their magic down his bicep and the inside of his elbow. "You taste exquisite."

Húlí groaned as his attentive lover peeled his shirt completely off and began working on his back, brushing his calloused fingertips over Fox's shoulder blades, down his spine, all the way to where the pants hung low on his hips. When Xiǎo Yīng's fingers slipped between the waistband and his skin, Húlí let out a tiny gasp of anticipation. His heart was drumming loudly inside his chest, and he could have sworn his blood ran hot inside his veins. Every inch of him was tight and tingling, screaming for release but not wanting to let go. Not yet. His lover's touch was too wonderful, too exciting. He didn't want it to end so soon.

Xiǎo Ying suddenly let go of his pants, and Fox groaned in disappointment. But Healer was not done. In one fluid movement, he pivoted Húlí around until they were facing each other. His mouth came down on Fox's with surprising gentleness, tenderly prying his lips open. Gods he tasted good, better than anything Húlí had ever known before. Was that what love did to you? It separated you from reality, ignored objectivity, and turned the object of your affections into some otherworldly perfect being.

No, Xiǎo Ying is *perfect. No illusion here. My man is perfect.*

What would have happened if Húlí hadn't met Healer? Well, he would most likely be dead, since the man had saved his butt more than once. But more importantly, he would still be living the empty life he had been before, running from one bed to another, alone and penniless, Ling Ling his only companion. Embarrassment burned inside him every time he thought about how much he had depended on his friend financially. There so many times he couldn't work, either because he was too weak or because he was on the run from the hounds. Ling Ling, with her inexhaustible source of energy, was always ready to do the legwork to keep them both housed and fed.

"What are you thinking about, A-Xin?" Xiǎo Ying asked, his lips pausing their trek down Fox's neck. "I'm a little jealous that you are so distracted while I'm making love to you."

Húlí laughed, cupping Healer's cheek with his hand. "Jealous? There's absolutely nothing to be jealous of. I was just thinking of how lucky I am to have found you. The gods in the heavens must be shining upon me to allow me such fortune."

Healer slid one hand over his lover's shoulder until it rested over his chest, the heat of his palm making Fox harder. "It goes both ways," he said. "Do you know how long I have been alone? You at least have Ling Ling. I had no one until you came along. Not since Master left." The man peppered kisses along the top of his chest. "But talk is cheap. Let me show you how grateful I am for you in my life."

When Healer's lips closed on his nipple and he ran his tongue over it, Húlí arched his back and moaned, sure he had never felt this wonderful. "You're a magician, A-Ying." His raspy voice sounded alien to his own ears. "Are you sure you're a doctor?"

Húlí felt the rumbling of Xiǎo Yīng's laughter against his chest. "*Bèndàn*. A divine doctor. Emphasis on the divine," he uttered, lips still working their magic on Fox's skin. "Everything I do is divine." It was meant as a joke, but Húlí couldn't agree more. His every touch, every word was divine indeed.

Xiǎo Yīng continued tracking kisses down the middle of Fox's chest to his navel and abdomen where he lingered long enough to fan the flames already burning there. When his mouth descended a few more inches, Húlí braced himself for the impending explosion of pleasure, but his lover stopped suddenly and straightened to meet Fox's bewildered gaze.

Healer's lips quirked at the corners. Was he amused by the obvious disappointment in Húlí's eyes? "How can you be so cruel, A-Yīng?" he heard himself say. Damn! He sounded like a lecherous idiot instead of a generous lover.

Xiǎo Yīng laughed in earnest then, throwing his head back. "You're so adorable when you're pissed." Húlí definitely didn't think so as he fought the urge to cross his arms over his naked chest and sulk like a petulant teenager. Healer laughed for a moment, his almost purple eyes twinkling with mischief. "You're too easy, my love."

What did he mean?

Húlí didn't have time to ponder for long because the man before him swooped him into his strong arms and carried him over to where their bedrolls were spread out. Fox took a minute to admire his lover's strength and power. Húlí was not a small man. He was tall with heavy lean muscle in his slim frame. Yet Xiǎo Yīng carried him as if he weighed no more than a sack of potatoes.

Still rendered speechless by the surprise move, Húlí watched as his lover dropped to his knees, still holding him up in his arms, and laid him gently on the bedroll. Fox blinked in astonishment and opened his mouth to say something, but was stopped once again by what Healer did next. Húlí's sharp fox eyes followed Xiǎo Yīng's hands as he stripped off his clothes, quickly and efficiently, each piece of clothing flying over his head to fall somewhere in the room. Húlí drank in each roll of Healer's chest muscles, every flex of his biceps, and the tightening of his abs. When the man stood up to get rid of his pants, half turning for a moment, Fox couldn't take his eyes off the powerful thighs and glutes of the divine doctor he loved.

The man was as ready for him as Húlí was in return. He gulped in anticipation. He was normally the one on top, but with this man, he wanted to find out how it felt to have him inside. A thought assailed him. "Fuck, no oil." Not that he would allow such a detail to ruin their first time. He was used to pain.

Xiǎo Ying chuckled, crouched by his bag, dug around inside it, and then waved a small vial in front of him. "I'm a doctor, remember? I always carry argan oil for skin rashes and to soothe inflamed scars." He dropped to his knees again and stole a glance at his mate. "Shall I do it or do you want to?"

Húli sat up and took the vial from his hand. "Both. I go first," he said, uncorking the bottle and pouring a few drops onto the palm of his hand. Then he handed it over to his lover. Leaning over, Húlí rubbed his hands together before reaching out to touch Xiǎo Ying, massaging the oil onto Healer's hard length, eliciting a deep groan from his lover. Gently at first, one soft stroke after another, the movement became more vigorous as Húlí's palms slid up and down over the man's sensitive skin. Xiǎo

Ying's skin was velvety and hot as if liquid fire ran through that part of his beautiful body. Fox hardened even further, anxious for Healer to touch him too.

Xiǎo Ying seemed to have read his mind and pushed him gently away. "Let me," he croaked, pouring some of the oil onto his hands. Fox gulped in anticipation and laid back on the bedroll, never once looking away from his lover.

Healer's hands shook, and Húlí's heart melted even more. The tough, ever-composed giant was nervous about making love to him.

"Turn around, A-Xin," he said in a whisper as if talking was becoming almost impossible. Húlí obliged, flipping over onto his knees. "You're sure about this?"

Húlí's chest was so tight with emotion and desire, he couldn't make himself speak, so he just nodded with a grunt. He couldn't see his lover now, but he didn't have to wait long. The warmth of Healer's large hands caressed his buttocks, cupping their hard curves and making him squirm. One of his hands slid toward the center, and before Húlí could blink, he had one well-oiled finger inside him. He moaned, and Healer moved it inside him, cautiously stretching him, getting him ready for his full length.

"Fucking heavens," Húlí exclaimed, dropping his head to the bedroll. "More."

Xiǎo Ying obeyed, moving his finger faster and wider. He curled his other hand over Fox's hip to reach around and caress him before burying himself in him. They both let out a surprised gasp that quickly turned into a moan of pleasure as Healer rocked against Fox's behind, gently at first and more demanding a few moments later. Húlí let out a scream as his lover plunged himself deeper inside him.

Xiǎo Ying stopped moving. "Are you alright? Did I hurt you?" he asked, panic in his breathless voice.

Húlí shook his head. "*Bù*, A-Ying," he assured him. "Nothing but pleasure, sweetheart. Don't stop now."

He wasn't lying. Waves of sensual bliss coursed through his body, threatening to make him explode like a supernova and scatter him throughout the heavens. He didn't want Healer to stop. Quite the opposite.

Xiǎo Ying hesitated for a moment and then resumed his rocking, riding them both to the brink, that narrow ledge that promised a thrilling free fall. The tension inside Húlí's gut grew momentum, and just as Healer slid his hand more tightly along his hardness, it burst out. Húlí vaguely heard his lover scream in release beneath his own howling as he spilled his seed over the bedroll.

Neither moved for a while, still connected and breathless, Húlí's muscles twitching in release, his lover's hand still wrapped around his shaft. He loved this closeness, Xiǎo Ying's hot breath on his bare back, his heart beating against his skin. It was intimate. It was exciting. It was everything he had ever dreamed and never thought he could have.

When their bodies finally separated and Healer spooned Húlí as they lay down to rest, Fox couldn't hold it any longer and burst out crying.

"What's wrong, my love?" Xiǎo Ying asked, peeking around to look at his face. "Are you hurt? Was I too rough?"

Fox sniffled and bit his lower lip, trying to control his weeping. "No, you didn't hurt me, A-Ying," he managed to say. "I'm not sad. These are tears of happiness." He turned halfway around to face his lover. "You just made me so very happy, sweetheart—so very happy."

And for once, he wasn't talking about the sex. He was talking about their closeness and how he felt inside. Being loved was a novelty for him. One he could totally get used to.

CHAPTER 22
XU MING & THE HOUNDS
XIǍO YING

Yè Yǐng ran ahead, his muzzle close to the ground on the trail of something—a rabbit, most likely. Even though he wasn't much of an eater, Xiǎo Ying wouldn't be opposed to roasted rabbit after almost a week of journeying through the dense woods without an ounce of meat in sight. The first snowflakes had fallen the night before, not sticking around for long but rendering a chill to the air. Winter came early this high in the Duǎnde Mountains, and most of the animals seemed to be already hiding from the cold.

"If I have to eat another batch of wild onions and rutabagas, I'm going to dig a grave and bury myself," Húlí exclaimed in his usual melodramatic tone.

"You don't hear Yè Yǐng complaining, do you?"

Ling Ling said, smacking him over the arm. "And he's a dog, a carnivore."

Húlí groaned. "I'm a carnivore too." He was careful to keep his voice down so his friend wouldn't hear him. Xiǎo Ying smiled, throwing him a sideways look. "You're my lover. Shouldn't you protect me from this woman?"

Ling Ling hit him again. Harder. "Your poor lover is the one who needs protection from your constant bellyaching. By the gods, you are worse than a two-year-old without his rattle."

The dog, still a few yards ahead, stopped suddenly, growling, his lips folded and sharp teeth on display. Xiǎo Ying raised an arm to stop his companions. "Shh, he must have prey." Húlí squinted and stared in the dog's direction. "What do you see, A-Xin?"

"Give me the bow," Fox answered, holding out his hand. "I can shoot it from here."

The words "Are you sure?" almost left his mouth, but he knew Húlí could see better than any human, and he was also an amazing shot with the bow and arrow.

Xiǎo Ying handed him the weapon, and he wasted no time in nocking the arrow and aiming it at whatever the dog was growling at. Fox released the bowstring, and the arrow flew in a perfect high arch, finding its target.

Ling Ling dashed to where Yè Yǐng now fussed over the fallen animal. She patted the dog's head. "Good boy," she said, bending down to pick something up from the fern-covered ground. She lifted a brown shape up in the air and turned to them. "It's a pheasant," she yelled. "A big one."

"*Yějī*!" Húlí exclaimed, his eyes twinkling with excitement. "We feast tonight, my friends."

They set up camp in the flattest area they could find, cleared the ground, and lit a fire. While plucking the animal, Xiǎo Ying watched as the dark dog walked some distance away to do his business and then came bouncing back to sit as close to Fox as he could.

His heart skipped a beat. More danger.

He glanced over at his lover who was oblivious to the fact that Yè Yǐng was once again glued to his side and engaged in banter with the female warrior. What was about Húlí that seemed to attract trouble? The memory of the incident in town when the powerful spirit attacked him came rushing back to the healer. What had all that been about? Húlí had just learned how to tap into his *yāomó* powers, and yet....

"What philosophical question are you trying to answer right now, A-Ying?" Fox's lips quirked into a smile. "That *yějī* will never be ready to cook at this rate."

Xiǎo Ying managed a smile despite the worry gnawing at him. "Sorry, I guess my mind wandered for a moment," he said, turning his attention back to the bird. "I'll have it ready in a minute."

Húlí scooted closer, the dog moving along with him. "Let me help you, A-Ying. I have the speed of a fox," he said.

"And the brain of a moth," Ling Ling offered with a grunt. She exchanged a knowing glance with Xiǎo Ying, nodding toward the dog.

She had noticed too.

Healer pulled his sword closer, the scabbard lying on the ground next to his feet, and the warrior did the same. "Come closer, my love," Xiǎo Ying said, pulling on Fox's arm. "I like having you close."

Húlí barked out a laugh. "You really think I haven't noticed our canine friend's sudden clinginess or the stares between you two?" he said. "I may be a little clueless at times, but I'm not stupid. Something is about to come at me again, right?"

Pride filled Xiǎo Ying's heart. "We don't think you're stupid," he protested with a soft chuckle.

"Just a little misguided at times," Ling Ling added, slipping her sword onto her lap. She looked at Healer and Húlí. "We probably should hurry with that bird or we are going to end up not eating at all today."

They all nodded in agreement, and between the two, they had the bird fully plucked, gutted, and ready to be roasted over the fire in no time. Now it would be a waiting game. They knew something was coming but had no idea what or when. They might as well make the best of it.

Dinner was delicious even though they kept an eye out for whatever danger was about to befall them, and despite their exhaustion, none of them dared sleep. Húlí, who was used to being on the run and had undoubtedly learned how to sleep under the direst of situations, fell asleep in the wee hours of the morning while the other three, humans and dog, kept a watchful eye around them.

The forest was so thick that moonlight barely reached the ground, bathing the area in ominous moving shadows as the wind played haunted tunes on the branches and leaves, flooding the air with creaks and moans. Healer had lived long enough alone in the middle of the woods not to be unnerved by it, but knowing something was coming for his lover made him jittery and overly aware of every sound, every movement.

Ling Ling suddenly jumped to her feet just as the dog growled. Xiǎo Ying started and looked around but couldn't see anything.

"What?" he asked.

The female warrior pointed at Húlí who still slept by the fire, her eyes round and unblinking. Healer couldn't guess what he was about to see, but *that* certainly wasn't it.

Curled into a ball on the ground, Fox was glowing like a star.

"What's wrong with him?"

Ling Ling's almost hysterical question summed up what he was feeling: panic, fear, and dejected helplessness. Not knowing whether what was happening to his lover was a good or bad thing made his insides burn with such intensity, he was surprised not to see smoke coming out of his mouth. He fell to his knees beside the curled-up form of Fox and cautiously laid his open hands on him. Xiǎo Ying expected Húlí's body to be hot, but instead his touch encountered nothing but coolness. He closed his eyes and reached out with his healing senses. Was Húlí in pain? Was he being attacked by some wicked spirit again?

Xiǎo Ying's eyes flew open. There was nothing wrong with Fox. Much to the contrary, he seemed to be in a state of serendipity, not a care in the world. So what was that glow that emanated from inside him and created a bubble around his body?

"A cocoon!" Healer exclaimed, gazing at the peaceful figure of his lover. "This is a protective shield." He turned to the female warrior whose eyes were still unnaturally rounded. "Someone—or something—is protecting him."

Ling Ling took a few steps in their direction. "So whatever is coming hasn't come yet?" she asked, regaining some of her usual composure. "And who is protecting him anyway?"

Laughter bubbled inside Xiǎo Ying's chest— pure joy at the realization that whatever was after his lover would have a real hard time going through all his protectors. Húlí, it seemed, had amassed quite a group of friends who would put their lives on the line for him.

"Why are you smiling?" Ling Ling asked, annoyed. "This is not funny. Too many unknowns make me itchy."

Healer shook his head. "His mother must be protecting him from the grave," he said. "Maybe even his father...." A thought took seed in his mind.

If Húlí was a full-blooded *yāomó*, then both his parents had to be as well. No surprise about his mother, but the father? He had been the emperor's favorite, the crown prince. How could the crown prince be a *yāomó* unless both his parents were too? Were demons part of the emperor's bloodline? And if so, why this uncensored witch hunt for every not fully human being that had been going on since he could remember?

"His mother? But how?" Ling Ling sat cross-legged beside them. Yè Yǐng still paced close to the prone figure of Fox, alert and ready.

"His mother was a *yāomó*, and most likely a powerful one—which was probably the reason why her marriage to the crown prince was kept so secret. It is possible that her spirit has evolved or morphed into something else and is now watching over her son." The words came out of nowhere but made all kinds of sense to him. After all, *yāomó* were themselves animals or plants that had evolved into enhanced humans. Why couldn't it be possible for them to change into something else once their human body was dead?

"Are you sure he's not hurt?" It was heart-warming to hear the concern in Ling Ling's voice.

With a shake of his head, Xiǎo Ying dismissed

the idea. He was not hurt at all—quite the opposite. But the danger was not gone. If his mother, or whoever was protecting him right then, felt the need to shield him, that meant something was still coming for him.

"Be alert." He threw a glance at the dog. "Yè Yǐng is still growling and baring his teeth." They both jumped to their feet and drew their swords, turning their backs to Húlí.

They heard them before they saw them.

The hounds.

Ling Ling snapped her head around to look at him. "Hounds? This far from the capital?"

The special bark could not be confused with any other, an eerie cross between the howling of a wolf and the bark of a dog—almost as if they were yelling. A shiver ran up his spine as he braced himself solidly on the ground. The canines wouldn't be alone. Who so wanted to kill Húlí that he was willing to come this far north?

Yè Yǐng, black fur raised along his spine, stood his ground, meeting the shrieks of the hounds with growling of his own. As soon as the first hound cleared the edge of the thick wall of trees, the dog pounced forward in warning. "Stay, Yè Yǐng!" Xiǎo Ying didn't want the dog to get hurt. The hounds were bred for strength and ferocity. Yè Yǐng was no match for them. The dog obeyed.

Both he and Ling Ling braced themselves for the attack, but the hounds stopped shy of where they stood. It was as if the hounds were waiting for someone, their teeth bared, drool dropping from the corners of their powerful maws. It took a moment or two for a human figure to appear from around a group of trees, his body and head covered in a dark green hooded cloak.

"Well, well, if it isn't Ming Xin's fan club," the man said, stopping right behind the hounds and leaning on a tree trunk, his arms crossed over his chest. "He always had a gift for charming people into doing his bidding."

Xiǎo Ying exchanged a glance with his female companion. This man, whoever he was, obviously knew Húlí and who he had been in the past.

"Who are you? What do you want with Old Fox?" Ling Ling yelled out, sword at the ready.

The mystery man cackled. "Old Fox indeed," he said once he stopped laughing. "So you're well aware he's a fox *yāomó*." He sounded mildly surprised. "Did he get you both to fuck him yet? He's good at that."

Healer's insides started burning. "Who are you? How dare you speak about our friend like that?"

The man uttered a mixture of a chuckle and a yelp. "Friend? That's precious. You really think that Fox cares about you? All he cares about is getting his *qi* replenished."

Xiǎo Ying had had enough. "*Gòule!*" he yelled out, pointing his sword at the man. "Uncover your face and identify yourself."

After a moment of hesitation, the man pulled his hood down. His face was vaguely familiar to Xiǎo Ying, but he couldn't quite identify him.

"Xu Ming," Ling Ling growled, raising her sword as well. "You again. When are you going to leave him alone? What did he do to you that warrants this?"

Xu Ming? Did she mean Fox's childhood friend and first lover? The one who had betrayed him and "outed" him as a *yāomó* to the imperial guards?

"Ling Ling, right?" Xu Ming said conversationally, as if they had just met at a teahouse. "You're still by his side? I didn't think he did women, but I stand corrected."

Healer chanced a look at the female. Her face was bright red, not from embarrassment but pure ire. "You fucking traitor," she spat out. "You're a rat who couldn't even stand by your childhood friend once things got choppy. How dare you chase him all the way here? What do you want with him?"

Xu Ming's smirk turned into a scowl. "Why, he survived once. I'm here to make sure that doesn't happen again," he snarled between closed teeth. "Unfortunately for you, that fate has now been extended to you too." Darkness filled the man's eyes as he narrowed them. "You all must die."

CHAPTER 23
WARRIORS & RATS
HÚLÍ

The voices were barely audible. They sounded as if they were coming from down a long tunnel; he could understand the words, but he couldn't tell who spoke. Húlí tried to open his eyes, but they were shut tight, as if someone had glued his eyelids with sticky rice mortar. Whatever held his eyes closed also prevented him from moving his body. What was going on?

"Stop fidgeting, Xin'er," a familiar voice echoed inside his head. "You haven't changed a bit."

His lungs must have stopped working for a second or so because he couldn't breathe. "Take a breath, A-Xin. Take a deep breath," Healer's voice whispered in his memory. He obeyed, exhaling a long, painful breath and then inhaling fresh, life-saving air.

"I have put a protective shield around you," the female voice in his head said. "Don't fight it."

Hesitation choked him for a moment. "*Mǔqīn?* Mom?" Was it possible? Was his mother talking to him from the grave?

"Hush, child," the voice admonished gently. "Your life is at risk, and I didn't die for you to get killed on this mountain."

"But...." The protest died on his lips as the other background voices grew stronger and more audible. All three voices sounded familiar, but he couldn't yet identify them.

"Weren't you supposed to be Húlí's childhood friend?" a male voice asked. The softening of his muscles as he heard it told him this was someone he cared for. "How can you turn on him like this? Who is behind you? What do you stand to gain from this?"

"Ming Xin is a threat to the imperial family," another male voice echoed. His chest ached at the sound, and if he hadn't been frozen in place, he would have pressed a hand to his heart. "He needs to be eliminated."

"It figures," a female voice exclaimed, anger

spilling out with her words. His heart slowed its frantic cavalcade. "Gōng Làn is behind this. What a despicable little weasel our emperor is."

"Just for that, Ling Ling, you need to die," the detested male voice replied with a growl. "Bad-mouthing the emperor is punishable by death."

"I want to see you try, asshole," challenged the voice he now knew to be his friend Ling Ling's. So much like her. Fearless. Belligerent.

The other male voice interrupted. Was it Xiǎo Ying's? "Why would he want his own nephew killed? Is it not enough that he's being pursued like a criminal?"

Húlí's stomach churned. He hadn't thought about it that way; he *was* indeed the emperor's nephew. Not that it mattered. Family loyalty and love didn't seem to exist in the imperial family.

"Are you stupid?" the other male answered with a dry chuckle. "If the public at large ever gets a whiff that the imperial bloodline is tainted with demon blood, everything the emperor has done in his reign will be questioned both by the populace and the noblemen. It will be chaos."

"You're calling the wrong person stupid, Xu Ming," Ling Ling said. "Who had the bright idea of criminalizing demons in the first place? Làn is the stupid one. Instead of accepting who he is, he decided to eradicate everyone who, like him, has demon blood."

There was a moment of silence before the one he now recognized as his lover said, "The emperor might have *yāomó* blood running in his veins, but he obviously has none of the power. That's what he's afraid of."

Xu Ming cackled again. "The emperor is not afraid of anything. He just wants to get rid of the rubble, the useless, dangerous *yāomó* who murk the waters of our grand dynasty," he declared.

"So you're telling me he's considering suicide, then." Ling Ling's biting remark must have had exactly the reaction she wanted, because she let out a pleased chuckle. "Not only has he demon blood, but he is the scum of the earth. I will support him on that though."

"Treason," Xu Ming yelled out in an outraged squeak. "You're talking treason."

"I'm talking common sense, you stupid minion." Ling Ling had never been one to mince words. "We'll make you go back to your master with your tail between your legs, *gǒu*." She paused. "No, no, calling you that is an insult to dogs. Sorry, Yè Yǐng."

Even in his haze, Húlí smiled at his best friend's

words. "*Mǔqīn*, let me go," he begged in his mind. "I need to help them."

"You need to help yourself," his mother replied in a soft but stern voice. "For you and the Xi family. Your friends can handle themselves."

"How do I know they're all right? I can't even see," he said, realizing he sounded like a spoiled child.

Immediately, his eyes snapped open, and he could see what was happening before him. Six hounds, their matted brown coats raised along their spines, lips curled to show sharp teeth at the ready. Closer to him, his friends stood their ground, one at either end of his body with Yè Yǐng in between them, forming a shield of sorts. Behind the hounds, a familiar face scowled at his friends.

Xu Ming had once been his best friend. His only friend. They had played together as children in the lonely confines of the palace, and they continued their friendship even after Húlí's life was destroyed and he became a fugitive of sorts. Húlí had loved and revered him. He had placed his heart and his trust in the hands of the only person who stood up for him. Until the day Xu Ming turned him over to the palace guards and their hounds. His betrayal had nearly destroyed Fox.

"What happened to make you turn on your childhood friend?" Xiǎo Ying asked again, his strong back turned to Fox.

Xu Ming smirked. "The emperor made me an offer I couldn't refuse."

"You sold out for power?" Ling Ling exclaimed.

"And money," Xu Ming added shamelessly. "And a spot in the emperor's bed. What could Ming Xin offer me? Other than his admittedly amazing bedroom skills."

Healer growled, anger pouring out of him. Húlí's heart melted a little more. "Do not speak of A-Xin in that way, you despicable human being. He has more value and character in his small finger than you have in your whole self."

His two friends looked at each other and then at the dog, who had begun growling loudly. Húlí's heart skipped a beat. They were going to attack, and he had seen firsthand what those hounds could do. They didn't stand a chance against six of them.

"Stop fretting, child," his mother's voice said, startling him. "Don't you think I have a backup plan? They'll be fine, trust me."

Húlí sighed. Whatever the backup plan was, it had better work fast, because at that moment, all three of his friends lunged forward in attack.

The hounds reacted first like Húlí knew they would. As soon as the three—humans and dog—charged forward, the hounds were on the move, bounding across the short distance between them.

Fox closed his eyes in panic. *Bù hǎo—not good at all.*

When he opened them again, he couldn't believe what he was seeing; Yè Yǐng, fighting side by side with his friends, was glowing. Had his mother done something to the dog too? Whatever that glow was, it seemed to give the canine extra strength, because he tore at one the hounds' necks as if it were a mere rabbit. A few steps away, Xiǎo Ying sliced the second hound wide open with a single strike of his spiritual sword, and next to him, Ling Ling had skewered the third hound with hers. The animals yelped in pain as blood spilled over the grassy land and their life force began to quickly wan.

There was panic in Xu Ming's eyes, if only momentarily, as Ling Ling pulled a second sword from her back scabbard and plunged it into a fourth hound that jumped toward her. Healer swiveled on his heels and sliced his sword through the neck of the fifth one, a splash of blood exploding into the air and falling on his lover, a scarlet rain shower that stained his clothes and his skin.

Húlí turned his gaze to Yè Yǐng, worried that the mangy dog wouldn't be a match for the last hound, but it turned out he didn't need to worry. The dog had dropped the first hound, now a pile of blood-matted fur, and turned to the oncoming one. The large canine closed his maw around Yè Yǐng's front leg, but the dog didn't even blink. With a jerk, he threw the hound a few feet away from him and then lunged at him with a growl. Blood was dripping from the dog's leg, but he didn't seem to notice as he latched his teeth into the backside of the creature. By all logic, the hound should have been able to overpower the smaller dog, but the opposite happened. In a few short moves, Yè Yǐng had total control of the fight, and within seconds there were no more hounds to worry about.

Xu Ming had retreated a few steps, his back against the trunk of a tree and his eyes wide open in disbelief. "No, no, no," he mumbled. "Not possible."

"Obviously very possible, idiot," Ling Ling commented, wiping her blade on the grass. "We absolutely won, so I suggest you hand over your sword, and we might consider letting you go."

After a moment of shocked paralysis, Húlí's childhood friend turned around and ran away so fast, he was but a blur between the trees.

"Shit," Ling Ling exclaimed. "I really wanted to give him a taste of my blade." Healer looked at her with an eyebrow raised in disapproval. "Just a tiny taste. I wouldn't kill him." She added under her breath, "Not that he doesn't deserve it."

Just as quickly as it came, the hold on Húlí's body was gone. "You're safe now, son," his mother's voice whispered in his ear. "Remember, I'll be with you and will protect you." Warmth spread in his chest. He didn't know how this was possible, but he wasn't going to complain.

"Look, he's not shining anymore," Ling Ling yelled, pointing at him where he was still curled on his side. "Old Fox, you were like a star in the sky: shiny but much uglier."

Húlí laughed, trying to stretch his stiff legs and sit up. "I can always count on you to tell me the truth, my friend," he quipped, shaking blades of grass and dirt from his clothes. "Even though sometimes I wish you'd be a bit nicer about it."

"You don't need nice," she replied, making another swipe of the sword against the grass. "You need honest support."

Fox opened his mouth to protest, but his lover jumped in. "She's right. You can never go wrong with the truth," he said. Then he smiled. "But she's wrong about one thing. You're not ugly at all."

Ling Ling made a retching noise. "Spare me, please. You make me sicker than the spilling innards of these hounds."

Húlí suddenly remembered how Yè Yǐng had been bitten by one of the dead hounds. "Come here, boy," he called out to the dog, who limped his way to him, all his earlier fierceness melted away into total submissiveness. Fox crouched and patted the dog's head before checking the injured leg. The dog yelped a little as Húlí's fingers explored the wound. "That hound did a number on you, but I don't think it's severe." He glanced at Healer. "Can you take a look?"

Healer joined them closer to the ground and gently studied the dog's leg. "It will heal," he declared after a minute or so. "Let me clean and bandage it."

A thought crossed Fox's mind. "Why can't he just lick it like he did with my wound?"

Xiǎo Yīng shrugged. "Not sure why. But I have a feeling your mom must have had something to do with it." He signaled Ling Ling to bring him his bag. "But for now he's just a regular dog."

For the next hour or so, they busied themselves

cleaning up the camping site while Healer treated the dog's wound. They didn't want to leave any traces behind just in case, so they buried the hounds as well. Morning had just broken when they resumed their journey up the mountain. By Húlí's estimation they should be less than two days away from their destination. He only hoped they had seen the last of danger. The emperor really didn't want them to succeed. Or survive.

Sometimes it sucked to be a *yāomó*. But even worse, it really rankled to be a Xi.

CHAPTER 24
MOUNTAIN TOP
XIĂO YING

Following Húlí was a challenge even for Healer. Fox was full of restless energy, his inner fox wanting to run between the trees and chase down the small creatures that inhabited the mountains. Even as his *qi* depleted, the remaining stamina was often exhausting for those around him. Xiăo Ying didn't want to be too far from him on the off chance he was attacked again, but Húlí made that simple task anything but. The man was unstoppable.

"I suggest you do not kiss him again for a few days," Ling Ling whispered at his side. "Let his *qi* deplete some more or he will definitely kill us with all that energy." So she had noticed too. "I too want to be close to him, but he never stops." Her voice had turned into an atypical whine.

Xiǎo Yīng threw a glance at his lover zigzagging between trees and bushes several yards ahead of them, his nose up in the air as if sniffing something and his nine tails unfurled. He was closely followed by Yè Yǐng, the only one in the group who could easily keep up with him.

"Can you slow down, Old Fox?" Ling Ling yelled out, uncharacteristically out of breath. The mountain was particularly steep at the top, and they expected the forest to soon give way to the plain rock they would have to somehow climb to reach the flat of the mountaintop where the temple stood. "Us non-foxes need to rest."

Húlí stopped and glanced back, confusion in his eyes. "I'm not even going that fast," he argued. "You guys are wimps."

"*Hǎo hǎo*, we're weak and lazy," Ling Ling conceded, obviously willing to agree to anything as long as they got to rest for a bit. "You're strong, handsome, and awesome, so please take pity of us mere mortals, will you?"

Healer hid a grin behind his hand. Ling Ling knew her friend well.

"All right, all right—we can rest for a while," Fox

agreed, turning around and joining the other two with Yè Yǐng in tow. "You'd think you're in no hurry to get to the top."

They all plopped down on the ground. Ling Ling let out a dramatic sigh as she slid all the way until she was flat against the brush that covered the forest floor. "We are, but we'd prefer to arrive with some of our life left. You're not like this when we're in town, Old Fox."

Húlí unstopped his water skin and took a quick sip. "The air here is energizing," he said, waving his tails behind him and wiggling his furry ears. Healer wondered whether Fox's mother had something to do with it. "I just feel...." He paused, turning his face upward. "I feel amazing."

He looked amazing indeed. Xiǎo Ying's heart just about exploded every time he glanced at his lover. Fox was stunning with his copper hair, liquid blue eyes, and the cute brown freckles that covered almost every inch of his pale skin. Not to mention the sexy, soft tails he unfurled every so often. Healer took a deep breath, controlling the urge to draw him in and hug him within an inch of his life. Who would have thought he would find this kind of love? His life since his family's massacre had been one of reflection, cultivation, and planning to bring his kin the justice they deserved. He had lived a life of isolation with no emotional attachments, his only human contact limited to the times when he talked to possible witnesses. Outside rare occasions when he visited the local pleasure house, he hadn't enjoyed human company in a long time. Then came Húlí with his deceptively shallow personality that hid a shattered heart and soul, and he was lost. Even though they had only known each other for a short time, Xiǎo Yīng couldn't imagine a life without him.

"Well, Mr. Amazing, we don't," Ling Ling said. "We're human and tired." She closed her eyes, and soon her breath had slowed down.

"How does she fall asleep like that?" Húlí asked, staring at his friend, a lopsided smile curving his lips. He scooted closer to Healer and leaned over to deposit a quick kiss on his cheek, gently touching him with the tip of one tail. "Well, what shall we do with this free time?" He wiggled his eyebrows, and Healer chuckled. "She sleeps like a rock and won't hear anything."

"No time, A-Xin," Healer said however reluctantly. Nothing would make him happier than making love to his man. But the sun was starting its descent, and they needed to get to the top before dark. He leaned in further and caught Húlí's mouth with his, gently pulling on Fox's lower lip with his teeth. Húlí moaned. "Can't wait to have you all to myself," Healer whispered over Fox's mouth. It had been a while since they had privacy.

Húlí scooted even closer, almost sitting on Xiǎo Ying's lap. "I've been doing a lot of thinking." Healer raised an eyebrow and Fox lifted his hand. "I do think, you know." His blue eyes twinkled in disbelief. "I've been planning for when we're finally alone again. I have a long list of things I want to do with you—to you." He winked, and Healer almost came undone. He couldn't lie to himself; he'd been having the same thoughts.

"Soon," Xiǎo Ying whispered, brushing his fingers along his lover's spine. "Maybe even tonight." He couldn't be sure of what waited for them at the top of the mountain, but he was so tired of the road that he hoped there was a comfortable room in their future. With a sigh that was half exhaustion and half desire, he drew his lover in and kissed him again, taking his time exploring his mouth and allowing his imagination to take him to a better place.

A place where the two could sleep peacefully at night in the knowledge their families had been vindicated and no one would hurt them.

Xiǎo Ying had never been so grateful to see the end of a forest. The sun had long given up emitting any significant heat and bathed the whole top of the mountain in its soft creamy light. They had arrived.

"There's nothing here," Húlí announced, his hands on his hips and a confused glint in his eyes. "Where the hell is the monastery Dān spoke of? There is nothing but grass and rocks up here."

Ling Ling swiveled on her heels just as Healer searched for something—anything—with his eyes. Had the old cultivator fooled them?

"Wait!" Ling Ling exclaimed, pointing toward a tall boulder just a few yards down from them. "There's something behind it."

Húlí took off running, his nine tails erupting behind him and Yè Yǐng in his wake. Xiǎo Ying smiled. It was always a pleasure to see his lover's lovely nine tails. "Hide your tails," he yelled out at Húlí. "We don't know what we're going to find here."

"Forget it," Ling Ling said, hurrying to follow him. "He has no control over those tails when he is this excited—or maybe scared."

A shiver ran through his body. Knowing that his

lover's tails only came out when he was excited made him swoon. A silly sense of pride made his chest swell. Those beautiful red tails always popped out when they made love, visual proof that Xiǎo Ying turned his lover on enough for him to lose control of his fox. He had never had any wishes beyond bringing his family justice, but now he wanted to be the one who made his lover smile and squirm with desire every time he touched him. He wanted to be the most important person in Húlí's life, and that was the most irrational, shallow desire he had ever had.

"Holy gods in heaven," Húlí exclaimed. The others had just reached him when he pointed in front of him. "I was not expecting this."

Xiǎo Ying wasn't either, and judging by the expression on the female warrior's face, neither was she. Sprawled in front of them, built on a natural dip in the terrain, was a small walled town. The monastery they had been imagining as a humble temple was only a small part of a much larger compound built around it. The red-roofed houses stretched outward from the colorful temple with its curved roof edged in what looked like spokes in a static wheel. Each house sported a small courtyard that would put many of the capital's to shame. A riot of flowers and blooming trees added even more color to the rainbow of buildings.

"What the fuck? This is what the old man talked about?" Ling Ling exclaimed, scratching her head with her index finger. "This is not a monastery. This is a freaking town."

"Might as well go check it out," Healer finally said, rubbing the stiffness from his neck. "The sun is pretty low already, and I would love to find a room for the night."

None of them disagreed, including the dog, who barked his assent. Together, they cleared the boulder and began the short descent to the town gates where one man stood guard. He wore a simple uniform with an unadorned chest plate over the brown tunic and pants. A sword was his only visible weapon.

"Who goes there?" the guard asked, not even bothering to unsheathe his sword. "Identify yourselves."

Xiǎo Ying raised a hand in the universal sign for peace before saying, "We're weary travelers sent here by Dānchún. We come in peace and need a room for the night." The guard squinted, taking them in. "I'm Xiǎo Ying and these are my friends, Húlí and Ling Ling."

305

The guard signaled to an invisible person up on the wall, and the gate creaked open. "Come in. You'll have to wait in our guest hall until our leader tells us what to do."

As long as it was a place where they could rest, Xiǎo Ying didn't really care where or what it was. He nodded along with his companions, and they all followed the guard into a small door just inside the gates. As soon as they entered, they were blinded by the bright light that flooded the space. Healer blinked a few times before he could see clearly. The room was a lot bigger than he expected, furnished with simple but tasteful furniture, but it was the expression on the guards' faces that surprised him the most.

The two men, the guard who had followed them inside, and one who was already there were staring at them, mouths wide open and a glow of wonderment in their unblinking eyes.

"Why are they all staring at us like we've grown a second head?" Húlí exclaimed, throwing Xiǎo Ying a glance.

Realization dawned in Healer's mind. "They're not staring at us," he said. "They're staring at *you*, A-Xin."

CHAPTER 25
BE OUR GUEST
HÚLÍ

Xiǎo Ying wasn't lying. The guards were staring at him so intently, it was almost comical. Except it was a bit unnerving. Húlí was used to being gawked at because of his natural fox beauty, but this was weird, to put it mildly. The two men's chins had dropped low, and Húlí could almost see the back of their throats.

"What are you staring at?" he finally asked. "Do I have something nasty stuck to my teeth?"

The guard who had let them in shook his head as if trying to snap out of an enchantment. "*Bù, bù,*" he uttered, waving his hands in denial. "You look so much like—" He was interrupted by the other guard with a punch to his upper arm. "Never mind. Sorry to stare. You just look like someone we know."

The second man stepped forward, his expression turned studiously into one of neutrality. "We'll go talk to our leader. Stay here, make yourselves comfortable, and we'll be back as soon as we can."

The two left, almost running, and the lock clicked behind them. Húlí exchanged glances with his two companions. "What the hell was that all about?"

Xiǎo Ying and Ling Ling both shrugged. "Who cares?" Ling Ling said, heading to a corner of the room where a table was set with a variety of dishes. "I'm starved, and they left us in a room with food. I'm digging in."

Despite his curiosity and a feeling of foreboding in the pit of his stomach, Húlí was hungry too, and the sight of all the delicious food on the table was too tempting to pass. Soon, they were all sitting at the table, enjoying the snacks left out for them.

"Whoever these guys are, they sure are hospitable," Ling Ling said, chewing on a chicken drumstick and dropping bits of meat for the dog.

Húlí had a feeling that the food had not been laid out for them but for the guards themselves. He let out a chuckle, thinking of the guards' faces when they came back to find most of their food gone. "Hopefully it's not poisoned."

Xiǎo Ying's lips turned up into a one-sided smile. "Always the optimist. There was no way they knew we were coming, and it's not like they get a lot of visitors up here on the top of the mountain."

He couldn't disagree with that, but after all the strange things that had happened to them on their journey, Húlí was not willing to discard any possibilities, no matter how paranoid they sounded. He dropped the last drumstick onto the floor for the dog to eat. Yè Yǐng had been attached to his hip for the whole trip up, but he seemed to finally have relaxed his vigilance. With his tongue lolling out of his muzzle, Yè Yǐng sat on the floor by Fox's feet and munched away on the chicken, letting out little whimpers of delight.

"Who do you think they thought I looked like?" Húlí asked, nibbling on crispy lotus root slices. Where could they have possibly had access to lotus this high up in the mountain? "They seemed pretty shocked, didn't they?"

The other two exchanged a look Fox couldn't quite decipher. They were worried about him, he knew. He hated that he had become such a burden to the two people in the world who cared the most for him. He knew they were in a constant state of anxiety about him. Even the poor dog didn't seem to be able to sleep in peace at night, always curling close to him and never straying too far. Nobody had ever cared about him like that, and if the thought warmed his heart, it also gave him pause. He was an adult, and he shouldn't be the reason his only friends lost sleep.

"Can you guys just relax and stop worrying about me?" he said. "I'm a big boy, and I can take care of myself."

"We're not worried about you," Ling Ling replied, bits of chicken flying out of her mouth. "We're worried about the poor dog who obviously loves you too much."

Húlí couldn't help it and laughed out loud. "What a great friend you are," he exclaimed. "But I'm serious. Stop worrying all the time. It makes me feel like a rat."

Healer slipped an arm over his shoulders. "*Bèndàn!* That's what friends and family do for you." Leaning over, he deposited a brief kiss on Húlí's cheek. "You have been alone for far too long and are not used to it. We love you, so we can't help but worry for you. It's not a bad thing."

Fox's cheeks caught on fire with pleasure. Friends and family. What a lovely set of words.

He opened his mouth to protest but was stopped

by the telling sound of a key turning. Both humans and canine glanced up at the door, not sure what or who would come through, but they needn't have worried; the same guard from before stepped inside, his eyes flying to the depleted food supply on the table, but—to his credit—showing no reaction.

"Come with me," he said. "Our leader wants to meet you, but you must be tired. I will take you to your rooms, and he will meet you in the morning."

None of them protested. Their bones hurt from the long climb, the fights along the way, and the scarcity of good nourishment. It had been a long journey, and not one of them would argue that a comfortable bed was what they most wanted at that moment.

Let the rest wait for the morning. Whatever the rest was.

THE ROOMS WERE SURPRISINGLY spacious and bright. Despite the darkness of the night that had fallen upon them, soft light illuminated each of the two rooms they were offered. Húlí couldn't tell exactly what was giving out the light, so he assumed it was some kind of magic. Each room had a bed wide enough to fit at least three people comfortably and were piled high with silk-covered linens in reds, blues, and purples. The same color scheme stretched across the room in small, interesting accessories that either hung from the walls or sat on top of furniture. Húlí's muscles instantly relaxed at the welcoming essence of the space as he stood, his head brushing the top of the doorway.

"These rooms are amazing," he heard Ling Ling exclaim from next door. "Yè Yǐng, you stay with me tonight. The lovebirds will be busy with other matters."

Húlí snickered. She was right. No matter how tired he might be, he'd never be too tired to love Healer with all his body and soul. "You're just jealous you don't have someone in your bed," he yelled back, stepping into the room and throwing his makeshift bag on a chair by the wall.

"I enjoy my freedom," she yelled in return. "Nothing like a big bed all to myself."

Húlí smiled. In all the years they'd been friends, he didn't remember a single time she had been in a relationship. It often filled him with guilt, afraid that he was the reason why. Ling Ling had always been protective of him, and he wondered whether she kept lovers at bay because of that.

Yè Yǐng dashed between Fox's legs and ran to the other room. "A great protector you are," Húlí said with a chuckle. He closed the door behind him and joined Healer, who was already disrobing. "Whoa, give me a second to catch my breath, A-Ying."

Xiǎo Ying chuckled. "Don't flatter yourself, my love. I'm covered in dust and tired to the bone. These cool sheets look a lot more attractive to me than you do right now."

Placing an open hand on his chest, Húlí affected a wounded expression. "Ouch, that really hurts, A-Ying. Not what you want to hear from your lover."

Healer laughed again, throwing his white tunic over the back of a chair by the bed. "Shut up and join me in bed," he said, dropping on the top of the covers and rolling to the side so he could unfold them.

There was no need to ask twice. Húlí was bare of any clothing in no time and tucked himself against Healer beneath the mountain of covers. Xiǎo Ying supported his neck with one arm as Fox glued himself snugly against his side with a loud, heartfelt sigh. "Did I die and go to the heavens?" he whispered, cheek comfortably resting on his lover's chest.

Xiǎo Ying's lips grazed the top of his head. "Are

you nervous about what we might find here?" he asked in a whisper as he brushed his thumb along the other man's jaw. "What you might find out about your true origins?"

He shook his head. Nothing could surprise him anymore. Húlí's life had been such a turbulent one, half of it lived in blindness of who as well as what he was, and the other half fighting those who hated him for it. What could possibly be worse than that? After being on the run for more than half his years, often hanging on to life by a thin, weak thread, there wasn't much that could shake him.

"I am," Healer admitted. Húlí tilted his head to look at him in question. "Once I have confirmation of what I suspect about my—our parents' deaths, I am nervous about what comes next, what to do with that information." He paused, and Fox cuddled closer, his hand closing on Fox's hip. "Now that I'm this close to the proof I have been searching for my whole life, I feel as if there's nothing else to live for."

With a jolt, Fox sat up. "What about me? What about us?" he asked, louder than he had intended. "Aren't we a good reason to live? To build a new life, free of chasing clues or being chased? Isn't that worth living for?"

A smile spread slowly across Healer's face, his

eyes glittering with something Húlí thought was joy. "You're right, my love. We are so worth it." He drew Húlí back down to him. "Nothing will make me happier than living for you, loving you forever. Sorry, A-Xin, I lost track of the truth for a second."

"It's easy to do after so many years focused on one thing," Húlí said. "I haven't thought of revenge much because I was too busy running for my life." It was true that he had never given revenge or seeking justice for his mother or himself much of a thought, either for lack of time or fear of what other dangers might lurk behind it. "What happens if we find out that I am indeed the son of the then crown prince? What does that mean?"

"Not much, I suppose, since you were never named as the rightful successor to the crown, but it does mean you have every right to be in the running like any of the other princes," Healer said. "Which must scare the crap out of them. You have powers they obviously don't. No wonder they wanted you dead."

They fell silent for a while, the warmth of the covers and their own bodies lulling them into a semislumber. Húlí raised his head and lowered his lips into the valley of the other man's chest, peppering it with butterfly kisses.

"Would you want to fight for the throne?" Healer asked him as he cupped the back of Fox's head.

Húlí didn't have to think about it. He raised himself onto his elbows and stretched to kiss his lover's mouth, long and hard.

Their eyes met. Húlí loved Xiǎo Ying so much, it was painful sometimes. There was no question in his mind.

"The only throne I want to occupy is the one in your heart."

CHAPTER 26
Lǎo Wei
XIĂO YING

Xiǎo Ying had always held himself apart from the rest of the world. Away from anything or anyone who could distract him from his life mission. His heart had been tightly shut to any emotional attachments, and even the forest animals he had often fed and cared for were carefully contained in a tiny walled corner within him, any deep feelings kept at bay. Now, he had given his heart fully and undeniably to this fox man. If asked, he would truthfully declare he had never loved anyone as much as this. He easily could survive on Húlí's kisses, no other nourishment needed.

The sun had peeked over this top of the world,

and its rays, ignoring the slats of the wooden shutters of the wide window, had invaded the room where they both lay in each other's arms. Húlí still slept, his soft snore a soothing melody to Healer's ears. Xiǎo Ying smiled as he brushed his fingers over Fox's cheek.

"*Wǒ ài nǐ*, A-Xin. I love you," he whispered. "How did I live all these years without you?"

A soft rustle against him widened his smile. "Poorly, I'm sure." Fox's slurred words were uttered between barely moving lips. "But once you taste this foxy deliciousness, you can never go back."

Xiǎo Ying tapped the other man gently on the cheek. "*Fàngsì*! I can walk away any time I want," he quipped, his upturned lips belying his words.

Húlí opened his eyes one at a time, ocean blue peeking from beneath his light lashes. "But you'd come running back in no time. Trust me. No one can resist the powers of a fox *yāomó*."

Fighting the urge to devour Fox's well-shaped lips, Xiǎo Ying squeezed him closer with a chuckle. "So that's what you've been doing—using your fox wiles to seize and keep my heart."

Blue eyes flew completely open, the cocky smile dying on Húlí's lips. "My wiles only work on your body," he breathed, his hand sweeping over his lover's hip. "I have no power over anyone's heart."

Healer's smile softened, his body responding to the other man's touch. "I'm glad," he whispered, leaning down over Húlí's mouth. "My heart has been dormant for so long, and I'm happy you're the one to awaken it." He covered his lover's lips with his, teasing them open with his tongue and welcoming Fox's. "If we continue this, we'll never get out of this room."

Húlí pecked at his lips a few more times before rolling out of bed with a grunt, his desire openly displayed as he walked across the room, gloriously naked. Healer moaned quietly, hardening at the sight. But his need would have to wait, for they had important things to take care of. Not that making love to his man was not important.

"Are you guys still going at it?" Ling Ling's voice seeped through the heavy wood of the door. "I couldn't sleep all night, listening to all your moaning."

Xiǎo Ying laughed quietly. The warrior was a breath of fresh air. Any time things got too serious, they could count on her to make them laugh.

"Hurry. Yè Yǐng is hungry, and someone just told me they have breakfast for us in the main room."

She knocked a few times for emphasis. "Are you guys awake?"

"Go save us a seat," Húlí yelled out, slipping into his pants.

"Don't think that'll be necessary," Ling Ling replied, her voice muffled. "I doubt if they have a lot of guests."

A few minutes later, they were all sitting in what looked like a modest court hall. It was a small space but gave out the impression of a much larger room. They sat at a round wooden table with a colorful mosaic top. There were a couple rows of chairs facing each other across a long, deep-blue runner that ended on a low dais crowned by another chair.

"Monks live here?" Ling Ling's question voiced what they were all thinking. This place was not at all what Xiǎo Ying had expected. What was supposed to be an isolated, humble building where a handful of monks lived and prayed turned out to be a whole settlement the size of a small city. And judging by the sounds coming from afar, a thriving one at that.

"Not in this particular building," a voice answered. They all turned toward it. Yè Yǐng jumped up and ran to the stranger who stood by the door, a tall bald man dressed in the typical ocher-colored tunic of the monks. He bent down to scratch the dog's ears with a smile. "This is our leader's meeting hall."

This mysterious leader had been mentioned several times since their arrival. "Who is this leader you speak of?" Húlí asked as the man walked in, followed closely by a tail-wagging Yè Yǐng.

"You'll meet him later today," the man said, his eyes fixed on Fox, studying him with curiosity. "May I ask who you are?"

All three stood up, belatedly bowing to the newcomer. "*Duìbùqǐ*," Xiǎo Ying apologized with a slight bow. "We're being rude. I am Xiǎo Yǐng, a healer." He raised his hand in the female's direction. "This is Ling-*gūniáng*, and this—"

He wasn't able to finish the sentence. The monk raised his hand to interrupt him. "You don't have to tell me who this is," he said, his eyes softening. "There is no mistaking his identity." Húlí exchanged a panicky look with Healer. "You're Xi Ming Xin." Surprising everyone, the monk bowed deeply, his hands folded over his chest. "Your Highness."

Húlí rushed to pull the man up. "I'm no high-ness," he said, a self-deprecatory chuckle punctu-ating his words. "Please call me Húlí or Fox, like my friend Ling Ling does."

Something in the respectful attitude of the monk

gave Xiǎo Ying the confirmation to his suspicions; Húlí was indeed the son of the former crown prince, and this monk knew it. The question was, how did he recognize Fox?

"Why do you call him that?" Ling Ling asked before Healer could. Not behaving like himself, Yè Yǐng fawned over the monk as if he was a long-lost friend.

The monk's eyes finally moved from Fox to the female warrior, and Xiǎo Ying noticed his lover's sudden sigh of relief. Being in the limelight was uncomfortable to Fox after a lifetime of running and hiding.

"It's written all over his face," the monk said. Unconsciously, Húlí wiped his face with a hand. "He's the spitting image of his royal father."

Húlí froze, eyes widening into perfect circles. "You knew my father?" There was such yearning in his voice, it made Xiǎo Ying's insides melt. The monk nodded. "How? How did you know him?"

"First things first," the man said, gesturing for them to sit down. "Our leader will tell you all about it. He's been delayed a bit, but he asked me to show you around town." He gasped as if remembering something. "I apologize. My name is Lǎo Wei, or Old

Gǒu, like most of my brothers call me." He chuckled softly. "We don't stand on ceremony around here."

They finished eating their breakfast and then followed the monk out of the building, the dog prancing beside the old man, his tail wagging.

"Are you a dog whisperer or something?" Húlí asked, a comically stunned expression on his face.

Old Gǒu laughed. "I was a dog once too." And with that enigmatic statement, the monk led them down the road into town.

THE TOWN WAS WAKING UP. Merchants carefully displayed their wares in stalls covered by colorful canopies along the main thoroughfare, a long cobblestone street that was straight as an arrow and bookended by two-storied buildings. Almost every doorway was brightened by splashes of color from hanging pots of flowers and paper lanterns. Doors opened and window shutters were lifted as they walked over the dark, shiny stones of the road.

"In another thirty minutes or so, this street will be crawling with people," the monk explained. "I'll take you to a local teahouse where we can watch the city waking up without being trampled by children and animals."

True to his word, Old Gǒu took them to the second-floor balcony of a large teahouse and sat them at a table overlooking the center of main street. From there they could see the street filling up with people of all ages and sizes, their clothing forming a rainbow that moved like a wave in and between the stalls. Children chased each other, shrieking as dogs joined in the fun, dodging chickens, ducks, and even rabbits, their fluffy ivory tails dotting the scene like giant snowflakes.

"How is it possible that there is such a town this high in the mountains and nobody knows about it?" Ling Ling asked, chomping down on a fried dough stick.

"It's by design," the monk answered, a mischievous smile curving the corners of his lips. "We want to keep our citizens safe and sound from the outside world."

"You mean from Gōng Làn," Húlí interjected, stopping the trajectory of his teacup halfway. "The outside world would be safe enough without the emperor."

Old Gǒu snorted. "You are not wrong, my friend. Our world has been cursed with terrible leadership since the old emperor died. But we're safe here."

Xiǎo Ying swallowed a bite of bread before talking. "You keep saying we're safe here. What do you mean by that?"

Both his companions leaned forward, waiting for the monk's explanation.

"I thought you knew," Old Gǒu said. "Our settlement here is a haven of sorts for people like you, Ming Xin." Húlí raised an eyebrow in question. "The *yāomó* kind, I mean. Most of the people living here are *yāomó* like you."

Healer shifted on his chair. Why would the investigation into his family's massacre lead him here? There were no demons in his family that he was aware of. The mysteries just kept piling up.

"When the old emperor died and the persecution of *yāomó* reached a feverish height, our leader started this community. It was very small at first, but it grew quickly as the word spread and the senseless discrimination escalated around the kingdom." The monk paused for a moment to take a sip of his tea. "And here we are now, a thriving city of outcasts." He swiped his hand through the air, pointing at the lively activity down in the street. "Welcome to Mófēng."

It was indeed a magical peak, a hidden jewel of civilization perched on top of a gorgeous mountain like a majestic eagle ready to fly.

"And who is this leader you keep talking about but whom we have yet to meet?" Ling Ling asked, her eyes following a group of young children down the street. "I'm starting to think he—she?—doesn't exist."

The monk's smile widened. "Oh, he certainly exists, and you'll get to meet him very soon. He holds complaint court every week, but as soon as he is done with it, he will call us to him."

"Complaint court?" Xiǎo Yīng shrugged as Húlí stole a glance at him. He had never heard of such a thing.

"He listens to any complaints people might have about pretty much anything, and then he tries to fix it if he can," Old Gǒu explained. "We don't use currency here, so we share our skills with whoever needs them. It works for us."

Xiǎo Yīng had to admit it seemed like a perfect way to live. No money meant less greed and less thirst for power, two of the main causes for war and discrimination. But he still couldn't understand what all of this had to do with his family.

The young server, dressed in a flowing white

robe, his silky raven hair falling over his shoulders, came back with more tea and, like the guards had, stared at Fox as if he had grown an extra head. After serving the tea—and almost spilling it over Húlí's lap—the server left, stealing quick glances behind him.

"What's with all the staring?" Húlí asked. "I was stared at by the guards, by the people in the street, and by the server. It's kind of creepy."

The monk's deep gut laughter filled the air. "You'll find out soon enough," he said after a moment.

Healer was curious too, but there was an even more pressing question in his head. "Lǎo Wei, I was sent here because it seemed as if there is someone here who has proof of what happened to my parents," he said, interrupting whatever his lover was about to say. "The kind of proof which will allow me to attain justice for my whole family. I don't understand how anybody here can help with that."

A male voice rang behind them, "You'd be surprised."

Xiǎo Yīng's eyes narrowed further as he turned around to look at the man who had spoken. Standing a few feet away from them, his black robes flowing in the breeze, was an exact, however older, copy of Húlí.

"We finally meet, A-Xin." The man's soft voice was an almost precise replica of Húlí's. "I finally get to meet my one-and-only son."

CHAPTER 27
FATHER
HÚLÍ

"*ùqīn?* Father?"

How was it possible? Húlí's father was dead. But there was no denying this man looked just like him. He must have looked so shell-shocked, Xiǎo Ying scooted closer and draped a comforting arm around him. "How? Can't be...."

The man who claimed to be Fox's father took a few steps forward, a slow smile stretching across his face. Húlí stared at what looked like his own reflection and blinked. The man was a good foot taller than he was, and his red hair was spotted with white, but there was no doubt they shared the same blood.

"It's a long story," the man said, bending down

329

to pet the dog that hopped enthusiastically on his hind legs. "I'll be glad to tell you if you allow me to sit with you."

Old Gǒu stood up, bowed briefly, and offered his seat. "Please, *Diànxià*, sit. I have a few errands to run." As the man accepted the offered seat, the monk nodded and left.

Ling Ling cocked her head to the side. "Fuck all the gods in the heavens," she said with her usual enthusiasm. "You are Húlí's spitting image. Are you really his father? I thought you were dead." She was about to say something else, but Xiǎo Ying touched her shoulder in warning.

Húlí snorted bitterly. "Tell me about it. I'm his son, and I was under the same impression."

"Son, you have every right to be bitter about this, but there is a reason," the man said, leaning forward over the table. "First, I must introduce myself to your friends." He looked at and bowed lightly to Ling Ling and Xiǎo Ying. "I'm Gōng Hǎoxīn, Ming Xin's father, and I am obviously not as dead as rumors have it."

Ling Ling laughed. "I can see the resemblance in the sarcastic tone," she said. "I'm dying to know how you came back to life."

Xiǎo Ying interrupted. "*Diànxià,* I'm sure A-Xin

deserves an explanation after a lifetime of believing you dead and gone forever."

The man nodded and settled his blue eyes on Healer. "You must be a *shényī*," he mused, rubbing his chin. "The prophecy was right after all." They all waited for further explanation, but the cryptic statement was all the older Húlí offered them. "Welcome to Mófēng, where everyone who comes in peace is welcome."

"I'm Xiǎo Ying." He pointed at Ling Ling. "This is Ling Ling, and the dog is—"

"Yè Yǐng," Gōng Hǎoxīn said, his gaze traveling to the canine. Húlí's mouth fell open. How in all the heavens did he know that? "We're old friends." More cryptic statements. The dog propped his front paws on the man's knee and wagged his tail in obvious recognition. "I'm guessing you were successful at your mission, my friend." The animal cocked his head to the side and barked once. Gōng Hǎoxīn rubbed his ears. "Good job."

"What's going on?" Húlí blurted out, his patience and curiosity winning over societal manners. "I am so confused."

"It's a long story, but let's start in the beginning, shall we?" Húlí couldn't agree more. Hǎoxīn waved the server to bring yet more tea and cakes. "Settle back and enjoy the tale."

Fox much doubted he'd enjoy any part of it, considering what had happened to his mother and his own life, but he was desperate to find out more about why his father, who had been believed dead for so long, was now sitting across from him very much alive. Warmth enveloped his hand as Xiǎo Ying wrapped it with his own. Their eyes met, and Húlí couldn't help but smile. His heart always melted a little under the warmth of his lover's gaze.

"The Gōng dynasty was almost 100 percent *yāomó*," Húlí's father continued. "It had been like that for centuries, our ancestors stemming from a demon sect so far back in history, no one was quite sure which or how it had come to happen. But the truth was, demons were well accepted as part of the general population, and no one even thought about it as worrisome or even strange. It was just as it was."

Ling Ling interrupted. "If that's the case, then why this persecution of demons? I mean, it started even before the old emperor died. If he was, like you say, a *yāomó* himself, why condemn his own kind to a life of misery and discrimination?" It was a good question. One Fox wanted to ask himself.

"I'll get to that, Ling-*gūniáng*." The former crown prince raised an appeasing hand. "Gōng Zhèng ruled with a firm but kind hand, defending the weak and keeping the powerful in check. Many of his ministers were demons like him, but he strove to have a well-balanced governing body with as many full humans as *yāomó* representatives. Life in the kingdom was good and peaceful for many years."

"What changed?" Húlí asked, his hand still firmly enclosed in his lover's. "How did things go so wrong that where there was no prejudice before, racial hate managed to sprout with such fervor?"

"It took some years for it to come to full fruition," the older man said. "Even before I married your mother, trouble had already been brewing. My mother, the empress, died young with me as her only descendant. My father, as was customary back then, had a few concubines to produce more heirs. Most of them were full human, and my brothers were born only half demons with diminished powers. Gōng Làn was the oldest and the most devious of all. He craved power and couldn't stand that I had been named crown prince when he was indeed older than I. So he started a long campaign of fear."

Xiǎo Ying shook his head. "He sowed fear in the hearts of the full humans against the demons." Gōng Hǎoxīn nodded. "He began a psychological war and turned the *yāomó* into the enemy."

"Exactly. He wanted the crown, and he was terrified and envious of demon power, since he had very little of it himself. By turning the population against the *yāomó*, he made sure he could hold on to the throne once he got it." It all made a sick, unfair kind of sense now. The prince continued. "It took a few years to take root, but the campaign of fear was mostly successful. It's not hard to instill fear into the hearts of humans. All it takes is a few well-placed rumors and lies, and it spreads like a wildfire. By the time you were born, Ming Xin, the tide had turned, and the full-human population was refusing to serve demons at their stores, locking the doors at night, and murmuring poison around the fireside. The *yāomó* went from being a respected race to the scourge of humanity, and thus the persecution began."

Húlí put his free hand to his chest, clutching at the clothes over his heart. The pain was real, but the anger was even more fierce. He had rarely experienced hate despite the life of hiding and running he'd led, but hate was nevertheless burning inside him at that moment. He didn't like it but seemed helpless against it.

His senior seemed to know how he felt, his blue eyes going softer, his lips tightening. "I married your mother in secret to protect her, since she was a demon as well. Only a trusted few knew the truth. Rumors in the palace claimed she was my concubine. We allowed it since it meant she wouldn't be viewed as a real threat by my brothers. After you were born, we started planning for the future. Things were not looking good for the demon sect or the emperor. My father knew that sooner or later his oldest son would make a move against him, and he wanted to assure that his legacy was well protected."

"Gōng Zhèng wanted to protect Húlí and his mother," Ling Ling muttered, her eyes lost in thought. "But why not protect all of you?"

With a shake of his head, the old prince replied, "He did have a plan to protect all of us, but things didn't quite go the way we'd hoped." He glanced at Xiǎo Ying, sorrow in his gaze. "Your family, the Xiǎos, were an honest and brilliant family of *shényī* who had no interest in the politics of court. They were loyal to the emperor because my father was fair to his people. The plan was that once my brother made a move for the throne, the Xiǎos would be able to prolong the emperor's life long enough to get my wife and my son out of the palace and hidden away in safety. But Làn got wind of the plan and attacked unexpectedly."

Hǎoxīn threw an apologetic glance at his son and shrugged almost imperceptibly before continuing. "My father had long sent me out of town under the pretense that I was squelching an uprising at the border. He then spread rumors of my death. Mófēng was his doing. His plan was to give me time to build a safe haven for my family and other demons and then send you and your mother to me. There wasn't much I could do when my brother sent his minions to our quarters. Thankfully, my father had a tiny window of time to have a loyal servant take you away from the palace disguised as one of Làn's men."

Húlí's face burned with anger as his heart galloped inside his chest. "Why not save my mother too?" he asked, voice choked by an onslaught of emotions. "If they took me away, they could have taken my mother too."

The older prince lowered his head, sadness clouding his eyes. "That will always be the biggest regret of my life even though I didn't know it was happening," he breathed with a long sigh. "That was the original idea. Your grandfather was as fond of your mother as I was. She was smart with a keen sense of fairness and spirit. He knew she would have made an amazing empress. When the servant came to rescue you both, she had been wounded already and had you enveloped in her arms to hide you from the murderers who had left, believing both of you dead. The assassins had set the court-yard on fire, and the trusted servant barely managed to get you out of there alive. In the end your mother chose to stay and smokescreen the enemy into believing we were all dead, giving us both time and space to get to safety. The courtyard burned to the ground, leaving no clues as to your true fate."

No wonder Húlí had always been so afraid of fire. He didn't recall the fire, which, just like all his other memories of that time, had grown hazy and disconnected, but his body hadn't forgotten, it seemed.

"But I was just a kid. I needed my mother." Fox hated the way his voice sounded, needy and hurt like that of a young lost child. He lowered his voice to a whisper. "I needed my mom." Xiǎo Ying squeezed his hand, a simple gesture that managed to slow his heart down, anger ebbing away like a wisp of smoke.

"Your mom is not gone." Gōng Hǎoxīn's statement shocked everyone. Húlí's eyes rounded, his jaw dropping. "Not really. As a demon she can exist without a human body. Your mother has been with you all along."

What exactly did his father mean by that? Waves of memories came flooding in: the voice in his head, whoever protected him when they were attacked, that feeling of warmth he often had when he meditated, an invisible hug he couldn't explain or define. Was that really his mother? He had hoped it was, but common sense kept telling him it was simply wishful thinking.

"You're kidding me, right?" Húlí exclaimed, the red of anger fading into paleness. "That voice in my head—that's really *Mǔqīn*? Not a figment of my imagination?"

His father shook his head. "That's your mother, son." He paused as if waiting for a reaction, but Fox couldn't speak. His thoughts were racing through his mind at such speed, he couldn't pin any of them down long enough to make sense of them. "When they killed her, she was able to transfer her soul into a plant in her garden where she stayed for a few years, hardly aware. After that, her cognition began to return, and she was able to free her spirit so she was mobile at least and could try to find you to make sure you were safe."

This outrageous story couldn't find a hold in Fox's brain. He was a man who could change into a nine-tailed fox. He, of all people, should be able to wrap his head around it, but he couldn't. Not yet.

"Eventually she will take on her fox form, but it takes many years," his father continued. "For now she sticks to her spirit form. That's how it works for us demons who are not born from other *yāomó*; we recreate ourselves through years and years of cultivation. Your mother's love has given her an edge."

Ling Ling coughed before speaking. "What do you mean?"

Hǎoxīn chuckled softly. "It's only been thirty-odd years. In terms of cultivation, that's a blink of an eye. The fact that she can already communicate with you is unheard of. Her love for you is truly performing miracles."

It was Xiǎo Ying's turn to speak. "She has done more than just communicate. She has been able to protect A-Xin when in danger." Húlí's father started. "She saved his life more than once already."

A soft, amused smile stretched across the old

prince's lips. "I shouldn't be surprised. Yuèguāng is an extraordinary woman, capable of love that transcends even death, I'm sure."

Húlí's heart skipped a beat. "Is that what my mother is called? Yuèguāng?" He had never known her name. For him, she had always been *Mǔqīn*.

His father nodded, smiling still. "Moonbeam, an appropriate name for her. She brought beauty, light, and softness to everything she touched." The man shook his head as if trying to break away from a spell. "The servant in question was able to take you to the man you know as *shūshu*. He was a great master of the martial arts. Some say he was a god who came down to the mortal world to help the old emperor. No one knows for sure. But he had been around for some years, the only individual my father truly trusted. The plan was to let him do whatever he could to protect you both and take you and your mother to me once it was safe to do so."

Húlí hung his head, the heat of his lover's hand the only thing keeping him from shattering. "In the end it was only me. *Shūshu* never told me his real name or where he had come from. He was a man of few words and even less emotion." He sighed, raising his eyes to his father again. "Not complaining. He brought me up the best he knew how and taught me how to survive in a world bent on killing me. But he vanished too soon. He never got around to teaching me much about my own kind."

"*Shūshu*'s real origins are a mystery to this day, but he seemed to hold a special place in his heart for my father and those he loved," Hǎoxīn said. "I can't speculate on why he disappeared, but maybe it was by design. The gods seem to have plans for all of us that they are unwilling to share."

"The gods be fucked," Ling Ling exclaimed, jumping to her feet and almost throwing the chair down. "What do they know about mortal living? What do they know about pain and suffering?" All eyes were on her now. Fox stole a glance at his father, thinking he would be shocked by his friend's blasphemous words, but instead an amused grin lit up the man's face. "What right do they have to interfere with lives they don't understand?" He had never seen Ling Ling so agitated. "Did Old Fox have to go through so much pain to get here? Why couldn't the gods just tell him, 'Go to Mófēng, that's where your father is.'?"

It was Xiǎo Ying who answered, "Then he would not have met you or me. Or Yè Yǐng, for that matter. He wouldn't be the man he is today. It's our experiences that make us who we are, and pain is part of that equation." He looked up at his lover and smiled. "I, for one, am so glad we met even if that means we both had to go through hell for it. In the end we have each other, and that's worth walking through fire if need be."

Ling Ling deflated a bit and sat back down, a sad smile on her lips. "You're right, of course," she said. "But it still rankles. Why did we all have to lose our families in the process?"

Húlí's head snapped toward her. "You lost your family too?" How did he not know that? What kind of friend was he? Someone who had been so wrapped up in his own misery that never once stopped to wonder about his best friend's past. For him, Ling Ling had always been the warrior he knew and loved, with no past, no history. "Why didn't you tell me?"

She shrugged, a lopsided smile curving her lips. "What for? It was in the past, and there was nothing I could do to change that," she said matter-of-factly. "I chose to move on."

A thousand questions buzzed inside Fox's mind, but he knew now wasn't the right time to ask them. It would have to wait for when they were alone.

"All of your destinies are entwined," Hǎoxīn said.

Húlí cocked his head in question. "All of your circumstances brought you here together."

He allowed a dramatic pause before continuing, "And from here you will go and change the world and save our people."

"Wait! What?" Had Húlí heard correctly? The others seemed as surprised as he was, their faces wearing sure signs of confusion. "Save the world? We can barely save ourselves."

"*Diànxià*," Xiǎo Ying uttered, leaning forward, still holding on to his lover's hand. "What do you mean by that?"

Hǎoxīn chuckled. "Don't be alarmed," he said, waving an appeasing hand at them. "It's not something you'll have to do tomorrow. More of a long-term mission."

Fox had had enough. Dropping Xiǎo Ying's hand, he hopped to his feet. "What in all the heavens is going on, Father? I went from being a wanted creature without much hope for the future to the savior of the world?" He raked his hair with his fingers. "What exactly am I supposed to save the world from? Bad eating habits? Poor fashion choices?"

Both his lover and Ling Ling were watching him closely, a mixture of admiration and amusement dancing in their eyes. A snort escaped Ling Ling's lips.

"As interesting as those issues are, you'll have to deal with matters of a more serious nature, my son." The sarcasm was thick in the older man's voice, mirroring his son's typical tone.

Húlí was not going to let his old man have the last word in snarkiness. "Eating habits are very important."

Hǎoxīn's squinting eyes twinkled. "No argument from me," he said, deadpan. "But I am speaking of getting this kingdom back to a good place where its people are not suffering from poverty, hunger, and discrimination. I'm talking about taking the throne back."

Ling Ling's narrow eyes rounded. "You're talking treason." No one could deny that. The old crown prince nodded. "*That* can get us all killed for sure."

"And how exactly would we do that?" Húlí asked, still standing. "We have no army, no supporters, and we are running for our lives. How can a band of outcasts overturn a mighty ruler?"

"We do have a small army here at Mófēng," Húlí's father said. "They are well trained and very motivated. They'll be even better trained once you and Xiǎo Ying teach them further. We have magic on our side and the rightful heir to the throne still alive and thriving."

"Still not enough to fight and win against the forces of the emperor," Xiǎo Ying exclaimed. "Gōng Làn has amassed an immense army and built up hate against the demon race for so many years now. Instilling fear is easy. Removing it is a whole other matter. The populace will not likely join forces with us despite being poor and miserable under the rule of the current emperor. Their fear of the *yāomó* over-shadows everything else."

They all fell silent, digesting Healer's wise words. He was right, of course. After years of being conditioned to hate anything to do with the *yāomó*, there was very little hope the common people would join the fight on their side.

Surprising everyone, Ling Ling was the one who spoke up. "We recondition the people." All eyes turned to her. "We start a campaign of reversal. It won't be as easy as causing fear, but not impossible. We use the enemy's own weapon. It can work."

"It *will* work." His father's words didn't stir the confidence Húlí was sure he hoped they would. But he couldn't deny that the kingdom needed a do-over. "And you, my son, are the man to do it."

After a moment of stunned silence, Fox burst out

laughing as he clutched his middle with both arms. "Me? The right man for the job? You don't know me, Father." He choked back his laughter before continuing. "I'm a good-for-nothing. I have spent my whole life jumping in and out of beds to replenish my *qi* and then running for my life. Ling Ling has provided me a roof over my head and food to sustain me for so long, she should ascend into heaven. I can't even hold a job long enough to matter." He paused for a moment, trying to repress the small sob that climbed his throat. "I'm useless. How can I save a kingdom?"

Hǎoxīn stood up slowly and crossed the space between him and his son with a couple steps. "You're not useless, Ming Xin." He grasped his son's upper arms and held him steady. "You are extraordinary. The son of a powerful fox demon and a dragon. You've been touched by the gods and brought here to vanquish the oppressor and his minions. You are not useless. You're my son, after all."

CHAPTER 28
THE PROPHECY
XIǍO YING

Xiǎo Ying had so many questions: how were his parents involved in this whole mess? Why had the former crown prince said the prophecy was true? What prophecy for that matter, and how was that connected to him? None of which had been answered by the time they retired for the night. Yè Yǐng had followed Ling Ling to her room, and Fox had made a direct dive onto the bed with a loud dramatic grunt.

"You can't be that tired," Xiǎo Ying mused, unwrapping his overcoat. The room was warm and cozy despite the almost frigid air outside. "We rested all night."

Húlí feigned outrage. "If that's what you thought we did, I must have done it wrong."

With a chuckle, Healer threw his outer garment on the top of a chair. "*Bù, bù,*" he said, shaking his head and kicking one of his boots across the room. "I don't mean it that way." After kicking the other boot away, Healer joined the other man in bed, lying on his belly next to him. "You loved me just right," he whispered, brushing his lips over Húlí's cheek. "Perfectly."

Their lips joined, gently at first until the sparks turned into a fire. Tongues slid together as they devoured each other, the flames licking every inch of Healer's body, awakening him in a way only his lover could. Once they took each other to the peak and back, they laid side by side, breathless and sated.

"What do you think your father meant when he talked about the prophecy?" Xiǎo Ying asked in muted tones, his voice already slurring from exhaustion.

Fox shook his head gently, eyes focused on the boxed ceiling. "I don't know. I'm still getting used to the idea that he's my father." He sighed, his hand seeking Healer's between them. "How do I even process that? He's been dead since I can remember, and now—" He turned abruptly to face Xiǎo Ying. "It hurts my head just thinking about it."

Xiǎo Ying shifted and brushed his fingers along his lover's face. He smiled, warmth spreading in his gut as Húlí draped one leg over his hip. "Then don't think about it for now. Let's sleep and talk about it tomorrow."

Húlí nodded, already half asleep, and closed his ocean-blue eyes, his red lashes fanning over his pale face. He was so beautiful. Xiǎo Ying's heart swelled with love as he slowly gave in to slumber.

LING LING WAS WAITING for them at the eating area the next morning, the dog curled by her feet. When Xiǎo Ying and Húlí entered the room, he jumped upright and rushed to greet them, tail wagging wildly.

"I may have eaten all the fried dough," Ling Ling said, barely looking up from her teacup. "You know what they say, the early bird catches the worm."

Húlí scratched the dog's ears. "It goes more like, the early bird selfishly wolves down everybody else's food," he quipped, dropping to a chair next to his friend. "You have absolutely no shame, do you?'

Ling Ling snorted, droplets of her tea flying out of her mouth. "I learned from the best, Old Fox."

Healer watched the exchange with amusement. He pulled out a chair and sat across from the female. "When did you lose your family?" There was no reason to be coy. Their lives seemed intricately connected in ways he still couldn't quite understand. They might as well be open about their pasts.

The warrior swallowed her bread, took another sip of tea, and locked eyes with him. "They went to sea one day like my father did every day and never came back," she said, her voice unnaturally level. "Their bodies and those of their fishing crew washed ashore a couple of days later. My mother specialized in herbs and certain plants and helped take care of the sick in our fishing town. She rarely went with my father on his fishing trips, but she did that time. She had told me the day before that they were heading to Chūntiān Island to collect a special flower for a customer. I never saw her again."

Silence filled the space between them until Húlí broke it. "Do you think your parents' death connected somehow to ours?"

"I can see how Healer's past is connected to yours, Old Fox," Ling Ling said. "But mine? They didn't live in the same city. They were not nobility or royalty. A fisherman and an herbalist. What could they possibly have in common with your family or the emperor's death?"

A deep voice startled them all into silence. "Your mother, Ling-*gūniáng*, might have been just a country herbalist, but she was familiar with plants that no one else was." Húlí's father stood in the doorway with Old Gǒu by his side. "She happened to know where to find a flower that the Xiǎos needed to make an antidote for the poison the emperor had been fed."

Ling Ling almost dropped her teacup. "She was killed because she was going to collect a flower?"

"Gōng Làn wanted no loose ends," Old Gǒu said.

A growl escaped Ling Ling's lips, and Húlí clutched her shoulder in support. "I'm going to kill him," she muttered between her teeth. "I'm going to grind him into a fine powder and feed him to the birds."

Hǎoxīn walked in and pulled a chair close to the table, but Old Gǒu stood behind him. "All in due time, Ling-*gūniáng*—all in due time."

"What's this prophecy you mentioned yesterday?" Xiǎo Ying asked, more curious than ever.

The former crown prince threw a glance at the monk behind him. "Want to tell them?"

Old Gǒu nodded. "It's simple. A few years after

Hǎoxīn settled here and many more of our people took refuge with us, I had a vision when I was meditating in the Hall of Frozen Waters." As curious as he was, Healer was not about to interrupt the story to ask questions about such a hall. "In my vision, the gods prophesied that three orphans, connected by fate and circumstances, would rise to save the kingdom." He cleared his throat. "A fox, a healer, and a warrior."

No one said a thing. Xiǎo Yíng had heard of and seen a lot of strange events, but it was one thing to hear about it and another to be part of it. After a moment of petrified stupor, they all glanced at one another.

Ling Ling broke the silence first. "Fuck! And what an unholy trinity that is."

It was all they needed to release the pressure kept inside them. It started as a rumbling and ended as an explosion of unstoppable laughter that rippled through the air.

Healer would think about the prophecy later. But now, he needed to join the tidal wave of mirth and just let go.

~

THEIR TOUR of the town ended outside the main hall where a crowd had gathered. As they walked past the people assembled there, a path opened up for them, and silence gradually replaced the muttering of voices. It was strange to be the focus of so many eyes, especially after a lifetime of living alone and only having sporadic interactions with other humans. Xiǎo Yíng stole a peek at his lover, who did not seem as uncomfortable as he was. But then again, that was Húlí, the man he loved and who, no matter what the circumstances, always gave off an aura of indifference. He smiled. His lover had built very effective sets of armor against the prejudice and persecution that had plagued him his whole life. Only Ling Ling and himself knew what lay beneath that veneer.

Climbing the white stone steps to the main hall, Healer felt rather than saw the crowd closing behind them, waiting. For what, he had no idea. He was still reeling from all the revelations of the past couple days. He had come here hoping to find definite proof of who his family's murderers were so he could exact retribution and had found—he still wasn't quite sure what he had found. A prophecy that hailed him as one of three to save the kingdom. All he ever wanted was to bring justice to his parents.

Who would have thought he was now charged with bringing justice to so many more people? Could he even do it?

Inside, a smaller crowd was gathered. Elders, Xiǎo Ying was certain, judging by the way their long hair was gathered in severe top buns with no ornaments whatsoever. Like those outside, the collected bodies in the hall dispersed to the side aisles to allow them a path to the dais. The mostly older men and women bowed to them as they passed.

He was used to it.

As a healer of certain standing, people tended to act very respectfully around him. But for Fox who had been chased and harassed his whole life, it had to be an odd feeling. A quick glance told Healer that Húlí was comically divided between ignoring the bows and bowing in return. Ling Ling had chosen to ignore it, walking purposely toward the raised platform, her head held high. After all the revelations, he wouldn't be surprised to find out she was some long-lost princess. Despite himself, he chuckled softly under his breath, belatedly remembering to hide it with his hand.

Extra chairs had been added to the dais, two to each side. As he sat down on the furthest one to the right, next to his lover, Xiǎo Ying wondered who the fourth chair was for. Yè Yǐng had followed them, tail wagging and tongue lolling out of his mouth, and settled by Ling Ling's feet. Old Gǒu stood behind Hǎoxīn's chair in the center, both friendly and menacing with his thick arms crossed over his chest and legs braced apart.

As soon as Fox's father sat down, the crowd went on their knees and chanted, "*Huángdì wànsuì, wànsuì, wànsuì.*"

Xiǎo Ying tensed. He knew now that Hǎoxīn was the rightful heir to the throne, but he was still surprised to see the town elders acknowledging him as the true emperor. A gasp escaped his lover's lips, and he had to fight the urge to reach out for Húlí's hand.

"Stand up," Hǎoxīn said with a wave of his hand and a smile. "We don't stand on ceremony here, remember?"

Old Gǒu didn't move but said, "Old friend, the occasion seems to call for some level of ceremony, don't you think?"

Hǎoxīn's chuckles were soon followed by everybody else's, and just like that, the mood changed from somber to relaxed, almost festive.

"We are gathered here today to officially introduce you all to my son and his two quest companions," the older man said. He turned his head in Húlí's direction. "This is Ming Xin, my son and rightful crown prince to the throne of Tiān Míngzhū." Húlí's gaze ping-ponged between his father and the rest of the room, his forehead furrowed and lips stretched into a thin line. Healer wanted to draw him into an embrace and assure him everything would be all right, but the old crown prince had moved on to Xiǎo Ying and Ling Ling. "These are his faithful companions, the youngest of the Xiǎos and Ling Ling, a female warrior from Dǎo." They both bowed their heads to the public. "The fourth chair is for my wife, who despite not being here in body is definitely here in spirit."

As if confirming his words, the lights flickered, and the empty chair scooted a half an inch forward. Ling Ling, who was sitting the closest to the empty chair, jumped to her feet, startled. "What the fuck!"

Hǎoxīn laughed. "No need for alarm. You have seen my wife's manifestation often in the past."

"Old Fox was the only who could hear or see her," she protested, smoothing invisible wrinkles from her clothes. Turning to the rest of the room, she bowed her head a couple quick times. "*Duìbùqǐ*, everybody. I was very rude." The crowd nodded their forgiveness while hiding their smiles behind their hands, and she sat back down, still throwing suspicious glances at the empty chair.

"My wife has been cultivating again," Hǎoxīn explained. "Her love for our son is so great that she was able to do what takes most everyone else a lot longer, sometimes hundreds of years; she has cultivated far enough that she's able to protect and communicate with Ming Xin. And myself." So that's how he knew about it. His wife had been keeping him abreast of all the happenings. "I wouldn't be surprised if she will succeed in cultivating fast enough to return to us physically very soon."

At that, Húlí turned his neck to his father. "She will? Like in human form?" he asked, voice strained. "How soon?"

Xiǎo Ying's heart tightened. There was such longing in his lover's voice. In that moment, Húlí was the young boy who had lost all who loved him when he needed them the most. Healer might have lost his parents too, but he had been older, and however hard it was, it could not possibly have been as tough on him as losing a parent at Húlí's young age.

"There are no guarantees," his father said with a warm smile. "But very possible, knowing my Yuèguāng." The older man reached out to touch his son's hand. "In the meantime, son, she is here with us. Never doubt it."

A sigh escaped Fox's lips, but he managed a sad smile he directed at the empty chair. "Knowing you're here, *Mǔqīn*, makes me very happy," he whispered.

Old Gǒu stepped forward, uncrossing his arms. "Our leader would like to invite you all for a celebration," he announced in a booming voice. "Tables have been set up on main street. Please eat, drink, and be merry." As people rustled to leave, the old man added, "But before we do, let's pay our respect to Xi Ming Xin, Crown Prince of Tiān Míngzhū and our future leader."

Much to their surprise, everyone fell on their knees again to kowtow to Fox, whose face had turned a bright shade of red while they all pledged their loyalty to him. Xiǎo Ying would have his hands full later that day, helping his lover come to terms with his newly acquired royal status.

CHAPTER 29

NINE TAILS
HÚLÍ

Air whistled in Húlí's ears as he bounded through the streets of town, wind on his face and all nine tails flapping freely behind him. He nearly flew around corners and between trees, dodging people and animals alike. As he neared the end of the steep cobblestone street, he made a sharp turn to the right, nearly squishing a clueless chicken that had unwisely crossed his path.

"*Duìbùqǐ*, chicken," he yelled out as the frantic clucking faded behind him. He wasn't going to stop now. He needed to run, to fill his lungs with all the icy cold air of the mountain until they felt as if they were going to explode. Nothing could stand in his way.

Except maybe that door.

Hoping it was unlocked, Fox didn't slow down, instead picking up speed as he aimed himself at the sturdy wooden door, reaching out for the door handle, a large metal circle too big for the humble abode. The lock gave in easily, and he was able to open the door wide before crashing into it. Momentum propelled him halfway inside the room until he came to a sliding stop by the blazing hearth.

"Still unable to knock, are you?" The familiar voice brought a smile to his face. "You could at least wipe your feet."

Húlí chuckled, shaking himself off like he so often had seen Yè Yǐng do, his reddish tails still unfurled behind him. "I keep miscalculating the distance between the corner of the street and our door," he said, sniffing the air. "I smell something good. What is it?"

Xiǎo Ying unfolded from his crouch by the fire, two smoking meat skewers in his hand. "Your favorite," he said with a wink. Húlí made a swipe for them, but his lover snapped them out of reach. "Nuh, not so fast, my love. You must pay for these."

A lopsided grin stretched Fox's lips. "Oh really? And how much must I pay for them?"

Healer pretended to think about it as he waved the skewers in the air, the scent of delicious meat wafting all the way to Húlí's nose. "I'm feeling generous," Healer finally said. "A kiss will do it." Húlí stepped forward, but Xiǎo Yīng stopped him with his outstretched hand. "But it has to be a good one. A *really* good one."

Húlí had never turned down a good challenge.

Stepping forward, he drew Healer into an embrace, one arm awkwardly hovering at his side and the other closing around his lover's neck. Teasingly, Húlí lightly touched the other man's lips with his own, once, twice, and then retracted for a moment to hear him catching his breath. With a groan that was as much mirth as yearning, he lowered his mouth to his lover's again, this time holding Xiǎo Yīng's lower lip between his lips and pulling gently before sucking on it.

"Is this good?" he whispered against Xiǎo Yīng's mouth, and he moaned and nodded. "I can make it even better." True to his promise, Fox slipped his tongue between Healer's lips, searching for his mate's, filling him with his taste, his fullness. His tails wavered behind him, stretching and curling as the heat in his belly intensified. Before he knew it, two of his tails had curved and closed around them in a furry hug, shortly followed by the other seven. They enveloped them both in a warm cocoon, their bodies melded together within.

"Hmm, this is a very good kiss indeed," Healer whispered once their lips pulled apart. "You can have your meat now."

As turned on as he was, Húlí was also a fox who had just run for miles on the mountain and in town. He was ravenous, so he grabbed for the skewers and devoured the meat while his tails were still wrapped around them both.

Healer laughed and planted a kiss on his cheek. "You love your food more than you love me," he quipped, unraveling himself from his lover's tails.

"Not true," Húlí said, cheeks swollen with food. "I love you both, but differently."

"What about me?" Ling Ling stood in the doorway, Yè Yǐng by her side. "You know, you really should close your door before making out. It just doesn't look good for heroes like us." It had been a running joke since Húlí's father had basically called them that in front of the townspeople.

Húlí snorted, spitting out a chunk of meat. "Heroes! What a joke," he said, turning his attention to the second skewer. "I don't know what makes them think we are actually going to save Tiān Míngzhū from the claws of the rotten emperor, my not-so-esteemed uncle." He snorted again, louder. "Have they taken a look at me lately?"

Ling Ling made a big production at pretending to study her friend's body. "You're right. There's not much to boast about, is there?"

Xiǎo Ying pulled his lover to him before he could react to her words. "I beg to differ, my friend," he said. "I see a lot to boast about. My man is handsome and amazing."

"And great in bed," Fox added with a greasy smirk.

"I'll take your word for it," the female warrior said. "You guys are impossible. I'm going to the main square to train a few people. Want to come?"

Ling Ling had been putting her warrior skills to good use, training many of the younger *yāomó* on how to fight. She had gathered a large following among the male population because of her beauty and strength even if her fierceness had them all just as terrified as they were infatuated.

Húlí shook his head, leaning it against Healer's shoulder. "I think I want to focus on my man right now," he said, triggering a frown from his friend. "My belly is full, I have exercised, and now I want some loving."

Turning her back on the two men, Ling Ling

walked out. "Too much information. I'm leaving. *Bǎozhòng.*" Yè Yǐng wagged his tail and barked once before following her.

Standing by the door, they both watched her walk away. Her dark-blue robes flapped behind her as she climbed the steep hill in the direction of the main square, the dog strolling along at her side.

"Why do you run every day?" Healer asked him quietly. "I would have thought that after being chased by the hounds for so many years, you would be tired of doing it."

Húlí, still leaning his head on his lover's shoulder, sighed. "It's different. Before, I was running from something bad. Now, I'm running to something wonderful." Healer cupped Fox's cheek, and heat quickly spread from that patch of skin and flesh to the rest of his body. His tails twitched in delight. "And now I can run freely with my tails unfurled and in plain sight. It's a wonderful feeling to be free at last."

They stood there for a while longer, watching the vanishing figure of their female friend in the distance and relishing each other's presence. The road ahead might be a bumpy one, but they had each other now. Not to mention a newly found family. Whatever the future held, Húlí knew everything would be all right.

"You know what, though?" he asked after a moment, raising his head to look at his lover. "There is one thing I don't understand."

Xiǎo Ying raised an eyebrow. "What's that?"

Húlí bit his lip before speaking. "Who or what in all the heavens above is Yè Yǐng?" He paused for a moment, thinking. "And how come I have a dragon for a father but ended up being a fox instead? Is there no justice in this world at all?"

WE HOPE you fell in love with Yi and Ayo's story. Please consider leaving a review on GOODREADS and your store of purchase.

If you're looking for more fantasy romance from Natalina, check out INFINITE BLUE or SLEEPING LOVE.

GLOSSARY
(IN ALPHABETICAL ORDER)

Bǎozhòng = take care

Bèndàn = idiot

Bù = no

Bù hǎo = not good

Buhaiza = I'm sorry

Bù kěnéng = impossible

Chóumì = dense

Chūntiān Island = Spring Island

Dānchún = pure and simple

Dǎo = island

Dà zhīzhū = big spiders

Diànxià = Your Highness

Duǎnde = short

Duì = right

Duìbùqǐ = sorry

Fàngsì = presumptuous

Fùqīn = Father

Ge = bro

Gǒu = Dog

Gòule! = enough!

Gūniáng = girl

Hǎiyáng = ocean

Hǎo = good

Hǎo ba hǎo ba = alright, alright

Hǎo kě'ài = so cute

Hépíng = peace

Huángdì wànsuì = may the emperor live many lives

Jīnzi = gold (in this case a piece of gold)

Jù shǔ = big rat

Lán = blue

Méiyǒu rén = no one

Mófēng = magic peak

Mǔqīn = mom

Nǐ kàn = You look

Nǐ shì shéi? = who are you

Nǐ zěnme gǎn = how dare you

Pipa = a stringed instrument similar to a guitar

Qi = inner energy/life force

Qǐng xiǎngyòng = enjoy your food

Qù = shoo, go!

Shan = (an open cross-collar shirt or jacket worn over the **yi**)

Shàoyé = young master

Shényī = divine doctor

Shūshu = uncle

Suhou = where Fox lives

Taihu = where Healer lives

Tiān Míngzhū = Heaven's Pearl

Wéi = hey

Wǒ ài nǐ = I love you

Xiānshēng = mister

Xiǎoqì = stingy

Xiǎoxīn = watch out

Xiǎozi = brat

Xièxiè = thank you

Xīwàng = hope

Yǎnlèi = tears

Yāomó = demon

Yěji = pheasant

Yi = (an open cross-collar garment)

Zhēn de = really?

Zuò = sit down

Zuò dé hǎo = well done

ACKNOWLEDGMENTS

I have always wondered whether the actors who receive Oscars ever forget to thank someone really important. How mortifying would that be, really?

In a much humbler way, these acknowledgments always make me nervous that I'll somehow hurt someone's feelings by accidentally leaving them out. So, if I do forget to thank you—you know who you are—I apologize profusely and swear there was no malice behind it.

First, I have to thank all the wonderful writers, producers, directors, and actors in Chinese fantasy dramas. You have brought another layer of wonderment to my creative mind by teaching me about Asian mythology and fairy tales. As soon as I learned about the legend of the Nine-Tailed Foxes, I had to write one into my stories. I have always loved foxes, maybe because of Aesop, who always painted these creatures as smart and wily. More recently I fell in love with foxes all over again as I watched them roaming the neighborhood—and even my school—

with their beautiful reddish coat and white puffy ears. And their eerie call that made me jump out of bed one night in alarm only added to the mystique —such heartbreaking emotion in its scream. I just had to use all that angst in a character, and thus Húlí was born.

As usual I have to thank my critique group, especially Karen, David, Ann-Marie, and Susan, for all their kind and helpful feedback. It's been invaluable.

A big thanks goes to Becky, my publisher, for having faith in my stories, and to her whole team of editors, formatters, graphic artists, marketing staff, and beta readers for the amazing work they do to release books I can be 100% proud of. Thank you so much. You've taught me so much over the years.

Thank you, Lisa, for always being willing to read my stories and give me feedback. It means the world to me.

So grateful to my family who, despite not being readers themselves, have always supported and believed in me. You guys rock.

And, of course, to my readers goes a huge bouquet of thank-yous. You make it all worth it.

About the Author

Natalina wrote her first romance in collaboration with her best friend at the age of 13. Since then she has ventured into other genres, but romance is first and foremost in almost everything she writes.

After earning a degree in tourism and foreign languages, she worked as a tourist guide in her native Portugal for a short time before moving to the United States. She lived in three continents and a few islands, and her knack for languages and linguistics led her to a master's degree in education. She lives in Virginia where she has taught English as a Second Language to elementary school children for more years than she cares to admit.

Natalina doesn't believe you can have too many books or too much coffee. Art and dance make her happy and she is pretty sure she could survive on lobster and bananas alone. When she is not writing or stressing over lesson plans, she shares her life with her husband and two adult sons.

Don't miss out on New Releases, Exclusive Giveaways and much more!

Join Natalina's newsletter: HTTP://BIT.LY/
REISNEWSLETTER
Join Natalina's reader group: HTTP://BIT.LY/
REBELSOUTCASTS

Natalina would love to hear from you directly, too. Please feel free to email her at CATARINADEOBIDOS1@GMAIL.COM or check out her website HTTP://BIT.LY/WEBNATALINA for updates.

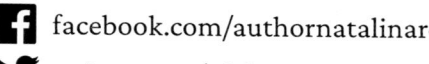 facebook.com/authornatalinareis

twitter.com/TichaB

 instagram.com/reisnatalina

bookbub.com/authors/natalina-reis

About the Publisher

Hot Tree Publishing loves love. Publishing adult romantic fiction, HTPubs are all about diverse reads featuring heroes and heroines to swoon over. Since opening in 2015, HTPubs have published more than 300 titles across the wide and diverse range of romantic genres. If you're chasing a happily ever after in your favourite subgenre, HTPubs have you covered.

Interested in discovering more amazing reads brought to you by Hot Tree Publishing? Head over to the website for information:

WWW.HOTTREEPUBLISHING.COM

Printed by BoD™in Norderstedt, Germany